BUM STEER

A BLANCO COUNTY MYSTERY

BEN REHDER

© 2015 by Ben Rehder.
Cover art © 2015 by Bijou Graphics & Design.
Print formatting by A Thirsty Mind Book Design

All rights reserved.

This novel is a work of fiction. Names, characters, places, and incidents are either the product of the author's imagination, or, if real, used fictitiously. No part of this book may be reproduced or transmitted in any form or by any electronic or mechanical means, including photocopying, recording, or by any information storage and retrieval system, without the express written permission of the author or publisher, except where permitted by law.

This novel is for Tommy Blackwell,
with much appreciation for answering
so many questions over the course of 13 novels.
Hey, I've got another one for you…

ACKNOWLEDGMENTS

Many thanks, yet again, to a lot of generous people for helping with this novel: Tommy Blackwell, Jim Lindeman, Becky Rehder, Helen Haught Fanick, Mary Summerall, Marsha Moyer, John Barber, Martin Grantham, Phil Hughes, Stacia Hernstrom, Linda Biel, Leo Bricker, Don Gray, and Eddy Mogollon. And thanks to my readers for understanding I do know the difference between a steer and an intact bull, despite the title of this book. Any errors are my own.

BUM STEER

CHAPTER ONE

At 11:42 p.m. on a Friday in late May, Billy Don Craddock took a deep breath and shoved approximately $142,000 in chips onto the blackjack table in front of him. The sizeable crowd around the table grew even louder than they'd been before. They pressed in tighter, oohing and aahing, giddy with anticipation, knowing they were about to see a great victory or a crushing defeat. They'd be happy either way.

Red O'Brien, meanwhile, standing tight behind Billy Don's left shoulder, was right on the verge of spewing. At the moment, he had at least a quart of cheap beer in his belly, and it was all he could do to stop it from rising up, up, up, and out onto the carpet between his lizard-skin Tony Lamas.

His nerves were shot. For good reason. Half of those chips were his. This was a fifty-fifty deal. Equals. They'd both end up rich—or right back where they'd started. A couple of rednecks living from odd job to odd job.

The blackjack dealer—an artificial redhead in her forties—tipped her head five degrees to the left and called something out to the pit boss, who was stationed in the inner circle formed by the ring of tables. The dealer had to get approval for a bet that large. The pit boss—whom Red had first mistaken for Dennis Farina, until he remembered that Dennis Farina was dead—sauntered over. No rush. Pit bosses didn't rush at Caesar's Palace. It was part of the job description. *Show as little emotion as possible. Appear indifferent, even if a fire breaks out. Be courteous, but never show anything that might be construed as warmth.*

"How much you think this guy spends every week at the tanning salon?" Trina whispered into Red's ear, her hand clasped around his left arm.

Under the circumstances, Red couldn't fully appreciate the wisecrack, but there was no doubt that he appreciated Trina. She'd been keeping company with Red and Billy Don for the better part of two days—ever since Red had spotted her playing Keno and bought her a drink. Then another drink. And another. Followed by dinner. Then more drinks. Tickets to a show. And so on. But she had turned out to be worth every penny, returning his generosity in ways Red could hardly recount to Billy Don without sounding like he was describing one of the many adult movies available in their hotel room.

Trina was a beaut, too. Former showgirl. Blonde hair. Green eyes. More cleavage than Red would see in a solid month back home in Blanco County. Trina might not have been the hottest gal in the casino, but she had to be in the top ten, considering how many of the female gamblers were driving Rascals or pulling oxygen tanks behind them.

The pit boss finally reached the table, surveyed the situation, and eyeballed Billy Don for several seconds. Then he muttered something to the dealer and gave a cool nod of his head.

Game on.

The crowd got even louder.

Every moment of Red's life had been building up to this one critical moment.

The dealer wasted no time, pulling cards from the shoe one at a time and placing them with great precision in front of the five players seated at the table.

Five of spades for the tubby dude in the Los Angeles Lakers jersey.

Queen of hearts for the sorority girl who was too drunk to add.

Nine of clubs for the Arab-looking guy who had been making Red uneasy all night by looking so Arab.

Two of diamonds for Horace Norris, who kept bringing up the fact that he and his wife had retired some years back and had been traveling the country in an RV ever since, and jeez, it was a great way to see America, because it provided the perfect combination of independence, comfort, and affordability.

But nobody cared about any of those people or their cards. None of those players had bet more than sixty dollars on this round. Everyone was waiting to see what Billy Don would be dealt. And here it came.

Bam!

King of spades.

The crowd roared. Good God Almighty, a king. Red's knees almost buckled from relief. He could've wept, he was so happy to see that face card. Trina gave his arm a little squeeze.

The dealer gave herself a card facedown.

Now the second round of cards.

Tubby dude got another five.

Sorority girl got a nine to go with her queen.

Arab guy got a six, for a total of fifteen. A crappy hand, but he deserved it.

Horace Norris got a seven, so he was sitting at nine.

And Billy Don got a four.

The crowd groaned. Red was devastated. Fourteen wasn't the worst possible hand, but it was close.

Then the dealer gave herself a second card, facedown, and flipped her first card up.

It was an ace.

Damn it, damn it, damn it.

Billy Don's odds to win this game had just gone from outstanding to horrible.

The dealer peeked at her second card but did not flip it over. Well, that was a small bit of luck. At least she didn't have a blackjack. If she had, the rules required her to flip it now.

She pointed at tubby dude, who took a six and stood. What an idiot.

Sorority girl, after a moment of blank-faced confusion, said she would stand, too.

Arab guy hit, got an eight, and busted. Good riddance, Osama.

Horace Norris hit, got a jack, and stayed with nineteen. He was beaming.

Billy Don swiveled his enormous head left and right in a show of frustration. He had no choice but to hit. He tapped the felt in front of him.

Red was lightheaded. Woozy. His face was flushed. The odds were good that this card would put Billy Don's hand over 21. They'd lose $142,000, and all their work and planning and effort would go down the drain. Red's dreams were about to come crashing down around him. Why hadn't they stopped one hand earlier? Wasn't $72,000 apiece good enough?

The dealer gave Billy Don a card.

A two.

Son of a bitch. Red couldn't stand this anymore. Now Billy Don had sixteen. No, he hadn't busted, and Red was grateful for that—but now Billy Don had the worst possible hand. Red had learned that unless the dealer had a low card showing—a two, three, four, five or six—you had to hit on a sixteen. If you didn't, more times than not, you'd lose. Of course, you were likely to lose hitting on a sixteen, too, but the odds weren't quite as bad if you hit. You were probably screwed either way, but you were less likely to be screwed if you hit.

So Billy Don tapped the felt again.

Red wanted to hold up his hands and call time. Or pull a fire alarm. Or vomit on the table. Do something—anything—to prevent the inevitable high card that was about to bust Billy Don's hand.

The dealer slapped it down. An ace.

Seventeen. Thank you, Lord, Billy Don now had seventeen.

"Stand," he said.

Red let out a long, beer-fouled breath. It was out of their hands now. Billy Don—bless his enormous heart—had done his part, just as he'd said he would.

Now it came down to the luck of the draw.

The dealer used her ace to flip her hole card over. It was going to be an eight or a nine. Had to be. And that would beat seventeen, and the game would be over.

But it was a three.

Red was starting to giggle with tension. He might just lose his mind.

So many low cards. Where were all the face cards?

The dealer gave herself another card. Another goddamn ace.

Now she had fifteen.

This was crazy.

The pit boss was watching. Actually showing interest. He couldn't believe it himself.

The dealer gave herself a fourth card.

There was no explanation for what Red was seeing. The dealer had just dealt herself another frigging ace. It was a six-deck shoe, so it contained 24 aces, but the odds that four of those aces would show up in one hand—and three for the dealer—were hard for Red to calculate. His stomach was seriously churning. He might have to make a break for the bathroom.

"This is insane," somebody said.

"Never seen anything like it," somebody responded.

Now the dealer had sixteen. She still had to hit. The rules required it.

She reached for the shoe, pulled her fifth card, and slapped it onto the felt.

CHAPTER TWO

19 days earlier

Rodney Bauer was woken by a gunshot at 2:17 a.m., but he stayed in bed, eyes closed, doing his best to ignore it. The shot wasn't close, like right outside his house, but it wasn't all that far away, either. Maybe a quarter-mile.

"You hear that?" Rodney's wife Mabel said, propping herself up on her elbows.

Just fucking great.

Rodney pretended he was still asleep, but he knew it wouldn't do much good, because Mabel was more obstinate than any creature alive, on two legs or four. But he loved her. He had to, right? Why else would he have put up with her for the past 17 years? It was because he loved her.

"Rodney!" she hissed.

He knew what would come next. She'd hiss his name once more, then give him an elbow to the ribs. Why did he always ignore her, knowing that he'd have to answer sooner or later? Didn't make sense. He supposed it was a matter of pride. Was he supposed to jump every time she barked at him? What kind of man would he be if he did that?

"Rodney," she hissed again, and then she elbowed him in the ribs.

"Goddamn, Mabel, what is it?"

"You hear that shot?"

"I heard it."

He and Mabel owned more than three hundred acres in Blanco

County, and it wasn't uncommon to hear a late-night shot now and again. Neighbors hunting pigs with spotlights. More power to 'em, that was Rodney's opinion. Shoot every damn wild pig you see. Destructive bastards. Invasive. Ugly. Smelly. A hazard to motorists.

"You gonna go see what's going on?" Mabel said.

"Wasn't planning on it. Pig hunters."

"Wrong direction for pig hunters," Mabel said. "That was either in our pasture or out on the county road."

Rodney didn't reply.

He hated to admit it, but she was right. Pig hunters accounted for most of the shots they heard after dark, but those shots came from a different direction. That shot a minute ago was probably—or at least possibly—a poacher. They'd cruise the county road, stick a rifle out a truck window, and pop a deer in Rodney's west pasture. Happened more often in the fall, when the bucks had antlers, but that didn't rule out a random bit of poaching in the springtime, when freezers were getting bare. The poachers were a genuine danger, too, because Rodney's house was just beyond the trees. A bullet could come thumping through one of the walls. Scary, for sure.

On the other hand, what the hell was Rodney supposed to do about it? Roam around in the dark and tangle with armed poachers? That's what game wardens were for. In fact, Rodney's tax dollars would be going to waste if he didn't let the game warden do his job. That was more than enough reason for Rodney to stay right here, in bed, under the covers.

Then he heard a second shot.

"Rod-NEY!" Mabel said, using that inflection that meant she was dead serious now, and he'd be in deep shit if he didn't get on the ball immediately.

"Okay," he said, hoisting his sizeable self out of bed. "Okay. Jesus. I'm going. But if I wind up getting shot, remember who sent me out there."

He could've walked the short distance to the pasture—it was no more than two hundred yards—but he figured he'd be safer, or at least he'd *feel* safer, if he drove his Chevy truck. He had a big Maglite flashlight on the seat beside him, along with his .357, plus a Q-beam million-candlepower spotlight. Shine that in some redneck's eyes and he'd be blind for a good, long time.

Rodney followed the worn caliche path that branched off from the driveway and made a mildly twisting route through the cedars and oaks between the house and the pasture. He had to pause at one point to wait for a cluster of three cows to get out of the way. Dumb animals. He had fifteen head of Hereford on his little ranch, and he hated dealing with them. You had to vaccinate them and worm them and feed them and protect them from predators. Wasn't hardly worth it. But if he got rid of the cattle and lost his agricultural valuation, his property taxes would skyrocket. Damn government.

The stupid cows finally lumbered out of the way and Rodney moved forward again, through the trees, and now the pasture came into view. He saw no lights. No shadowy figures running for the county road. No poachers. No nothing.

He slowed and turned sharply to the right, so the pasture was to his left, and he stopped there for a moment. He grabbed the Q-beam, turned it on, and began to slowly sweep the field with it. Damn, that sucker was bright. Rodney saw nothing but tall grass and a cluster of seven or eight cows, standing and waiting, expecting to be fed, even though it was the middle of the night. Idiots.

Then the light passed over something odd, and Rodney went back to it.

A cow on the ground. Wait, not a cow. His bull. And it wasn't bedded down, it was flat in the grass from horns to hoof. Something wasn't right.

Rodney whipped the wheel left and drove toward the bull. When he got within ten yards, he saw blood on the animal's head. Lots of it. Well, for fuck's sake. What was going on here?

Rodney edged closer, getting nervous now, and wondering if some asshole had shot his bull. Seemed obvious that's what had happened. He came to a stop fifteen feet from the bull, with the headlights bathing the animal in a harsh glow.

Before getting out of the truck, Rodney once again swept the surrounding pasture with the Q-Beam, to make sure nobody was lingering in the darkness, ready to pounce. He saw nothing.

So he got out of the truck, flashlight in his left hand and .357 in his right, and approached the bull. It wasn't merely wounded, it was stone dead. No question about that. No movement at all. No ribs rising and fall. No twitching.

The bull was lying with his back to the truck, hooves pointing in the same direction as the headlights, so Rodney began to circle around the fallen animal.

That's when he saw an object sticking out from under the bull's sternum.

Rodney froze.

It was an arm.

Blanco County game warden John Marlin stood twenty feet from the two dead bodies—the massive Hereford and the still-unidentified woman underneath it—and said, "No gun. Unless it's underneath the bull, too."

He was answering Sheriff Bobby Garza, who just moments earlier had said, "What's the first thing that pops out at you?"

The sun hadn't yet risen above the nearby treetops, but there was plenty of light now for the team of responders to see what they were doing. Hours earlier, Garza had made the decision that they wouldn't process the scene until they had more light.

He had called Marlin an hour ago and asked him to stop by to offer his opinion on what had taken place. After all, Marlin was one of the few law-enforcement officers in the county with more experience than the sheriff. Marlin was happy to oblige, because he and the sheriff worked well together. Garza often asked Marlin to take an active role in larger investigations, and this could very well turn into just such a case.

At the moment, Henry Jameson, the young and meticulous crime-scene technician who served five counties west of Austin, was taking dozens of photographs. Lem Tucker, the medical examiner, was waiting patiently nearby, chatting with Chief Deputy Bill Tatum, who had been first on the scene.

"If we don't find a gun," Garza said, "that means at least one other person was here. And why didn't they call it in?"

Marlin could hear the low rumble of a diesel engine coming from the direction of Rodney's house.

He said, "Guess that depends on what they were doing out here. And on what kind of injuries she might have. Was she crushed by the bull or was she dead already?"

"Meaning she might have been shot, too? Or she shot herself?"

"Who knows?" Marlin said. "Maybe she shot the bull and it fell on her."

"Rodney said there were two shots. Looks like the bull has only one wound."

"Are we even certain that wound is from a shot?" Marlin said.

Garza shook his head, meaning he didn't know what to think.

"I'm seeing blood, or what looks like blood, on the tip of this bull's left horn," Henry called out. "Not spatter. A consistent coating from the tip of the horn and down to about four inches."

"Ouch," Garza said to Marlin. The unspoken assumption was that the bull had gored the woman. Or someone else. Or some other animal.

"Did Rodney have an opinion on whether it was a rifle or a handgun?" Marlin asked.

"He couldn't tell," Garza said.

The rumble was getting louder.

"Guess we might as well hold off on the speculation for now," Garza said. "We won't have to wait much longer."

Henry Jameson stepped back and gave a wave, meaning he had processed the scene as much as possible with the bull in place. Right on cue, Deputy Ernie Turpin pulled up on a John Deere tractor they were borrowing from a nearby neighbor.

"Looks like he knows how to drive that thing," Marlin said.

"Ernie runs a tractor on his uncle's place from time to time," Garza said.

"What's the plan?" Marlin asked.

He knew they couldn't simply drag the bull off the body. Evidence might be destroyed.

"We're gonna see if we can lift him straight up," Garza said.

"That sucker's gotta weigh two thousand pounds," Marlin said. "Can that little tractor handle that much weight?"

"I sure hope so."

Tatum gave hand signals as Turpin backed the tractor into place, with the backhoe positioned directly over the bull. Then Turpin hopped from the driver's seat and he and Tatum clamped cables around each of the bull's legs, plus one more around his neck. The process took a good twenty minutes.

Turpin returned to the driver's seat and looked at Garza, who gave a go-ahead nod. Turpin began to slowly lift the bull, and it appeared that it was going to go smoothly—until the tractor's front wheels began to lift off the ground.

Tatum approached the tractor and said something to Turpin, but Marlin couldn't make it out over the diesel engine. Then Tatum walked around to the front of the tractor and stepped onto the shovel, which was just a foot or so off the ground. The chief deputy was broad and heavily muscled from years of lifting weights. His two hundred pounds would act to counterbalance the lifting of the bull.

It worked. The bull rose, legs first, then its sagging midsection, and now the carcass was completely off the ground. The tractor's front wheels stayed put.

"Who says country cops can't get the job done?" Garza said to Marlin, grinning.

Turpin slowly toted the bull away, but all eyes were focused on the corpse that remained. She was facing Marlin and Garza. Her eyes were open and fixed in a vacant, faraway stare.

Marlin's immediate assessment: Young woman. Mid- or late twenties. No more than five feet tall. Ninety pounds. Medium-length bleached-blond hair. Dressed in faded blue jean shorts and a white T-shirt with a Luckenbach logo on the front. The center of the shirt was soaked with blood, which was now reddish-brown.

"You see a gun anywhere?" Garza said.

Henry stepped closer to take more pictures, sketch the scene, write some notes, and collect any evidence he might find. Everyone else kept their distance for the time being. Henry was in charge.

"Nope," Marlin said. "No gun."

"See a gun, Henry?" Garza called out.

"No, sir."

"Any shells?"

"Nope."

"Footprints?"

"Sorry, no. Ground's too rocky."

Now Henry studied the body for several moments, looking the woman over from head to toe. Checking for other injuries or defensive wounds. Noting lividity. Taking more photographs.

"Looks like she has a wound to the abdomen," Henry said. "Her shirt is torn, and there's blood around the tear."

"Can you see the wound itself?" Garza asked.

"Nope."

Could be a bullet wound. Could be a gore wound. Could be something else entirely. Lem Tucker would shed more light on that later.

"Got a small tattoo on her right wrist," Henry said. "It's the Texas flag, about an inch wide."

Another series of photographs.

Henry was meticulous, and Marlin was hoping the technician would find some evidence of obvious value. But that didn't happen.

Eventually Henry stood upright and looked toward Lem. "She's all yours."

CHAPTER THREE

Billy Don was almost ready. Red could feel it. For seven months now, they had been practicing blackjack—morning, noon, and night—and Billy Don was almost ready.

"You ain't nowhere near ready," Red said.

"Why the hell not?" Billy Don said, looking a little miffed.

Billy Don was seated in his regular spot on the couch, sunk way down low because he was so damn big. Six foot four and three hundred pounds. Maybe three hundred and ten now, because they'd been consuming so much junk food and beer during their card sessions. Not getting much exercise. What they call a sedimentary lifestyle.

Red was sitting in a chair he had drug in from the kitchen dinette way back in October, so he could deal to Billy Don across the cable-spool coffee table. Since then, they had played thousands of hands. Maybe tens of thousands. Worn through several decks of cards. And Billy Don was almost ready.

"You almost forgot to split those eights," Red replied.

"Did not. I'd do that in my sleep."

"Then why did you pause for a second?"

"Was thinking about supper."

"You just had lunch."

"Exactly. So thinking about supper is only logical. It wouldn't make any sense if I was thinking about breakfast, would it?"

Red shook his head. "You can't get distracted for even a second, Billy Don. Do that in Vegas and we'll be dead meat."

"Sorry, what? I wasn't paying attention."

"Funny."

"Come on, Red. I'm as ready as I'm ever gonna be. Time to fish or cut bait. When are we gonna do this?"

Red started to argue, but then he tossed the remaining cards on the table and leaned back in his chair. "Maybe you're right."

Billy Don appeared startled. Wasn't often Red admitted Billy Don might be right. Red tended to be a skeptic about most things the big man said. In fact, when Billy Don first mentioned that he was a damn good blackjack player, Red assumed it was nonsense—just some drunken bragging. But at the time, both men were sitting on the better part of $25,000 after winning a contest involving a bounty on a particular wild pig, and Red had been looking for a promising investment opportunity.

Like gambling.

So he'd decided to see if Billy Don was exaggerating about his card-playing skills. Wouldn't take more than a few hands to figure that out. Except, lo and behold, it turned out Billy Don was telling the truth. He was a smooth player, and faster than hell at adding up the numbers. Billy Don would tap the table, meaning he wanted another card, or wave his hand over his cards, meaning he wanted to stand, just a split second after a new card had hit the table. It was impressive.

"Where the hell did you learn how to play?" Red had asked on that first day.

"When I was a kid." And that was all he said.

"And...?" Red said.

"My old man was a gambler. Used to make me deal to him all damn day. I hated it, but I learned the game inside out. Passed math that year 'cause I learned to add real fast."

In the years that the two men had known each other, not once had Billy Don ever mentioned either of his parents. Red had gathered from vague comments that Billy Don hadn't spoken to them in years. Or maybe they were dead. Or in prison.

"How old were you?" Red asked.

"Ten or eleven."

"Ever go gambling with him?"

"Once."

Red waited. Billy Don said nothing.

"And...?" Red said.

"And what?"

"What happened?"

"We went to Vegas when I was about sixteen. I was big enough they didn't card me. Hell, I was drinking beer the whole time.

Acting like a big shot, even though I was nervous as hell. My old man drug me along 'cause he said I was a better player than he was, and he was right. See, you learn when to hit and when to stay, when to split, double down, and all that stuff. There are charts you can memorize that tell you what to do. But there are other times when you're operating on nothing more than a gut feeling. Sometimes you gotta go with it. I was always good at that part."

"So you ignore the charts?" Red said.

"Not really. Sometimes. Or you don't. Maybe you follow the chart but increase your bet, because the cards are falling in your favor. Sometimes you just know a face card is coming your way, or at least an eight or a nine—enough to give you a winning hand."

"You talking about counting cards?" Red said.

"Hell, no. They'll toss you for that. I'm talking about having a feel for the shoe—knowing when it's running hot and you should ride it as long as you can. That's about the only way I can explain it."

This was a side of Billy Don that Red had never seen before. Billy Don could hardly follow the directions on a jar of instant coffee. How in the hell could he kick ass at something as tricky as blackjack?

"So what happened?" Red said.

"When?"

"In Vegas with your daddy."

"Oh. Well, we rented a big ol' Cadillac and drove straight to Barbary Coast, because that was the only place he'd go. He gave me a thousand bucks to play with, and I think he was playing with three or four grand. Two days later, he was up by about ten grand. The next day, he lost it all. Gotta remember, this was a lot of money back then."

"It's a lot of money now."

"No shit."

"And how'd you do?" Red said.

"I turned that thousand bucks into seventy-three hundred."

"No, you didn't."

Red was mesmerized. He couldn't help it. Billy Don had a hidden talent. It was like suddenly learning your basset hound can ride a bicycle.

"Sure as hell did. Daddy went back to the car rental place and offered 'em five grand for that Caddy. They took it, and we headed for home the next day, feeling like we owned the damn world."

Red was intrigued. And an idea was taking shape. What if he

and Billy Don went to Vegas with their pig-bounty money? Was it unreasonable to think Billy Don might be able to double or triple it? It would be like something out of *Rain Man*.

"Didn't last long, though," Billy Don added, "because Daddy couldn't resist stopping in Laughlin later that night. He lost the Caddy and most of the money we had left."

Of course, Red was willing to concede there might be some risks involved. What investment didn't have risks?

"Was that the only time you played?" Red asked.

"Oh, hell, no. I played eight or ten times a year for a couple of years. I'd fly out one morning, play all day and all night, then come home the next day."

"Did you win most of the time?"

"Overall," Billy Don said, "yeah. I came out ahead. Way ahead. Got lucky."

Red ignored those last two words. He figured a gambler couldn't win consistently because of luck. Had to be skill—and the good grace of God Almighty shining down on you, wanting you to win.

Ever since that conversation, seven months ago, Red's opinion had not changed, because Billy Don had done nothing but play more skillfully with each practice session. Now it was late in May, and Billy Don was ready.

Red was about to tell him that when he heard a vehicle coming up his rutted caliche driveway. Judging by the sound of an oilpan scraping on a rock, it was a low-riding vehicle—a car, not a truck. Now it sounded more like two vehicles, judging by all the noise.

Red got up and went to the nearest window.

It wasn't two vehicles. It was a battered Ford Ranchero. Beige with a gold stripe. Cracks across the windshield caught the sunlight. No license plate in front. The fan belt was emitting an annoying squeal. It was towing a shiny new livestock trailer.

"Who is it?" Billy Don said. He had managed to extract himself from the sinkhole in the couch and was now at Red's side.

"No idea."

"Expecting anyone?"

"Nope."

Red didn't get many guests, and most of his unexpected visitors were driving cars owned by the government.

"He's gonna have a hell of a time getting that trailer back down the hill," Billy Don said.

Red opened the front door and stepped out onto the porch. He couldn't make out the driver. Too much glare off the glass. But it looked like just one person in the car.

The driver pulled right behind Red's truck as if he belonged there. Then he got out of the car. Skinny guy. Scraggly blond hair past his shoulders. Needed a shave. Sallow complexion. Wearing a stained T-shirt and blue jeans.

"*Hola!*" he called. "*Cómo estás?*"

"Howdy."

The man waited a beat, then said, "Hell, I expected more of reception than that. I know it's been ten or twelve years since I seen ya, but damn."

Red squinted at him.

"You don't recognize me, do ya?" the stranger said. He pulled his sunglasses off. "That help?"

"'Fraid not."

The man stepped closer, now about fifteen feet away. "I lost about thirty pounds. Let my hair grow out."

Red looked closer. Studied the man's face. And suddenly Red had to grin. "Shelby?"

The man spread his arms, presenting himself. "In the flesh."

"Been a long time," Red said. "Goddamn."

"It has. How the hell are ya?"

"Doing great. Come on inside and take a load off."

As Shelby came up the porch steps, Red noticed that the stains on his tank top weren't just dirt or oil.

"Where'd all the blood come from?" Red said as the men shook hands. "You okay?"

Shelby laughed. "That, my dear cousin, is a long story—but I'll tell it in exchange for a cold *cerveza*."

CHAPTER FOUR

It was ten minutes after two and Marlin had just sent a text to Nicole—*How are you feeling?*—when Sheriff Garza appeared in his office doorway. "Got a minute?"

"Sure. What's up?"

"Got a little bit of personnel news this morning," Garza said, taking a seat in the chair across from Marlin's desk. "Brace yourself. Bill is retiring."

"Wow. Seriously?"

"He gave notice this morning. One month. He warned me at the start of the year that he was thinking about it. But still…"

"Man. It'll be weird around here."

Bill Tatum had put in more years at the Blanco County Sheriff's Office than anyone who had ever worked there. He had slowly worked his way up from reserve deputy to full time to chief deputy. He probably could've been elected sheriff at some point, if he had been interested.

"Won't be easy to find a replacement," Garza said. "I've been keeping a list of possible candidates, just in case, but most of them have already landed somewhere."

"You want to hire or promote from within?" Marlin thought Ernie Turpin would make a solid chief, but he kept that opinion to himself for the time being.

"I've been putting some thought into that," Garza said. "If I promote, I'll still need to hire a new deputy. In fact, we could really use two, but you know how the budget is. In the meantime, Bill has a lot of loose ends to wrap up, so I'm wondering…" Garza grinned at him.

"If I can help with that new case."

"Mind reader. You got time? What is it, turkey season? I know you're busy with that."

"No, I can help." Marlin enjoyed assisting with cases that didn't typically fall within his capacity as a game warden.

"That would be great. Fortunately, I have some good news right off the bat. A guy on a Harley was riding down A. Robinson Road this morning when something in the ditch caught his eye. He turned around and saw that it was a woman's handbag. So the guy brought it in about an hour ago. You know where I'm going with this."

"It belonged to our Jane Doe," Marlin said. "And now we have an ID."

Garza was already nodding.

Up to now, the woman found underneath the bull had not been identified. When Lem Tucker had gotten her to the morgue, he'd found no wallet or ID in her pockets. No keys or phone. Nothing on her that could be used to reveal who she was. There had been no worried phone calls about a missing woman. Henry had run her fingerprints and come up empty.

Lem, however, had confirmed that the woman had suffered a gore injury. No gunshot. She had possibly bled out from that wound, but Lem would have to conduct an autopsy to determine whether being crushed by the bull had contributed to her death.

Garza said, "April Elaine Thornton. Twenty-nine years old. Married at twenty-one, divorced at twenty-three. No kids. Lives several miles south of Goldthwaite."

"In Mills County or San Saba County?"

"San Saba. No warrants, no record. That's all we have right now. I just left a voicemail for her father. Waiting on a callback."

Marlin knew how that would go. Break the sad news. Extend sympathy. But Garza would have to ask some questions. Who were April's closest friends? Any idea who she was with yesterday or last night? When was the last time you communicated with her? Who did she live with? Did she have a boyfriend? A girlfriend? Where did she work? What did she drive? Any idea where her vehicle is right now? And lots more.

Obviously April had been out in that pasture with somebody, and they needed to figure out who that person was. It was possible that person had contributed to April's death.

"Any guesses as to what they were doing out there?" Garza said.

"Could've been a lot of things," Marlin said. "Poaching. Looking for a place to fool around. Planning a burglary, because

Rodney's house is set behind all those trees. They could've been rustling."

"Don't see much of that."

"Yeah, but it happens. You know as well as I do that people will steal anything that isn't bolted down."

"And if it's bolted down, they'll steal some bolt cutters."

"That's about right. Not just livestock, but trailers, saddles, feeders, and whatever else they can get their hands on. I remember a time maybe twenty years ago when a couple of idiots tried to dig a cattle guard out of the ground over near Round Mountain."

"So how does the average rustler go about it? Stealing a cow. Or cows."

"Couple of ways," Marlin said. His phone vibrated in his hand. "They usually bring their own trailer, but they'll use the owner's loading chutes. They'll look for cattle already penned for market, then cut fences to drive the trailer over there. Then they just run the cattle through the chute, load up, and drive away. It can be a pretty elaborate operation, where they steal 10 or 15 head, or it can be a quick deal where they grab one and go."

"But in general these are people who've worked cattle before, right?" Garza said. "It's not like somebody spontaneously says, 'Hey, I know what we can do tonight. Let's go steal a cow!'"

"No, but I did catch some college kids with a heifer in the back of a Suburban once. That's the exception. They had about fifteen guys in that vehicle, plus the cow, and their rear axle broke. Good times."

Marlin glanced at his phone. A text from Nicole. *Feels like the flu. Weird this time of year.*

She was probably right, but Marlin couldn't help worrying, considering the surgery Nicole had had late last year.

Garza said, "What do you do with a stolen cow? Sell it?"

"If you can, yeah," Marlin said. "Try to sell it at an auction barn, maybe after altering the brand. Or keep the stolen cattle for breeding, then sell the calves."

His phone vibrated and he snuck another look.

Just took my temp. Mild fever.

"This here's my friend Billy Don Craddock," Red said, ushering his cousin into the mobile home.

"Hey, there," Shelby said.

Billy Don shook Shelby's hand. "How you doing?"

"Damn, you're a big ol' boy, ain't ya?"

"Big enough for most things," Billy Don said.

"Shelby's my cousin," Red said. "One of many."

The three men stood silently in the living area for a moment. Red was wondering what had brought his cousin to his house after all these years. Shelby lived just north of Cherokee in San Saba County, a good hour's drive away, and the last thing Red had heard through the grapevine, going back several years, was that Shelby was facing charges for stealing a deer rifle out of a rancher's hunting cabin. Red wasn't going to ask about that, because he didn't really care how it had turned out.

"How 'bout that beer?" Shelby said, grinning again. He seemed to grin a lot.

"Help yourself," Red said, pointing toward the ice chest resting on the floor beside the couch. He and Billy Don always kept cold beer nearby whenever they were playing cards. Or hunting. Or watching football. Or just sitting around.

Shelby raised the lid and grabbed a Keystone tall boy. "Y'all need one?"

"Sure," Red said,

"Why not?" Billy Don said.

Shelby passed beers around and the men got settled—Billy Don back on the couch, or really *in* the couch, Red in his recliner, and Shelby on the dinette chair.

"Y'all been playing cards?" Shelby said, nodding at the deck on the coffee table.

"Just goofing around," Red said, not inclined to share their Vegas plan with his cousin.

"Cool," Shelby said, nodding.

"So let's hear it," Red said.

"Huh?" Shelby said.

"The long story," Red said. "About the blood on your shirt."

Shelby began shaking his head and grinning some more. "Yeah, that's kind of a weird deal. See, this ol' boy offered to buy that trailer from me. Only problem is, he moved to Blanco a couple of months ago, so I had to shag my ass all the way down there, which is a hassle I don't need. Anyway, I get to his place and he starts saying he never wanted the trailer, that I must've been confused. So I play him the voicemail he left, where he offers me two thousand bucks, and he says it don't matter, he's changed his mind. I might've called him some names after that, and he took a swing at me, so I got him in a headlock and punched him in the nose. Bled like a sumbitch."

Red waited for the conclusion.

"Then I left," Shelby said.

"Wasn't really a long story," Red said.

"Yeah, I guess not."

"But at least you got to kick the guy's ass."

"Guess so."

"That trailer's worth more than two thousand," Billy Don said.

"Yeah, I know," Shelby said. "But times are tight. You wanna buy it? Make an offer."

"I'm all set for livestock trailers," Billy Don said.

"What's his name?" Red said.

"Huh?"

"What's the guy's name? Maybe I know him."

Shelby lifted his beer and drank about half of it. Then he said, "Oh, I doubt it. His name is Tom."

"Last name?"

"I don't even know."

Red thought that was odd. This guy Tom was going to buy a trailer and Shelby didn't even know his full name?

"Where's he live?" Red asked.

"Huh?"

Shelby was bouncing his knee up and down. Fidgety.

"Where does Tom live?"

"Out off one of those county roads west of Blanco. Don't remember which one. I already tossed the map out the window."

Red didn't know how to reply. Something wasn't quite right. Red was known to fabricate a story on occasion, and being somewhat of an authority on it, he got the feeling Shelby was fabricating his ass off. Why? Better question: Did it matter? Why should Red care if a cousin he hadn't seen in years wanted to tell some weird story about punching some dude in the face?

"Well, it's good to see you," Red said. "You look like you're doing okay."

Which was an example of Red doing some fabricating himself. Shelby didn't look all that great, despite losing thirty pounds. His hair was thin, his teeth were in bad shape, and he had a couple of infected bug bites, or some kind of sore, on his cheeks.

"I was in the neighborhood, so I thought I'd drop by," Shelby said.

Red drank some beer. So did Billy Don.

"Actually, I also need to ask a favor," Shelby said.

Here it comes, Red thought.

"Yeah?" Red said.

"Somehow I ran off yesterday without my wallet. And since the trailer deal fell through, I'm flat broke. Any chance you could loan me a few bucks?"

Red did his best to keep the irritation from showing on his face. "How much?"

"I don't know. Maybe fifty? Gas to get back home. I really hate to put you out, but I'm in a tight spot. Don't know anybody else in Blanco County."

Red resisted pointing out that Shelby could get home to Cherokee with just fifteen or twenty dollars' worth of gas, even pulling a trailer.

"Guess I wouldn't mind getting a bite to eat, too," Shelby said, as if he'd picked up on Red's thoughts. "Haven't eaten since lunch yesterday."

"We got some leftover pizza," Billy Don said.

"Where'd you stay last night?" Red asked, quickly changing the subject. He didn't want Shelby hanging around and eating all their food.

"Slept in the Ranchero. Wasn't sure what to do, and then I remembered you about an hour ago."

"Lucky me," Red said.

Shelby grinned.

"You ain't got a credit card?" Red said.

"I'm over my limit," Shelby said. "Been a rough year."

Red pulled his wallet out and snuck a look inside. Two twenties, a ten, three fives, and four singles. "All I got is a twenty," Red said, holding a bill out toward Shelby. "Sorry."

"Oh, hey, better'n nothing," Shelby said, taking it from Red's hand. "Really appreciate it. I'll mail you a check when I get home."

Yeah, right. "Don't worry about it."

"I got a better idea," Shelby said. "Hang on a sec." He turned and went out the door, then came back a minute later carrying a plastic Walmart sack. "Here you go," he said. "It's all yours."

Red peeked inside and saw a Reconyx trail camera.

"That sucker costs six hundred bucks brand new," Shelby said. "Top of the line model. Infrared and all that shit. High-def video. That's a fair trade, ain't it?"

"Where'd you get it?" Red said.

"Just an extra one I don't need," Shelby said.

"Don't I need a computer to make this work?" Red said.

"Well, kind of, but it's got a built-in viewing screen, so you can get by with that for the time being. All the little extras are in there, including a card viewer."

Red wasn't sure what a card viewer was, but he wasn't interested enough to ask.

The men made small talk for a few more minutes, then Shelby downed the last of his beer and said, "I gotta take off. You mind if I grab a roadie?"

"Help yourself," Red said, sounding anything but hospitable.

Shelby pulled another tallboy out of the ice chest, thanked both men, and then went outside and climbed in his car.

Red and Billy Don moved out onto the porch to watch him go.

"Dude's on meth," Billy Don said.

That thought had never occurred to Red, but now that Billy Don had said it, Red realized it explained everything about Shelby's behavior—the way he seemed jittery and nervous. The weight loss. The bad teeth. The sores on his face. The money problems.

"Well, duh," Red said. "It was obvious."

Shelby was doing his best to maneuver back down the hill, and it wasn't working out so well.

"Bet that trailer's hot," Billy Don said. "So is that trail camera."

That hadn't occurred to Red, either, but it would explain why Shelby was willing to sell the trailer so cheap, and why he gave Red an expensive trail camera in exchange for $20. Not that Red had any qualms about possessing a stolen item.

"Way ahead of you on that one," he said.

"Hundred bucks he backs into a cedar tree," Billy Don said.

CHAPTER FIVE

All the way back to San Saba County, Shelby had thoughts of hauling ass, just as he'd had those same thoughts all night long, sitting in the Ranchero, trying to wrap his mind around what had happened. Simply run. Take off. California. Montana. Mexico. Somewhere far away.

Could he assume a new identity? Start over? Was that even possible these days? How would he go about it? He had no money—in his pockets, at home, or in the bank. How do you make a fresh start with nothing? How do you stay hidden for years at a time?

It wasn't the cops he was worried about. Hell, no. If the cops were his only concern, everything would be peachy. Might have to serve some time, but that sure beat the alternative.

No, the problem—or the threat, really—was the man Shelby was about to meet with face to face. Knox.

April's brother.

Shelby turned on the deteriorating county road that led to Knox's trailer. Three miles to go, and the road now went from pavement to gravel. Like driving over a washboard. Running on fumes right now.

A list of crazy things Knox had done in the past year alone:

Poisoned his neighbor's donkey for braying too much.

Threw a guy over the back rail of the bleachers during a San Saba High School football game.

Silenced a witness. Permanently.

Where Knox lived, way out in the boonies, it would be easy to make someone disappear. Gone without a trace. Shelby knew that could happen to him. And how hard would the San Saba County sheriff's department look for a guy like Shelby? Answer: Not real hard.

Shelby did have a plan, of course. Not the truth. Fuck, no. If he told the truth, he'd probably be dead within the hour. Instead, he was going to tell a story that was close to the truth, but not quite. The idea had come to him on the drive home.

Two miles to go.

He popped open another beer. Number five. He'd bought a cheap six-pack and used the rest of the money for gas. Had to get a buzz to do what he needed to do. Alcohol would have to suffice, because he didn't have anything else.

One mile to go.

He stopped for a moment—right there in the middle of the county road—and took a massive piss. Then he drove on. Slowly. Had to get his head right. Keep his story straight. And hope he made it through to the other side. Then the time had come. Knox's driveway was just up ahead. Shelby eased off the gas and made the turn, with the livestock trailer still following behind him.

Knox had heard him coming and was waiting on the porch, which didn't surprise Shelby at all. He and April should've been home hours ago. Knox had probably been calling her phone. Thinking they'd been caught.

Shelby parked in the gravel turnaround in front of the trailer and slowly got out. He was scared. Didn't need to fake that.

Knox was already coming down the steps. Didn't offer a greeting. Simply said, "Where's April?"

Not worried at this point. Curious. Confused, maybe. Impatient, for sure.

"I got some bad news, Knox. Real bad news." Shelby was stuck between the Ranchero and the mobile home. If things went south, he had nowhere to run.

Knox stopped. Frowned. He wasn't a big man, but he had a way of seeming larger than he really was, and of making you understand that you'd have to be an idiot to take him on. You could always see it in his face. In the way he carried himself.

"What happened?" Knox said.

"We had a problem."

"I got that, but what happened? She get arrested?"

Shelby was shaking his head. On the verge of crying. "Worse than that. I don't... Knox, I'm afraid to—"

"Spit it out, Shel."

"There was an accident. She's dead, Knox. April is dead. I'm so sorry."

For a brief moment, maybe three seconds, Shelby saw a Knox he'd never seen before. The confidence was gone. The withering glare evaporated. He was knocked back, breathless and panicked by what he'd just heard.

Then, in an instant, his face transformed into rage, and now he was coming at Shelby fast.

"It was my cousin," Shelby said just as Knox grabbed him. "He screwed everything up."

CHAPTER SIX

The following afternoon, John Marlin was heading for the break room, preparing to grab some coffee before a meeting with Bobby Garza. He stepped into the doorway just as a woman was coming out.

"Pardon me," Marlin said, expecting the woman—tall and brunette—to move left or right and let him pass. But she didn't.

"Hey, there, John Marlin," she said, grinning. "Fancy running into you."

He took a closer look at her face and recognized her instantly. It had been a long time since he'd seen her—decades, actually—but she hadn't changed much. Still a beauty. Same blue eyes he remembered. Slender. Athletic. And those dimples. A few crow's feet, but otherwise, the years had hardly touched her.

"Lauren?"

"Good memory. Dang, you're even more handsome than you used to be, if that's possible. How about a hug?"

Marlin moved forward and embraced her—friendly, but professional—then stepped back. Her scent lingered. The same perfume she'd worn way back when?

He said, "So you're—"

"Good. You two are meeting," Bobby Garza said from the hallway behind Marlin.

"Morning," Marlin said, somewhat confused.

He moved aside to let Garza pass. At the same time, he studied the badge on Lauren's shirt. It was round, with the head of a longhorn bull superimposed over a five-point star. Now he understood why she was here.

She was a special ranger with the Texas and Southwestern Cattle Raisers Association—fully commissioned as a peace officer through the Texas Department of Public Safety. Special rangers investigated cattle theft and other agriculture-related crimes. Just last year, the TSCRA had appointed the first and only female special ranger. Marlin had read the news, but he was only now realizing that Lauren Gilchrist was *this* Lauren. The new last name had prevented him from making the connection. Garza had texted Marlin earlier to see if he could sit down with a special ranger from San Saba County.

"Oh, we met a long time ago," Lauren said, in response to Garza's remark.

"Yeah?" Garza said, proceeding into the break room to get some coffee of his own. "You work together before?"

Lauren looked at Marlin and raised an eyebrow. *You want to answer that?*

"Uh," Marlin said, "no, it was back in college. At Southwest Texas State."

"Oh, right," Garza said. "I bet you had some of the same criminal justice classes."

Lauren was still looking at Marlin, to see if he'd spill the beans.

"Yeah, we did," Marlin said, "and we dated for a while."

"And look at him blush," Lauren said. "It's okay, John. Young people date. Hell, even old gals like me date. You got anyone to set me up with? A twin brother I don't know about?"

Now Garza had turned and was eyeballing Marlin, amused.

"I'm guessing you don't need any help in that department," Marlin said to Lauren. "You look great."

"Thank you. So do you."

Garza said, "Ranger Gilchrist is here to—"

"Please call me Lauren."

"Okay, Lauren is here to talk about the April Thornton case. You probably pieced that together." To Lauren, he said, "John is a very skilled investigator. Quick on the uptake."

"I don't doubt that. He always excelled at everything he did."

Was that a double entendre? Marlin wasn't sure. Lauren's expression didn't indicate that it was. Garza didn't seem to notice anything.

"Why don't we adjourn to my office?" Garza said.

"Lauren, here's where we are so far," Garza said. He was seated behind his desk, with Marlin and Lauren across from him. "John, you already know most of this, so bear with me."

Lauren took a small notepad from her breast pocket and was prepared to jot anything useful down. She was dressed in the unofficial Texas Rangers uniform: crisp, white button-down shirt, pressed jeans, and boots. But she wasn't wearing a Stetson or sport coat, as many of the rangers did. It was a good look on her.

Garza said, "I spoke to April Thornton's parents yesterday afternoon, and it was clear they didn't have contact with their daughter on a regular basis. The family lived between Goldthwaite and San Saba, but the parents retired to Dallas six years ago. The dad told me April had been making bad decisions for too long—partying, not working, that sort of thing—and when she started dating a guy named Shelby Roach, they basically washed their hands of her. This guy Roach has a record for theft and burglary."

"Oh, I'm very familiar with Shelby Roach," Lauren said. "Real winner. But don't let me interrupt."

Garza nodded. "No problem. Jump in whenever you have something to add. We've been trying to track Roach down, but no luck so far. Nobody knows where he is. We've talked to most of April's friends, her brother Knox, coworkers at the bar where she was a waitress, and so on. None of them had contact with her in the 24 hours before she died, and nobody can shed any light as to why she was out in Rodney's pasture—except, I hope, maybe you, Lauren."

Lauren said, "Okay, some quick background, just so you know. April Thornton, her brother Knox, and Shelby Roach all went to school together—first grade all the way through high school. April wasn't a bad kid, but as they say, she ran with the wrong crowd, meaning guys like Shelby, who is your basic garden-variety punk. We're pretty sure he's been involved in a string of thefts in the past few years in San Saba, Mills, and Brown counties, and a handful over in McCulloch and Coleman counties. Most of the thefts have taken place on farms and ranches, the most recent one being a livestock trailer worth about six grand. Most of the time, the thief has been able to just drive in and grab all kinds of stuff. People don't lock things up the way they should."

"Is Shelby Roach any relation to a man named Jeremy Roach?" Marlin asked.

"That was his dad," Lauren said. "He died several years ago. Did you know Jeremy?"

"I knew of him, back when he was one of the few decent deer processors in that area. I think he operated out of Goldthwaite, right?"

"Yes, back in the seventies and eighties. Worked from his ranch."

"I hadn't heard his name in a long time," Marlin said. "Anyway, how did Shelby Roach end up as a suspect in your thefts?"

"His past record, combined with word of mouth, mostly," Lauren said. "People have seen him in the area just prior to stuff going missing. Unfortunately, we have zero physical evidence. No tire tracks, no fingerprints. No eyewitnesses. And Roach learned from his earlier arrests to keep his mouth shut. Now he says talking to cops only gets him in trouble."

"Funny how that works when you're a thief," Garza said.

"Right," Lauren said. "You can understand why my ears perked up when I heard that his girlfriend April was found dead in a cattle pasture. You want my theory, I'd say Roach was out there to steal something—and April was either helping or simply along for the ride—when things went south. Oh, and for bonus points, Roach has a meth habit, so we knew it was only a matter of time before he did something really stupid. I just wish April Thornton hadn't ended up paying the price for associating with such a lowlife."

Blunt talk. Marlin remembered that, too, about Lauren. She spoke her mind, regardless of the subject or the audience.

"Well, Henry did find Roach's fingerprints on the purse," Garza said, "so he might've been with April on Saturday night, but those prints could have been there for days or even weeks."

"Or he put 'em on there when he tossed the purse out the window," Lauren said. "I'm sure he was freaking out, so he wanted to get rid of any evidence that they'd been together that night."

"I assume you're tracking Roach's bank cards," Marlin said.

"Yep, and nothing yet," Garza said. "I've asked Mills County to send a unit past his place a couple times a day to see if they can spot him."

Lauren said, "I'm guessing he hauled ass, pardon my French. He's probably three states away by now, scared to death, and not just of getting busted. Did you happen to check Knox Thornton's background?" She was addressing Garza.

"I saw that he got popped a couple of times for possession of a controlled substance, but both charges were dismissed. He cooperated when I talked to him on the phone yesterday, but he wasn't particularly helpful. He said he had no idea who she'd been hanging with the night she died, and he hadn't talked to Shelby for a couple of days."

Lauren was shaking her head. "Don't believe anything he says. Knox is probably the biggest scumbag in San Saba County, but he's smart enough to stay out of prison. He moves meth, but we don't know where he gets it or whether he has a lab. On one of those possession cases, a witness named Grant Bender disappeared. Bender was a small-time dealer who got some of his inventory from Knox Thornton, and when he got busted, he agreed to testify against Thornton in exchange for a lighter sentence. Then he vanished without a trace. This was about seven months ago. It's still open as a missing-persons case, but I'd bet my life savings Knox buried the guy somewhere. The sheriff has never made any headway because everybody's too scared of Knox to even talk about him, including Shelby."

"Shelby would be scared enough of Knox to hightail it?" Garza said.

"Oh, absolutely."

Marlin said, "If Knox deals and Shelby uses, safe to assume Knox is Shelby's dealer?"

"That would be my guess," Lauren said.

"Any chance they're also partners in crime?" Garza asked.

"We're not sure about that. I don't think Knox would make the mistake of working with Shelby. They're on different levels—that's the best way to describe it. Knox is a pro. Shelby would be the weak link that got everybody busted."

"Okay, good. This has been very helpful," Garza said. "John, Lauren is prepared to hang around for a few days, and I'm hoping y'all can team up and work on this together. That sound all right?"

Marlin could feel Lauren looking at him. And Garza was eyeing him, too, with an expression that seemed to say, *If you don't want to work with your old girlfriend, now's the time to bail out. Sorry to put you on the spot.*

"Sounds good," Marlin said.

Red and Billy Don had taken a break from practicing blackjack, and they were on their way to Johnson City to stock up on groceries when Red noticed something peculiar in his rearview mirror.

"Billy Don, you remember that Ranchero my cousin was driving yesterday?"

"Yep."

"What color was it?"

"Light brown."

"You positive?"

"Well..."

Red waited. Billy Don was leaning his head left and right, as if he were trying to remember.

"So you don't know for sure," Red said.

"Guess not. Why? Who cares what color it was?"

"You think that's it behind us?"

Billy Don glanced in the passenger-side mirror, which was caked with mud, then struggled to turn his great bulk around in the seat and peer out the smudged back window.

The Ranchero—or *a* Ranchero—was fifty yards behind Red's truck. Maintaining the same speed, so it wasn't getting any closer. Red couldn't see if the windshield had cracks running across it, like Shelby's.

"Don't know," Billy Don said. "Why would your cousin still be hanging around? Wasn't he going back to Lampasas?"

"San Saba," Red said, "and, yeah, he was."

He let off the gas and decreased his speed by five miles per hour. After a full minute, the Ranchero had gotten no closer. Red dropped his speed five more miles per hour. The distance between the two vehicles stayed the same. Red sped up, and so did the Ranchero.

"Do you see a front license plate?" Red asked.

"Nope, but I don't remember Shelby's Ranchero missing a license plate."

"It was," Red said, and he was fairly certain he was right.

"Just pull to the shoulder and let him pass," Billy Don said.

So Red did. Used his blinker and everything. Came to a complete and legal stop. Both men turned around and watched.

The Ranchero kept coming, and as it got closer, Red could see that the windshield did have horizontal cracks in it, just like Shelby's Ranchero had.

But when the vehicle passed, it was plainly not Shelby behind the wheel. Some other dude with stringy hair. He glanced casually in the direction of Red's truck. Red gave the dude a nod, but the dude didn't nod back.

"That's so weird," Red said after the Ranchero had gone by. "I would swear that's the same Ranchero."

Billy Don said, "Different color."

Red didn't argue, but Billy Don plainly wasn't sure what color

Shelby's Ranchero was.

"Ain't like you see Rancheros every day, or even every month. When was the last time you saw one before Shelby came over the other day?" Red said.

"Saw an El Camino not too long ago."

"El Caminos are for rednecks. I'm talking about Rancheros."

"Don't know," Billy Don said. "Don't care."

Red pulled back onto the highway.

Why had it seemed like the dude in the Ranchero had been following Red's truck?

Strange, but it had to be a coincidence.

CHAPTER SEVEN

Bobo Baldwin never expected to find $46,000 stashed in a suitcase, but he'd been running his pawnshop for more than three decades, and he'd found some crazy shit over the years.

Like a Dallas Cowboys NFC championship ring buried under a bunch of greasy wrenches in a toolbox.

Half of a mummified human finger stuck in the blade guard of a circular saw.

A Polaroid photo of a '70s-era female pop star snorting coke off her drummer's shaved chest.

Now this.

Bobo had been in the back room—the storage area—rearranging some items because things were getting cramped back there, when he noticed the suitcases. It was one of those three-suitcase sets, where a small case nests inside a medium one that nests inside a large one. Nice luggage, too. Delsey was the brand. Nothing fancy, but sturdy and well made. Derek, Bobo's only employee, must've written the ticket on the suitcases, because Bobo didn't remember doing it himself.

Bobo had been meaning to get himself a decent suitcase for the cruise he and his girlfriend were taking in July. First real vacation in years. Couldn't wait to see Traci in a thong bikini. Half his age with four times his energy.

So Bobo bent down to the lower shelf to pull the nested cases out, just to take a look-see, and he had to move a lot of shit out of the way, and by the time he'd gotten the job done, he was out of breath. Understandable, since he weighed two-ninety and the only exercise he got—other than trying to keep up with Traci—was looking up from his crossword puzzle whenever a customer came through the front door.

But the suitcases. Odd. Heavier than he would've expected, even considering the quality.

So he unzipped the large case and there was the medium case, just as he'd expected. He unzipped the medium case, and there was the small case. He took it out. Yep, there was definitely something in there. Derek was supposed to give every item a thorough inspection after receiving it, because you didn't want to sell someone a power tool with a dried-up appendage attached, or accidentally give away an NFL ring. Plus, it was just good business to sell a clean product, as opposed to a suitcase that might be filled with stinky old clothes or a dead raccoon or who knows what.

Bobo unzipped the small case and saw cash.

Lots of cash.

Most of it in strapped bundles, but some of it loose.

Other than sucking in a breath, he didn't react. Just stared for a long moment. He'd seen large sums of cash before, of course. He kept large sums on hand for some purchases that were off the books.

But this was different, because this cash had fallen into his lap.

Bobo shut the case, waddled quickly into the front room, and locked the door. He scrawled a note and taped it on the glass. *Back in 30 minutes.*

Then he returned to the back room. Opened the small suitcase again. Just eyeballing it, he'd say there was easily thirty grand here. Maybe forty.

Before he touched the cash, he unzipped and checked inside the various other storage compartments on the outside of the case. Empty. Same with the zippered pockets inside the case. Then he did the same thing with the medium and large cases. There was nothing here.

Well, nothing except the tag Derek had attached to the handle of the large case, with a receipt number that would be linked to the owner's name, address, and phone number, along with the date the suitcase set had been brought in. But that information was irrelevant at the moment.

Bobo slowly reached into the small suitcase and began to remove the cash.

Two bundles of hundred-dollar bills.

Three bundles of fifty-dollar bills.

Four bundles of twenty-dollar bills.

Two bundles of ten-dollar bills.

And a bunch of loose fives and ones.

Total amount: $46,408.

Holy fuck. How did this get here? Bobo figured some geezer died and the kids didn't look through everything thoroughly. That's the way it usually happened. Who wants to sort through a bunch of dusty old crap? How would anyone know that nutty old Dad stuck some hundred dollars bills between the pages of a bible, or that Mom put her diamonds in a box of old dishes for safekeeping?

And did it matter how it got here?

The important thing was, Bobo had a decision to make and some questions to answer. Do the right thing or the wrong thing? What were the odds of getting caught? Could anyone ever prove what had happened? Would he be placing himself in danger? He mulled all this over for a grand total of about thirty seconds.

Then he went to his small office and rooted through the drawers in his desk, where he found a paper sack from a liquor store purchase earlier in the week. He returned to the back room, bagged the cash, and put the nested suitcases back just as they had been before. Then he went back to his office and stuck the plump paper sack into the wall safe. Slammed the door shut and spun the dial. Not even Derek knew the combination.

He returned to the front room, removed the note, and unlocked the door.

Act natural, he told himself. *Nobody will ever know.*

Marlin got home at six-fifteen with to-go taco plates. Geist, the pit bull, met him at the door, excited that he was home, and then immediately refocused her attention on the bag in his hand. Marlin left the food on the kitchen countertop and made his way to the master bedroom.

Nicole was in bed, the lights out, the TV on, a humidifier on the dresser quietly humming. She gave him a weak grin. "Hey," she said.

"Hey. How're you doing?"

He moved toward the bed, but she said, "Stop there, okay? I don't want you to catch it."

Marlin stopped five feet away. "Any idea what *it* is?" he said.

"Like I said, it's gotta be the flu, or just a bad cold." She sounded congested.

"Fever the same?"

"Yeah."

"Headache?"

"A little."

"Runny nose?"

"Yep. Throat's a little sore."

"You sure you don't have some kind of allergy?" It was, after all, late spring in central Texas. The air was thick with all manner of pollen.

"None that I know of."

She didn't look horrible, but she was obviously not feeling well.

"Screw this," Marlin said, and he stepped to the bedside. He bent and kissed her on the forehead. She was covered by a thick bedspread. "Aren't you hot?"

"You always tell me I am," she said.

He laughed. At least she was well enough to joke.

"Need aspirin?"

She shook her head.

"You hungry?"

"Maybe a little."

"I brought home tacos, but in hindsight, maybe that wasn't the best choice."

She made a face suggesting that she did not find tacos appealing at the moment. "Could you make me some scrambled eggs?"

"You bet."

Forty-five minutes later, they were both finished eating, and Marlin was lying in bed right beside Nicole. If he caught whatever she had, so be it. That would almost be a relief, because then he'd know it was in fact something contagious, as opposed to a sign that the major surgery she'd had the previous year had somehow compromised her long-term health. He knew that was ridiculous—that the surgery couldn't lead to flu-like symptoms seven months later—but that didn't stop him from ruminating about it. Like most people, sometimes he worried about things that weren't worth the time.

Like now. He was anxious about telling Nicole what had happened today. Why was he nervous? Silly.

He began by describing the discovery of April Thornton's body, and the connection to Shelby Roach, which led to the investigative involvement of Lauren Gilchrist, the TSCRA special ranger. He could tell that Nicole was doing her best to appear interested and attentive, but it was obvious she was a little loopy from antihistamines, and he doubted much of what he was saying was sinking in.

So he finally said, "I figured I'd better mention that Lauren and I went to Southwest Texas together. In fact, we used to date."

Nicole pulled her eyes from the TV and looked at him. "Wait, Lauren? She's the special ranger?"

"Right."

"You dated?"

"We did, back in school."

She rolled onto her side to face him. "For how long?"

"I think it was about a year."

"Then you called it off and broke her heart?"

"Of course. That was my standard practice back then. Leaving women shattered and inconsolable. A real cad."

She was grinning at him. Amused that the conversation was making him squirm. "Were the two of you serious?"

"Oh, not really," Marlin said. "Just dated. It was college."

"Why did you break up?"

"There's no big story to it. It was a casual thing that had run its course. That's all."

"Does 'casual' imply no sex? Oh, I guess not! You're turning red."

"Well, it's an awkward conversation," Marlin said.

"You're so funny. That was ages ago. Why would you feel uncomfortable telling me?"

He shrugged. "I don't know. Just because we'll be working together, I guess. Wanted you to know."

She was studying him closely. Still grinning. "Is she gorgeous? Is that it?"

He was ready for a question like that. "She's no Nicole Marlin, that's for sure."

She jabbed him playfully with an elbow. "That means she *is* gorgeous."

"I don't know about *gorgeous*," he said. "I guess she's pretty. She hasn't been disfigured in an industrial accident or anything like that."

"If you decide to run off with her, will you do me a favor?"

"Sure. What is it?"

"Leave the humidifier behind."

CHAPTER EIGHT

Marlin ran into Chief Deputy Bill Tatum in the hallway of the sheriff's department the next morning. He hadn't seen Tatum since Bobby Garza had shared the news about Tatum's pending retirement.

"So it's true?" Marlin said. "You're bailing on us?"

"Yeah, after only 26 years."

"Has it been that long? You're making me feel old."

Tatum shrugged. "It was time."

"What're you going to do with yourself?" Marlin felt like he was reciting a script: *What to say when a longtime coworker retires.*

"Oh, I don't know. Hunt. Fish. Travel. Sit around and drink beer. Whatever the hell I want, really. Sounds horrible, doesn't it?"

Marlin noticed Lauren in the hallway beyond Tatum, who turned to see what had caught Marlin's attention. Lauren gave a wave and ducked into the coffee room.

Tatum turned back around and raised an eyebrow. "Who was that?"

"Special ranger from San Saba County," Marlin said. "Down here on the Thornton case."

"She, uh, looks a little different than most of the rangers I've known."

"Meaning female?" Marlin said.

"Well, that, too, but I meant a whole lot prettier. I know I'm not supposed to comment on such things, but what the hell. I'm retiring."

Red emerged from his bedroom at nine o'clock, and as he was walking through the living area, on his way to the kitchen for a Dr Pepper and some cold pizza, the window beside him made a cracking sound, followed immediately thereafter by the sound of a nearby gunshot.

Red dropped to the floor as tiny shards of glass were still bouncing off the carpet.

What the hell?

For a moment, Red was puzzled by the sequence of events. The window broke, *then* he heard the shot. Wasn't that the way it had happened? Oh, duh. Now he remembered that sound traveled slower than a bullet did.

Red remained as flat as possible, waiting. Was it a stray shot? Maybe an idiot neighbor target practicing? If so, why only one shot? And none of his neighbors were close enough that their gunfire would be that loud. Sounded more like it had come from the direction of the road. Or somewhere on Red's property, on the slope down to the road.

Now Red heard the groan of floorboards—Billy Don getting out of bed—followed by the squeal of unoiled door hinges.

"The hell was that?" Billy Don said from down the hallway. He was wearing nothing but enormous athletic shorts. It wasn't a pretty sight. Too much hair in places where hair shouldn't be.

"Bullet came flying through here a second ago," Red said.

"For real?"

"Yup."

"The shot woke me up. Didn't know what was going on."

"You might want to get down," Red said.

"On the floor? If I do, I ain't gonna be able to get back up."

Red listened for any sound at all. He thought he might've heard a vehicle on the road. Yeah, he could definitely hear a vehicle. Sounded like they were zooming away, but some of the people who lived on this road tended to drive too fast.

"What was they shooting at?" Billy Don said.

"I got no idea," Red said, but he did have one idea. Just a theory. He was hesitant to mention it, but he did. "Starting to wonder if they was shooting at me," he said.

Billy Don snorted. "Here we go again."

"What's that mean?"

"You've got a paranoid streak."

"Hell if I do."

"'Member last fall when you thought the sheriff was investigating you for murder?"

Red didn't answer. He had been wrong about that, and Billy Don had been right. Painful to admit it.

"Besides," Billy Don said, "why would anybody shoot at you?"

Red was still flat on the carpet. He was noticing a sour smell. Could use a good cleaning. "I mighta made a few enemies over the years," he said.

"Oh, good night," Billy Don said. "Nobody wants to kill you."

By now, nearly a full minute had passed with no more shots.

"Never know," Red said. "People ain't always rational."

"Like right now," Billy Don said.

"Better safe than sorry."

"If you're so worried, why don't you call the cops?" Billy Don said.

"Because this country wasn't built by people who ran to the government every time they had a little trouble."

The floorboards groaned again as Billy Don shifted his weight impatiently. "I gotta pee."

"Then pee already," Red said. "What're you waiting for?"

Billy Don turned to his left and went into the bathroom. After a pause, Red heard Billy Don peeing with great force and for a very long while. Gross. Red was glad they each had their own bathroom.

A moment later, Billy Don stepped back into the hallway. "Gonna lay there forever?"

Red had to admit he was starting to feel a little stupid. He pushed himself off the floor and stood up, careful not to present a silhouette in front of the window.

"Did that sound like a rifle or a handgun to you?" Red said.

"Handgun," Billy Don said. "Had to be."

"Nothing too big," Red said. "Maybe a thirty-eight."

"Sound's about right."

Red edged over to the side of the window and peeked outside. Nothing to see but his caliche driveway flanked by a bunch of cedar trees. The upper pane of the window had a neat, round hole in it, with cracks spider-webbing outward from it.

"BANG!" Billy Don yelled, and Red jumped sideways, away from the window.

"Goddamn it!" Red said.

"Now *that* was funny."

"Jerk."

"Why so jumpy?"

"*You* come and stand in front of the window if you're so brave," Red said.

Billy Don walked over and stood in front of the window. He began to stroke his hairy chest, as if inviting the shooter to unleash another round.

"You look like a moron," Red said.

"It was just a stray shot," Billy Don said. "Don't get your panties in a twist." He walked into the kitchen.

Red went outside and stood on the porch for a minute, just listening. Then he went down the steps and began to walk down the driveway slowly in his bare feet. Looking left. Looking right. Didn't know what he was looking for.

But he spotted it just the same—an item reflecting the light of the morning sun, about fifteen feet from the edge of the driveway. Red walked over and saw a handgun shell nestled in a clump of bluestem grass, right behind a small cedar tree. Thirty-two caliber. Nice and shiny. No tarnish. Hadn't been out here long.

Red didn't own a .32, and neither did Billy Don. Besides, Red wasn't in the habit of shooting handguns in his front yard. He was more likely to shoot a .22 rifle from his back porch at anything edible that might visit his deer feeder.

Red bent to pick up the shell, but stopped and shouted, "Billy Don! Come take a look at this!"

"So you're married?" Lauren said.

"Yep," Marlin said.

"Happily?"

"Oh, yeah."

"What's the secret to doing that? Never mind. I'm already getting into your business. You probably remember how nosy I am. I'm happy for you. How long've you been married?"

"A few years."

"Any kids?"

"No."

"First marriage?"

"Yeah."

"Wow, you held out a long time. Bet you had every available woman in Blanco County after you. Probably some married ones, too."

Marlin laughed. "Any man with all his teeth and no criminal record is considered a catch around here."

"You're stretching it."

"Only a little."

They were in Lauren's truck, a blue Ford double cab issued by the state. Looked like a personal vehicle, except for the county radio mounted under the dash and the red-and-blue strobes hidden behind the grill. The interior of the truck was a mess. Fast-food wrappers. Empty soft drink cans. A thick layer of dust over the dashboard and the instrument console. All of the windows were crying for a wipedown with Windex. This was exactly how Marlin remembered the beat-up Bronco Lauren had driven in college. She was always too busy having fun to bother going to a car wash.

They were on their way to Rodney Bauer's ranch. Lauren had suggested that they start at the scene of April Thornton's death and work from there. Marlin had no problem with that approach, although he doubted he and the deputies had missed anything at the scene.

"We really need to get ahold of Shelby Roach," Lauren said. "Or at least prove he was with April when she died. Or that he wasn't with her."

"From what you said yesterday, I'm guessing he won't talk when we find him."

"Probably not. We're gonna have to interview all his sleazebag buddies, or figure out some other way to track his movements."

They were on Highway 281 going south. It was a beautiful morning.

"Tell me about your wife," Lauren said.

"Well…her name is Nicole. Her talents include yodeling, carving soap, and running backwards."

Lauren was smiling. "You still have that goofy streak. Come on. The real stuff."

"Like what?"

"How old is she?"

"About ten years younger than me."

"I bet she's a knockout, right?"

"Why do you say that?"

"That's just your style, John."

He wasn't sure what to make of that. So he said, "She's the best person I know."

"Yeah? How so?"

Lauren slowed and turned right on a county road between Johnson City and Blanco.

"She's willing to help just about anybody," Marlin said. "She's compassionate. She's the county victim services coordinator, and there was a woman she was helping who was having major health problems last fall. Nicole gave her a kidney."

Lauren made an expression that said she was impressed. "Whoa. That's commitment. How'd that go?"

"Smoothly, fortunately. I was pretty freaked out beforehand."

"I bet."

"And I still wonder how it will affect her long term. Like right now, she's sick, and I keep wondering if it has anything to do with the surgery, even though I know damn well it doesn't."

"What's she sick with?"

"A cold," he said. "She was feeling better this morning than she did last night."

"What on earth made her decide to donate a kidney? Did she have some special connection to this woman?"

"No, she's just...that's just the type of thing Nicole does. I was reluctant as hell to let her go through with it, but I'm glad I did."

"*Let* her go through with it?" Lauren said.

Marlin laughed. "Figure of speech," he said, "and if you knew Nicole, you'd understand what a poor choice of words it was."

"She sounds like a great lady," Lauren said.

"She is. I take it you were married, too, since your last name has changed."

"I was," she said, "for about eight years. But it didn't work out."

Marlin figured that explained her earlier question about the secret to a happy marriage. "Kids?" he said.

She shook her head. "Nope."

CHAPTER NINE

"Yeah?" Billy Don said, out of breath from coming down the slope.

Who gets winded walking downhill? Red wondered.

"See that?" he said, pointing.

"The shell? What about it?"

"From a thirty-two. Looks fresh to me."

Billy Don didn't appear particularly interested. "Coulda bounced out of Shelby's vehicle."

Red thought that was dumb. What were the odds of that happening? He said, "I touched it a second ago and it was still warm from the barrel."

Billy Don believed the lie. He said, "You really think someone took a shot at you?"

"Don't you?" Red said.

Billy Don looked downhill, over the tops of the cedar trees, toward the road. Then he said, "I gotta admit, if somebody I knew was gonna get shot at, it would probably be you."

"Oh, thanks."

"Who'd you piss off?"

"No way of knowing," Red said, "but something else occurred to me. How much cash we got in the house?"

"All of it," Billy Don said.

"Exactly," Red said. "That's my point."

The men weren't big fans of banks. Or savings and loans. Or even credit unions. Red knew that the international banking system was nothing but a sucker deal designed to funnel more and more money into the hands of rich people.

Red and Billy Don preferred to keep their cash in their own hands. Red had all of their Vegas gambling money—nearly $50,000—stashed at the bottom of his gun safe, which was bolted to a wall in the closet of his bedroom. Fireproof. Waterproof. Burglarproof. Somebody would have to steal the entire damn trailer to make off with that money, or at least spend several hours hacking away with various power tools, and then they'd need to tote the safe away, which would take at least four men, or three Billy Dons. It was a losing proposition. Didn't mean nobody would try.

"Let me ask you something else," Red said, squinting into the morning sun. "And be honest. How many people have you told that we're going to Vegas? And that we're taking a lot of cash with us?"

Red could tell from Billy Don's expression that he wasn't going to like the answer.

"A couple," Billy Don said.

"Couple dozen?" Red said.

"I could go for a breakfast taco," Bobo Baldwin said, standing behind one of the glass jewelry displays in the showroom of his pawnshop. "How about you? You want a couple of breakfast tacos? My treat if you'll go get 'em."

Derek was at the desk doing paperwork—he was always working on a mountain of paperwork, because that was one of his tasks—but he paused and looked up. He appeared surprised, but in a good way. Not often that Bobo offered to buy a meal for his employee. Never, in fact. Not once.

"Sure, yeah, I could go for that," Derek said, slowly rising from the desk.

Bobo was already checking his wallet for a ten. That would cover four tacos and a small tip at the little Mexican joint next door in the strip center.

"Get me a couple of bacon, egg, and cheese," Bobo said. Crap. He couldn't find a ten. He'd have to give him a twenty and count on Derek to return the proper amount of change.

"Cool," Derek said, taking the bill. He was young—somewhere in his twenties—and skinny as a golf club. Bobo remembered those days, back when he could eat tacos galore and not gain an ounce.

"And a black coffee," Bobo said. That would make the order take longer and give Bobo more time.

"Be right back."

Once Derek was gone, Bobo trundled to the desk, sat down, and began to thumb through the monthly logbook. He hadn't fooled with this book in ages—since he'd hired Derek, in fact. Bobo hated maintaining the logbook, so he'd made it another one of Derek's tasks long ago. If Bobo had rooted through the book while Derek was there, it would've seemed unusual and raised Derek's curiosity. It had been *that* long since Bobo had even touched the logbook.

The book contained a record of every item in the pawnshop. Well, every *legal* item. Back in 1979, when Bobo had first opened his doors, he'd had every intention of running an honest operation. Why wouldn't he? There was plenty of legit money to be made, as long as you knew what things were worth, and you didn't offer too much to the customer. One third of the sales value—that's what you shot for. Or less.

Say a guy wants to pawn a diamond ring that might fetch $900 if you were to sell it out front in the display case. You offer maybe a $300 loan. Most of the time, the customer takes it, feeling confident he'll be back to reclaim the ring by repaying the money. In reality, many of the customers did not come back to reclaim their property, which allowed Bobo to make a very nice living for himself. Even the customers who did return to claim their merchandise padded Bobo's wallet, because they were paying a steep interest rate and additional fees. All legal, too. Sweet.

There were detractors who said guys like Bobo preyed on desperate people who were in financial difficulty and had very few options. Bobo, not surprisingly, didn't see it that way. He felt that he offered a worthwhile service that was in demand precisely *because* his customers were in financial difficulty and had very few options. Bobo *was* their option—often their easiest and most reliable one. Sometimes their only one. Many of the customers were grateful, or, at a minimum, indifferent. They certainly didn't hold Bobo in any sort of contempt. If they liked the arrangement, why should anyone else care?

Bobo had operated within the legal constraints of this business model for a good ten or twelve years before he succumbed to temptation and began to accept an occasional piece of questionable merchandise. Stolen. That's what "questionable" meant. And there was just *so* much money to be made in questionable merchandise.

Take the diamond ring that would sell for $900. If some shifty-eyed crackhead brought that ring in with no receipt or other proof of legitimate ownership, Bobo might offer the guy $50—and not for a loan, but an outright cash purchase, with no paperwork. The dude would take the offer every damn time. He'd take it and bolt out of there on quivering legs, straight to his dealer for another fix.

The one big drawback that became obvious to Bobo after he began to accept stolen merchandise—other than the need to sell it without getting busted—was that it encouraged an entirely different type of clientele to frequent his pawnshop. Burglars. Scammers. Con artists. Drug dealers. Bookies. Loan sharks. Thieves. Pickpockets. Garage sale enthusiasts. And the like.

That's why Bobo had been reluctant, even afraid, to check the logbook. What if the customer who had brought those cases in was a hardcore thug?

The logbook might answer that question.

Bobo's shop, like all pawnshops, was required to generate a detailed transaction report for every incoming item—customer name, address, phone number, driver's license number, height, weight, and eye color, along with identifying information about the pawned item, such as a serial number—all of which had to be uploaded to a national law-enforcement database within 24 hours.

Cops took this shit seriously, too. They checked the database with great frequency and enthusiasm. Pain in the ass—but in this case, it might be helpful. Bobo had come to the conclusion that, despite his apprehension, he *should* check the logbook and see who had brought the suitcases in. Maybe it would be a one-time customer—some nobody—and Bobo could set his worry aside. If they came looking for the money Bobo had found inside, he could say, "Cash? There wasn't any cash. Don't know what you're talking about."

Bobo flipped the logbook pages backward, homing in on the item number written on the tag attached to the suitcases. Back…back…back…getting closer.

He slid his finger along, tracking.

Found it.

Now he ran his finger to the right, to the name of the customer.

Holy crap. Son of a bitch.

Marlin instructed Lauren where to park on the shoulder of the county road, not far from a gate that opened into Rodney Bauer's pasture.

"You can see the pen and loading chute right over there," Marlin said. "They cut the lock on the gate, so I figure they were going to drive in with a trailer, after they herded some cattle into the pen. That sound about right?"

Lauren killed the engine. Several buzzards were circling just fifty or sixty feet off the ground.

She said, "Some of the scumbags bring their own portable chutes nowadays, but yeah, either way, they could've loaded up and been gone in ten or fifteen minutes. The problem is, lots of ranchers build their pens close to the road, just for convenience, but that makes it convenient for the rustlers, too."

They both got out of the truck. Rodney had already put a new lock and chain on the gate, so they climbed over. Marlin noticed that Lauren was as agile and athletic as she'd been when she was in college.

Marlin led the way into the pasture. After they'd walked about twenty yards, they could see the area behind Rodney's pen, where the carcass of the bull still lay. A dozen buzzards were busy pecking at it, but they hopped away and eventually took flight as Marlin and Lauren got closer.

"The body was right here," Marlin said, stopping short of the darkened patch of soil.

"Is that her blood or the bull's blood?" Lauren asked.

"A little of both, best we can tell."

"Any chance she was gored after the bull was shot? Maybe the bull gored her when it fell on her."

"Doesn't seem likely," Marlin said. "We think the bull died immediately. There's nothing to indicate that the bull thrashed or moved at all after it fell. And since April Thornton's torso was completely under the bull, nowhere near the horns…"

Lauren was nodding. Marlin didn't need to continue. "Can you email me the photos your forensics guy took?" she asked.

"Sure. I'll forward those."

Lauren was looking around the pasture now, hoping to spot something that might somehow shed more light on what had happened here. Marlin knew she wouldn't find it, but he understood why she felt the need to visit the scene herself. He would've made the same request.

"One thing that puzzles me," Lauren said, "is why two shots? That's what this guy Rodney said, right? Two shots?"

"Yeah. About thirty or forty seconds apart."

"Whoever shot the bull—what, they missed the first time?"

"I agree that doesn't seem likely, especially since there was powder residue on the bull's hair."

That meant the gun was fired from close range, likely a foot or less. The bull had essentially been executed.

"Do we know what caliber of handgun?"

"It was a through and through," Marlin said, "which suggests something fairly powerful."

"No shells found?"

"Nope."

Probably a revolver. If it had been a semi-automatic, the shooter had picked up the empty brass.

Lauren was about to ask another question when her cell phone rang. She answered, and after listening for a few seconds, her body language began to change. She was hearing something she liked. She thanked the caller and hung up.

"The credit card company," she said. "Someone tried to use Shelby Roach's Visa earlier today at a gas station in Johnson City."

CHAPTER TEN

Red dealt Billy Don a five of hearts on the first round, followed by a four of clubs. Red's up-facing card was a seven of diamonds. Despite what had happened—the gunshot earlier—they had to keep practicing.

"I've been thinking about this Vegas trip," Red said.

Billy Don reached out and added more chips to the small stack on the table in front of him. He was doubling down. Red gave him another card laid sideways—a final card, because you couldn't hit again after doubling down—and it was a queen of spades. Nice. Now Billy Don had nineteen.

"Maybe we should just go ahead and go," Red said, adding a six to his seven. "You're obviously ready." Red gave himself another card, an eight, for a total of 21.

Billy Don had lost.

"Or maybe I ain't," Billy Don said.

Red tossed the remainder of the deck onto the table. "Can't win 'em all. You're ready."

"Just the other day, you said I wasn't ready."

Billy Don looked around for a beer that wasn't there. Too early in the day.

"I was giving you a hard time," Red said. "That's my job. Truth is, you're ready as hell. You're gonna bring that town to its knees. If we're gonna do it, this is as good a time as any."

"You know what I think?"

"Hardly ever," Red said.

"I think you just wanna get out of town."

"Well, shit, why not? Wouldn't you?"

Billy Don's gaze lifted to the window, where Red had placed strips of duct tape over the bullet hole and the resulting cracks. If they had curtains, they'd be drawn shut at this point. "Yeah, I guess. Does seem weird that you found that shell."

Red had been thinking hard on it, trying to figure out who might be angry with him. It was a fairly lengthy list, but he couldn't think of anybody who'd be so upset they'd want to turn his lights off for him. Regardless, even if nobody in particular came to mind, the bottom line was that somebody *had* taken a shot at him, and that was a real good reason to take some precautions.

"Okay, then," Red said. "Why not leave tomorrow? Or even this afternoon? I say we get packed and get the hell outta Dodge."

"Still planning on flying?" Billy Don said.

"Yeah." Red would prefer to drive, but he wasn't confident his truck could make it.

"You know airplane tickets cost a shitload when you don't buy 'em a week or two ahead of time?"

"Can't be that much more," Red said, not answering directly, because he didn't know anything about the cost of air travel. He hadn't been on a plane since he was a teenager, when he and his parents went to an uncle's funeral in Arkansas. Poor guy was servicing a septic tank when he slipped and fell inside. Didn't drown, but came down with some sort of horrible disease.

"Pretty sure it's a bunch more," Billy Don said.

Red pulled his cell phone from his pocket—a cheap Korean brand that worked most of the time. He did a quick Internet search for the Southwest Airlines phone number, and in less than a minute, he was talking to a live human being. It was not a long conversation. Billy Don was right. Flights the next day were more than twice as much as flights a week from now. All told, it would cost them nearly a thousand dollars more to go immediately. That wasn't even including a motel. Could they even get a room on short notice? The nice lady on the phone was telling him how to get the best price, which was a package deal, hotel and flight combined, but you had to plan in advance. Then she began asking whether he needed a rental car, which was something he hadn't even thought about. Red was in no mood to deal with all that bullshit right now, so he hung up. Who knew it'd be so complicated to go to Vegas?

"Guess we'll keep practicing," he said. "Sharpen your game. We'll fly in a couple of weeks."

And in the meantime, keep an eye out for some nutcase with a grudge.

"We could take the bus," Billy Don said.

"You familiar with the type of person that rides a bus?" Red said, making a disgusted face.

"Yeah," Billy Don said, starting to smile. "People like us."

"You wanna be cramped up in a bus halfway across the country with a bunch of trailer trash?" Red said. "Not me. We'll fly."

"Hey, Chris," Marlin said to the clerk behind the counter at the convenience store. Local kid. Maybe twenty years old. Had been working there for about a year. Always friendly and helpful.

"How's it going?"

The store was empty at the moment, which was convenient.

"Need a favor," Marlin said.

"Shoot."

"Can we have a look at your security video from this morning? We need to see who came in at 8:23."

"Sure thing. Come on around."

That was another good thing about Chris. He wasn't the type to ask a bunch of questions.

Marlin and Lauren joined him behind the counter, where he already had the feed from the store's security cameras brought up on a monitor. The screen was divided into four quadrants, but one was black.

"We have three cameras," Chris said. "Two inside, one outside. But you can see that, I guess. You said 8:23?"

"Right."

"I've been working since six this morning. It's been busy. Let me see what we have."

Chris opened a menu that allowed him to plug in a specific time and choose which cameras he wanted to view. He selected ALL.

The feed began at 8:22.

"There's Barney," Chris said, pointing to Barney Weaver, a local, in one of the quadrants.

Barney was at the counter, completing a purchase. Another quadrant showed a woman in a business suit near the back of the store, grabbing something from a shelf.

"She was buying a can of pears," Chris said. "I remember that, because it seemed like an odd purchase at that time of day."

The last quadrant, which showed the gas pumps outside, was

void of activity—until a few seconds later, when a vehicle pulled into the frame.

Lauren immediately leaned closer to the screen. She was smiling.

"Something?" Marlin said.

"Shelby Roach drives a Ranchero," she said. "Can you enlarge that screen? Forget about the other feeds."

Chris punched a few buttons, and now the outside shot filled the entire screen. The Ranchero had pulled up on the far side of one of the gas pumps. Unfortunately, the pump itself was now obscuring the view of the driver. Marlin could see just the blurry top of the driver's head as he attempted to buy gas. Brown hair? Dirty blond? Sandy colored? Hard to tell.

Ten seconds passed. Then twenty. Then the driver got back into the Ranchero and drove away. The poor quality of the video, combined with reflections on the driver's side window, made it impossible to discern anything more about the driver.

"Well, that sucks," Lauren said.

"At least we know they were driving a beige Ranchero with a darker stripe," Marlin said. "Chris, can you email that clip to us?"

"Sure. How much of it do you want?"

"Just one second on either side of the Ranchero coming and going."

Marlin placed one of his cards, complete with email address and cell phone number, on the counter. Lauren did the same.

"If you see that Ranchero again," Lauren said, "please give one of us a call."

"Will do. Can you tell me what's going on? Were they trying to use a stolen credit card?"

"We just need to talk to the driver," Marlin said.

Colin Kelly's phone began to ring, but he was too busy posing shirtless in front of the mirror—really liking what he saw—to answer. Besides, the ring tone told him who was calling, and she could go fuck herself.

After a moment, the phone stopped ringing, and Colin continued flexing, standing there in the bedroom he'd converted into a weight room several years ago. His torso was waxed and glistening. He spent upward of forty dollars a month on baby oil, but it was worth it.

Damn. Just look at that shit. Totally fucking ripped.

Sure, he had testicles the size of small grapes, oily skin, and acne like buckshot spread across his back. His hair was thinning rapidly on the crown of his head. His blood pressure was routinely 160 over 110, his cholesterol hovered around 300, and his liver enzymes were elevated. The last time he tried to jerk off, his penis remained semi-flaccid and he couldn't achieve an orgasm, which he blamed on the mild depression that had settled over him recently. Still, though, he looked damn good, especially in nothing but a pair of spandex shorts.

The phone began to ring again. Same ring tone. Charmaine. Bitch. He ignored it.

At his current weight, 245, Colin had it all: Mass, definition, proportion, symmetry. Not that he cared whether he met judging standards or not. He only wanted to be jacked beyond all reason, and after struggling for several years to reach his peak form, he'd finally achieved it.

There it went again. The damn phone. Why didn't she just leave a voicemail?

Colin couldn't stand it anymore. He gave in.

"The hell do you want?" he said.

"Hey, baby," Charmaine said.

"Don't do that. Just tell me what you want. You're calling for a reason."

She made that pouty noise she sometimes made. He hated that particular noise. He hated all of the little noises she made. She got on his nerves big time. Always had.

"Do you have to be so mean?" she said.

"Do you have to be such a slut?"

He expected her to hang up after that insult, but she said, "That's not fair. I warned you for months that I was unhappy."

"So you cheated on me. Nice. That's what a non-slut would do, right?"

She didn't answer. Never date a cocktail waitress. That would be a hard and fast rule for Colin from now on. Especially not one who works at the same bar where you're a bouncer.

"What do you want?" he said.

Now a sigh. Whatever it was, she was building up to it. She *would* tell him what she wanted. Eventually.

"I came by this afternoon, but my key wouldn't work."

"I changed the locks, to keep whores out."

"But how am I supposed to get the rest of my stuff?"

"You're not."

"What?"

"You're not getting the rest of your stuff."

He sat down on the weight bench and slipped his free hand down into his shorts, cupping his privates. Just a habit he had. Something he did without really thinking about it. He'd cupped himself in public a few times and caught angry or disgusted glares from people passing by.

"But I need some of those things," Charmaine said. "Right away. Like, tonight. It's urgent."

"Ha. Life's hard, ain't it?"

"Colin, come on. You can't just keep it all."

"Oh, I'm not keeping it. I didn't keep it."

"What does that mean?"

He had been looking forward to this. He was about to pay her back for the pain she'd caused him. It wasn't going to be an equal amount of pain, but it was a start.

"I trashed a lot of it," he announced. "Pawned the rest."

Now she made a new sound. A quick intake of breath that was a combination of surprise and—what? Panic?

"Tell me you're bullshitting, Colin," she said. "Please, *please* tell me that's not true."

"You left eleven days ago and I hadn't heard from you since. What was I supposed to do with all your crap?"

It hadn't been crap. She didn't own crap. She always insisted on good stuff. Expensive stuff. Name-brand stuff. Her wardrobe alone probably had a total value well into the five-figure range. Did a 23-year-old cocktail waitress really need designer dresses that cost $300 each? Ridiculous.

"Oh, Colin," she said. "Oh, my god."

He knew she wouldn't be happy, but she was taking it harder than he had expected.

"Don't know why you needed all those clothes anyway," he said, "seeing as how you always take 'em off every chance you get."

Charmaine was crying now. He could hear her on the other end sniffing and sobbing. Screw her. He was *not* going to feel guilty about it. She had always managed to manipulate him in the past, but no more.

"Colin," she said.

"What?"

"Colin."

"*What?*" He was ready to hang up.

"There's something I need to tell you," she said. "This is really bad."

CHAPTER ELEVEN

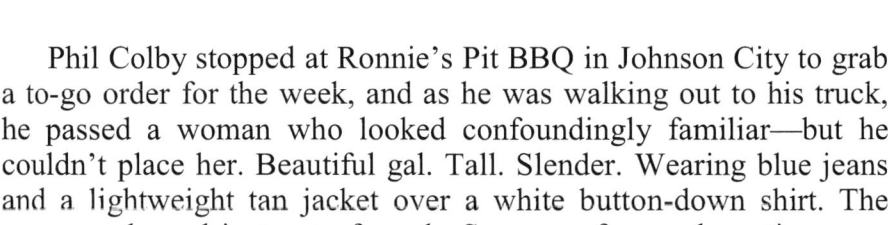

Phil Colby stopped at Ronnie's Pit BBQ in Johnson City to grab a to-go order for the week, and as he was walking out to his truck, he passed a woman who looked confoundingly familiar—but he couldn't place her. Beautiful gal. Tall. Slender. Wearing blue jeans and a lightweight tan jacket over a white button-down shirt. The memory danced just out of reach. Someone from a long time ago. Not a local. He was going to let it go—and then it came to him.

When he turned around, the woman had just reached the door to the restaurant.

"Lauren?" Colby called.

The woman turned.

Colby began to walk toward her.

She hadn't given him more than a glance when they had first passed, but now she was studying his face and she began to grin.

"Good lord. Phil Colby?"

"I *knew* I knew you," he said, "but it took me a minute to figure it out. Dang, you haven't changed at all. How are you?"

They stepped closer and exchanged a quick hug.

"I'm doing great," Lauren said. "Just, you know, working—and running into all sorts of people. First John and now you."

"Yeah? You saw John?"

"We're working a case together." She pulled her jacket aside, revealing a badge pinned to her shirt underneath. Colby recognized it immediately.

"You're a special ranger? That's outstanding."

"Thanks. I'm enjoying it. It's only been a couple of years."

"That's great."

"It's pretty cool, I'll admit. I was a deputy before that."

"You look fantastic," Colby said, and it was true. She seemed even prettier now than she had been when she was younger.

"You, too," she said.

Colby hated that the exchange felt awkward. There was no reason for it to be awkward, despite everything that had happened. Back in college, he and Lauren had always clicked, both when she was dating Marlin—and afterward. He remembered long late-night conversations peppered with near-constant laughter. And alcohol. Plenty of alcohol. Then things took an interesting turn.

"So are you married? Got kids?" Colby said.

"Divorced," Lauren said. "No kids. You?"

"Nope on both."

"Never married," Lauren said, "or divorced?"

"Never married."

"Really? A guy like you?"

A group of customers exited from the restaurant. Colby and Lauren moved aside to let them pass.

"I was engaged once," Colby said. "Hey, you probably remember Terri."

"Oh, that's right. I liked her a lot. We had some classes together. What happened?"

"We dated for about six years, then got engaged, but it didn't work out."

"'Didn't work out.' That's very vague, Phil." She was teasing him. "Did you run her off with your strange predilections?"

He laughed. Now they were warming up. He remembered her wicked sense of humor. "Well, she wasn't the first and she won't be the last."

"I bet that's right."

"Where are you living nowadays?" Colby asked.

"On a small place outside San Saba. Got a few acres out in the middle of nowhere. Just peace and quiet, you know?"

"Sounds nice."

"It is. What about you? Your family still have the ranch?"

She remembered. He wondered if she would. But how could she not?

"I do, yeah," Colby said. "My parents passed away quite a few years ago. Doing my best to hang on to the place. Between cattle and leasing it out for hunting, I get by."

She nodded. "Good to hear. I remember it's a beautiful place."

She gave him a knowing grin.

"Driving home tonight?" Colby said.

"No, I got a room at the motel. Just grabbing some supper before I head over there."

There was a pause then. He had an idea, and he was fairly certain the expression on her face—the way she was looking him dead in the eye, waiting—was saying, *Well, are you going to ask or not?*

"Hey, listen," Colby said. He lifted the plastic bag hanging from his hand. "I've got five pounds of brisket, ribs, and sausage in here. Why don't you come over and help me eat some of it?"

On a chilly October night, they drove to the Crystal Chandelier in New Braunfels and paid ten dollars a head to see a rising country star named George Strait. Marlin couldn't have known this would be one of those special nights that etches itself into your memory with razor-sharp clarity, and that he'd look back on it in years to come with a sentimentality that would make his heart ache for a chance to relive it, even for a moment or two.

It was their fifth date, though neither of them was counting. Phil and Terri met them there, and it wasn't long before the beer and the laughter were flowing like the Guadalupe River after a spring thunderstorm.

Marlin could recall the way the jeans hugged Lauren's hips, and the light scent of perfume on her neck when he leaned in close to speak above the music. Every so often, she would catch his eye and hold it for the longest time, squeezing his hand or rubbing his thigh, as if the night held endless promise.

On the dance floor, she'd place one hand on the small of his back, firm, but allowing herself to be led by his cues. He pulled her close during "Amarillo By Morning," and with her warm body against his, he began to wonder if he was falling in love—or was he letting himself get carried away by the alcohol and the company of a lovely young woman?

Between sets, she pulled him outside for some fresh air, and in a private spot under a waxing moon and the canopy of a towering oak tree, they began to kiss. She was more insistent, more aggressive, than she'd been on previous occasions, and that in turn created an urgency he couldn't contain. He slipped one hand up the front of her sweater, and this time, unlike earlier times, she did not stop him. He released the front clasp on her bra and found the warmth of her breasts. After a few moments, she began to rub the front of his jeans and he almost couldn't bear the pleasure it brought. He didn't know if he could last. They were both breathing heavily.

"We should go," she whispered in his ear. "Very soon."

"Where?"

"Your apartment."

Marlin led her to his truck and they began the drive up the interstate to his place on the south side of San Marcos. On the way, she slid over beside him and repeatedly kissed his neck as her hand tugged at his belt buckle. He was having difficulty focusing on the road ahead.

His roommate was out of town. He was so grateful for that. He wouldn't need—

"Where are you?" Nicole said.

Marlin snapped back to the moment, here, now, in his living room.

"What?"

"Your eyes were on the TV, but you were a million miles away," Nicole said. She was in her usual spot at the far end of the couch, under the lamp, with a magazine in her lap. "And you were smiling like you'd just won the lottery."

His face began to get warm. "I don't know. Just thinking."

She was looking at him suspiciously, but grinning. "Uh huh," she said.

He focused on the TV, and after a while, he felt her gaze leave his face.

Half a minute later, he looked at her again, watching as she read, and his heart began to swell. In just a few years, she had given him more treasured memories than he could count. The best ones of his life.

She glanced over again and caught him. "What?" she said.

"Nothing."

"You're being weird tonight."

"We should go dancing sometime soon," he said.

She licked her thumb and flipped the page, studying him playfully, and knowing full well that something had prompted that suggestion. "Sounds good," she said, "but I'm still wondering about that smile."

Red's plumbing wasn't all that reliable, so the general rule was to flush the toilets as infrequently as possible. Need to take a leak? Step outside. That's what Red was doing at nine-thirty in the evening—just about to pee off his back porch—when he heard movement in the cedar trees near the back of his property. Something walking across dry leaves. It was a still night, so the sound carried.

Could be anything. Deer. Wild pig. Raccoon. Coyote. But damn, after what had happened that morning, Red was jumpy, despite the fact that he had consumed the better part of a 12-pack. He zipped his fly and stood perfectly still, waiting. And there it was again.

Crunch. Pause. Crunch. Pause. Crunch.

Something was picking its steps slowly and carefully. Not close, but not all that far away, either. Maybe forty yards. Far enough that whatever it was—had to be a deer, right?—wasn't aware that a human being was standing on the porch in the darkness. There was no moonlight and Red couldn't see squat. But he continued to hear it—something plainly making its way from right to left. Red knew from experience that it wasn't necessarily a large animal. Even an armadillo could make a lot of racket by rooting around in the grass.

Red took a careful step backward, closer to a washing machine that sat snug up against the house. The washer hadn't worked in years, so now it served as a handy place to set things down, including the high-powered spotlight he and Billy Don used to shoot pigs—legally—and the occasional deer—not so legally—at the feeder after sundown.

Red grabbed the spotlight, leveled it, and waited.

The crunching continued, and Red began to hone in on it. The source, whatever it was, was now at the one o'clock position. He heard more movement. And yet again.

Red pulled the trigger on the spotlight, and the powerful beam cut through the darkness. Red heard more leaves crunching and caught a glimpse of rapid movement on the periphery of the lighted area, so he swung the spotlight in the direction. Something or someone was running, but there were too many trees in the way to get a good look. Then nothing. Red continued to sweep the area with the light for a full minute, but there was no more movement. Whatever had been out there had fled the area. Or it had ducked behind a tree and was waiting for Red to turn the light off.

"Pig?" Billy Don was standing in the doorway to the trailer.

Red killed the beam.

"Don't know," he said quietly, not wanting his voice to carry. "Might've been a person. I think it was."

Billy Don started to say something else, but Red held a hand up to silence him. They both waited. No more crunching sounds.

"You're seeing things," Billy Don said.

"Because there was something to see," Red said.

Red blasted the light again, hoping to catch somebody sneaking around in the open, but there was nothing out there.

"Whatever it was," Red said, "pretty sure it was kind of brown. Or brown and black."

"Probably just a pig," Billy Don said.

"On two legs?" Red said.

"A talented pig," Billy Don said.

CHAPTER TWELVE

Colin Kelly walked through the door of the pawnshop at one minute past nine in the morning, the first customer for the day, and Bobo Baldwin immediately felt a sense of panic deep in his belly.

Holy crap. Son of a bitch. Act natural.

Colin Kelly, who was a steroid junkie—essentially one humongous collection of bulging muscles from head to toe—had been a sporadic customer over the years. Not a friendly one, either. The guy had a temper, and he liked to give you the feeling that he was about to lose his shit and snap your head off. Always making smart-ass remarks, or bitching about the amount Bobo offered for his items.

About ten days ago, Colin Kelly had brought in a large quantity of merchandise in his car. Mostly women's clothing, but a lot of other shit, too. Jewelry. Perfumes. Kitchenwares. And, yes, those Delsey nesting suitcases. Bobo had figured that out when he'd checked the logbooks.

Colin Kelly walked straight to the counter and, as usual, Bobo felt dwarfed to be standing in front of him. No small feat, considering that Bobo had to outweigh him by fifty pounds. But where Bobo was round, soft, and short, this guy was a towering rock. A beast. Barely human. Like one of those drawings—a caricature. A freak. Plus, his rippled arms were always coated with something shiny. Looked like baby oil. He left horrible smudges whenever he leaned on the glass counter. Bobo had once rejected a beautiful Armani suit Colin Kelly had brought in because the fabric was saturated with oil.

"How's it going?" Bobo asked, trying to sound as casual as possible.

"Shitty," Colin Kelly said, trying to sound as casual as possible. But the truth was, he was on the verge of a nervous breakdown. He placed a solitary pawn ticket on the counter. "Need to get this back."

The only good news in this whole situation was that Colin had pawned all of Charmaine's belongings instead of selling them outright. He would have received more money from Bobo by selling, but Colin had realized that pawning would allow him to stick the knife into Charmaine good and deep. He'd been planning to make her pay a shitload of money for the pawn tickets to get her possessions back. Well, that had been the plan before she'd called yesterday and screwed everything up. What she'd told him had really taken the wind out of his sails.

Bobo grabbed the ticket off the counter and was taking a look. Meanwhile, Colin was checking around for the skinny guy, Derek. He was the one who seemed to do all the work, while Bobo mostly sat around drinking coffee or working on a crossword puzzle.

"Delsey suitcases," Bobo said, doing his best to sound as if he'd never heard of that particular brand until this very minute. "Going somewhere? Taking a little vacay?"

"Maybe so," Colin Kelly said, "or maybe not. Can I get the suitcases?"

"I'll need twelve-twenty," Bobo said.

A paltry sum, but the loan value of an item—what a customer got when he pawned it—was even lower than the amount for an outright purchase. That $12.20 consisted of the original ten-dollar loan, plus 2% interest and a 20% fee.

Colin Kelly handed over a ten, two singles, and two dimes.

"Gimme a sec," Bobo said.

He turned and went into the back room on shaky legs. This was not good. Of course, he had the option of simply giving the cash to Colin Kelly. Bobo could say he'd found the money and put it in the safe for security purposes. And, yeah, by the way, he'd been meaning to call and tell Colin all about it, but it had been so damn busy around here that Bobo had forgotten. The monstrous freak wouldn't believe it for a second, and he'd get pissed that Bobo had tried to rip him off, but it might be even worse if Colin didn't get the money back.

Bobo went to the same shelving unit as two days before, bent down, and retrieved the nested suitcases. Lighter now. As he came back into the showroom, he did his best to appear calm and collected. He went around the end of the counter, rolling the nested cases, and he passed the handle off to Colin Kelly.

"There you go," Bobo said, desperately hoping the bodybuilder would take the luggage and leave, without opening them.

Colin lowered the telescoping handle and lifted the entire set into the air by the hand grip. He made a little up-and-down motion with the cases, as if gauging their weight. It was obvious what he was doing.

Bobo could feel sweat beginning to pop on his forehead.

Colin was fucked. He knew that already, before he even opened the cases. He could tell they were lighter now than when he'd brought them in. He set the cases on the countertop and began to unzip the large case, revealing the medium case inside. He unzipped that one and exposed the smallest case. He unzipped that one, took a deep breath, and flipped it open.

Empty.

It was as devastating as measuring his bicep and realizing he'd lost an inch in circumference.

Fucking empty. Fucking pawnshop. No fucking surprise, right?

He looked at Bobo, who was looking right back at him, like *Something wrong?*

Colin started to speak, but his throat was dry. He swallowed hard. He wasn't angry. He wasn't irritated. He was scared.

"There was cash in here," he said. His voice did not sound like his own.

"Huh?"

"There was cash in this suitcase. Lots of it."

Bobo frowned. "Why would you pawn a suitcase with cash in it?"

"I didn't know there was cash in it at the time, genius," Colin said. "But there was."

Bobo made sort of a shrugging gesture, like *What do you expect me to do about it?*

"I need that cash," Colin said.

"I don't know what to tell you," Bobo said. He held Colin's receipt up. "Ticket says one set of Delsey suitcases, not one set of suitcases plus contents. How'm I supposed to know there was cash in there? Maybe you stashed it somewhere else."

"No," Colin said. "No, I didn't stash it somewhere else. It was in here. Now it's gone."

"How much money we talking about?" Bobo said. "If it's a few hundred bucks, well, I might be able to—"

In one surprisingly swift and nimble move, Colin reached over the counter and grabbed Bobo by the shirtfront.

This behemoth was about to beat Bobo to death. Who could blame him? He'd lost $46,000. Bobo would be upset, too.

"Take it easy," Bobo said.

"Where'd my money go?"

The man's breath smelled like onions.

"Let me just, uh, remind you that you're on camera," Bobo said.

Colin Kelly glanced upward at the security camera over the counter. Then he pulled Bobo halfway over the counter.

"I don't give a shit," Colin Kelly said, his face an inch from Bobo's. "Somebody took that goddamn cash and I'm gonna get it back. I *have* to get it back."

The enormous man drew one beefy fist back.

"Hang on, okay?" Bobo pleaded. "Just hang on a second. Let me tell you something. Here's the situation. I didn't wanna bring this up, but I feel like I have no choice, you know, because it's plain you didn't make some kinda mistake. The cash was in the suitcase. I believe you. No question. But the problem is—you know my clerk Derek? He's been acting a little weird lately. And shit's been going missing. That's why I fired him this morning. If there's a problem here, it's gotta be Derek. I'm not saying he took your money for sure, but we're the only two people who could've done it, and I know it wasn't me."

"Got any brilliant ideas?" Lauren asked.

"Well, I don't know about brilliant," Marlin said.

They were seated on opposite sides of a booth at the Kountry Kitchen, drinking coffee and trying to decide how to proceed with the case.

"Okay, strike brilliant," Lauren said. "Got any ideas at all?"

"One," Marlin said.

The waitress stopped at the booth to refill their mugs. After she left, Lauren said, "Pretty gal. Sure is taking good care of you." She looked at Marlin and smiled.

"There are only so many hunks in Blanco County," Marlin said, deadpan. "It's like an exclusive club. We get special attention."

"Probably broke her heart when you got married," Lauren said.

"Well, it's true that every woman in a fifty-mile radius was devastated."

"I believe it," Lauren said.

"They recovered, with time."

Marlin chose not to tell her that he had dated the waitress several years earlier. That was one of the drawbacks of living in a county with fewer than ten thousand residents. It could get claustrophobic, seeing the same people over and over again. Lauren had suggested meeting at this particular café, and Marlin hadn't been able to come up with a reason to go somewhere else. And, really, was it worth the bother? He had a past. So what? He couldn't alter his daily routine to avoid anyone he might not be in the mood to see. This list would include not just old girlfriends, but plenty of locals Marlin had cited for hunting or fishing infractions over the years.

"So what's your idea?" Lauren said.

"What I've been wondering," Marlin said, "is why Shelby Roach is hanging around in Blanco County. Assuming that was him at the convenience store this morning, why is he still here? Why hasn't he gone back to San Saba? He and April Thornton came down to steal some cattle, and it went badly, but now he's still here. I don't get it."

"That's a good point," Lauren said.

"If that wasn't him at the store, who was it?" Marlin said. "Who was driving his Ranchero and trying to use his credit card?"

"And where have they been staying for the past two days?" Lauren said. "That's your idea, right? Dig around and see if we can figure out where they've been staying."

"Exactly. It's starting to seem a little odd that nobody has had contact with Shelby Roach in the past two days. We need to figure out why that is. Agreed?"

"Absolutely."

CHAPTER THIRTEEN

The trail camera!

That was the first thought that popped into Red's head when the sun rose high enough to shine into his bedroom window and wake him up. The trail camera that Shelby had given him! After Shelby had left, Red had mounted the camera on a tree not far from the feeder behind his trailer. Red figured there was a good chance the trespasser from last night might have stepped right in front of it.

Red sprang out of bed and walked down the narrow hallway into the living room, where Billy Don was sunk deep into the couch, watching *The Price Is Right*.

"Check this out," Billy Don said, "This dumb lady just bid eight hundred bucks for a—"

But Red went right out the back door, down the steps, and toward the rear of his property, where the deer feeder sat. He was lucky that his back-fence neighbor was a third-generation rancher with more than a thousand acres, so Red didn't have to worry about a subdivision popping up directly behind him anytime soon. He could continue to hunt right off his back porch.

Red navigated through oaks and cedars, over rocks, around a cluster of cactus, and pretty soon he was standing beside the trail camera, which was mounted about three feet off the ground, not far from the deer feeder. The little digital counter on the front indicated that it had taken 178 photos in the three days it had been out here. Not surprising, because Red had set it to take two photos every time it was tripped, and to sit idle for only one minute before it would reset and take additional photos.

He unhooked the bungee cord holding the camera in place and

popped the door open. It took him a few minutes to figure out how to view the stored photos, but the instructions were printed right there on the inside of the unit. Handy. Pretty soon, the two-inch LED screen was showing Red the first of the 178 photos. The camera was aimed at the deer feeder ten yards away, and the photo showed half a dozen white-winged doves beneath the feeder, eating corn, in mid-afternoon.

Red hit a button with his right thumb and advanced to the second photo, which was a nearly identical shot of the doves under the feeder. He went to the next two photos. More doves, but later in the day. Then some deer showed up at dusk. Red clicked faster and faster, speeding through three days' worth of photos. Deer. Doves. Raccoons. An occasional wild pig. A possum. A fox.

Then a person.

"Billy Don!" Red yelled. "You're wrong again!"

Colin Kelly owned a Mini Cooper, and when he was behind the wheel, he looked as ridiculous as a bear riding a tricycle. He was simply much too large for such a vehicle. He actually developed cramps if he drove for more than fifteen or twenty minutes. He had to tilt his head to the left or right because the roof was too low. As with many other circumstances in Colin's life, the car was Charmaine's fault. She'd talked him into the Mini Cooper, despite his repeated objections.

"Oh, those cars are adorable!" she'd said after seeing one in the parking lot outside of the gym where they were members. That was her favorite word. Adorable.

"You kidding?" he'd said. "Way too small for me."

"But they're so cute!"

"Then *you* get one," he'd said.

"I already have my Miata. It's adorable, too!"

He had to admit that was true, especially with her in it, with the top down. She was a head-turning blond, and when men pulled up beside her at a stoplight, they stared, and sometimes the more aggressive ones attempted to initiate a conversation.

When she'd first gotten the Miata, he'd wondered how she'd been able to afford a new car, but he hadn't pressed it. Later he learned how. One of the other men she'd been seeing behind his back—and there had been several—had given her the down payment. It figured. She always seemed to get what she wanted, one way or another. Like the Mini Cooper. She'd wanted one, and since she already had a Miata, she did the next best thing. She badgered Colin until he bought one. That meant she could drive it—without making the payments! Best of both worlds. Genius, really. What a conniving bitch.

The Mini Cooper served as a constant, painful reminder that he had allowed her to manipulate him, and for that reason, he intended to sell it very soon, even if he had to take a big loss. But, for now, he was crammed in the driver's seat, feeling conspicuous as hell, as he waited for Derek to emerge from his apartment.

Which unit? No way to be sure. Bobo had given him an address, but Colin hadn't known it was an apartment complex until he'd arrived. So then he'd called Bobo to get the unit number, but fucking Bobo hadn't answered. Shithead. Too scared to answer the phone. The only good news was that Colin had spotted Derek's Dodge Charger, so he knew Derek was home. Somewhere in Building C of Del Luna Azul. Or maybe Building B. But the Charger was parked closer to Building C.

He settled in, getting as comfortable as was possible, and waited. Even in the best of circumstances, Colin wasn't good at waiting. Under these particular circumstances, he was particularly impatient, and his emotions swung from dread to agitation to a bone-deep fury that made him want to tear the steering wheel from its column.

"You got a library card?" Billy Don asked.

"Oh, sure," Red said, pulling into a spot in the small parking lot. "You know me. Always hanging out at the library. Right now I'm reading the classics. I can't get enough Edward Hemingway."

He hopped out and Billy Don followed him toward the library. Nice place, built from limestone. Had a high-quality metal roof. Red had to wonder how many tax dollars were spent on construction. More important, why should every citizen in the county have to foot the bill for a library? Some people, like Red, didn't think books were all that important. So why should he have to pay for them? Same thing with public schools.

Billy Don said, "Reason I ask is, you remember that last time we was here?"

"Nope."

"When we needed to see pictures of the chupacabra?" Billy Don whispered, just as they stepped through the front door.

That remark refreshed Red's memory. It had been several years, but he and Billy Don had made a trip to the library to research the mythical chupacabra, back when there was supposedly one on the loose in Blanco County. But the main reason the previous trip to the library was memorable was because—

"May I help you?" said the old woman behind the front counter.

This lady. This cranky old bat. She was mean and nasty and a stickler for the rules. She was wearing a small nameplate that said MARTHA CRAIN, perfectly centered on the left breast pocket of her linen jacket.

"Uh..." Red said. "We, uh..."

He was freezing up. Stern old ladies did that to him. All he wanted was a chance to get a better look at the photos on the trail camera. The little LED screen was handy, but he hadn't been able to make out much about the person who had appeared in four consecutive photos, because the shots were just too small. If Red could see them on a larger screen, he might be able to figure out who had been sneaking around on his property, and that was probably the same person who had sent a bullet through his front window.

"We was wanting to use a computer," Billy Don said.

Martha Crain lowered her head and looked at them over the rim of her glasses. "One of you has a library card?"

It was obvious she assumed the answer was no. How judgmental was that? Of course, the answer *was* no. And that meant this dusty old fossil was going to be a problem. Why was there always a bureaucrat like Martha Crain standing in the way every time Red tried to get something done? It wasn't fair.

Red was just about to tell the old biddy what he thought of library policy when Billy Don said, "I was hoping to apply for a card today, ma'am. Right now. And then I'd be able to use a computer, right?"

"First things first," Martha Crain said. "I'll need to see your driver's license."

"Uh, well," Billy Don said, "I don't have a driver's license, but I do have an ID card from the National Weapons Alliance. Good as gold."

"Is that a photo ID?"

"No, ma'am. But you've got something better than a photo. You've got me, in the flesh, standing right in front of you. Lucky you."

Billy Don was joking around, but she didn't smile.

"I'm afraid you'll have to provide a photo ID."

"I've got a driver's license in the truck," Red said, hating the fact that he, as a sovereign individual, was having to jump through hoops to make this government enforcer happy.

"Is it current?" she asked.

"It's currently in my truck."

"But is it current?"

"I ain't following you."

"Does it state your correct address?"

"Yes, ma'am."

"Is it expired?"

Damn! "Well, it's a coupla months out of date, to be honest," Red said. "I been meaning to get that taken care of."

"How many months?" Martha Crain asked.

"About thirty," Red said.

"I'm sorry," Martha Crain said, obviously not sorry at all, "but without a photo ID, there's simply no way I can issue a library card."

Red was on the verge of really getting ugly. He said, "Lady, has it ever occurred to you that a policy like that stops people like me and Billy Don from educating ourselves?"

"Is that what's stopping you?" Martha Crain said.

CHAPTER FOURTEEN

They started with the motels, because if Shelby Roach was still hanging around Blanco County, he had to be sleeping somewhere at night. Sure, he could be staying with someone he knew—a friend or a relative—but that was unlikely, considering that most of his known friends and relatives had been contacted, and nobody admitted to knowing where he was.

The clerk at the Best Western in Johnson City had no registered guest named Shelby Roach, and he didn't recognize a photograph of Roach. Same thing at the Hill Country Inn, the only other motel in town.

"I guess we could check B-and-Bs," Lauren said, driving aimlessly for the moment, "but there were vacancies at both motels, and if you were Shelby Roach, what're the odds you'd choose a bed and breakfast over a motel?"

"Zilch," Marlin said. "Not even one percent."

"But if we don't check..."

"And he's staying at one, we'll feel like idiots later. The nearest one is over on Nugent." He pointed the way.

She pulled onto Highway 281 and went north, but had to stop immediately at the traffic light at the Highway 290 intersection.

"How's your wife feeling?" she asked.

"Much better," Marlin said. "Thanks for asking."

"I'd like to meet her sometime," Lauren said.

The light turned green and she turned left.

"That would be nice," Marlin said, although he wasn't sure he meant it.

"She from around here?" Lauren asked.

"Seguin, originally. Then she got a job here as a deputy."

"She went from deputy to victim services coordinator?"

"Yep."

"Interesting. I went from deputy to special ranger."

Marlin's phone vibrated with an incoming text. It was from Phil Colby.

Hey give me a call when you get a minute, no rush.

"You said Nugent?" Lauren said.

"Yeah, the next right."

They stopped at the bed and breakfast, with the same results they'd had at the two motels. The owner had not seen Shelby Roach.

Back in the truck, Marlin said, "Let's do convenience stores next, and after that, I guess we'll have to repeat the process in Blanco."

"Which way?"

"Go down to the light, then take a right. Nearest store is four or five blocks down."

Inside the store, the owner, a middle-aged Iranian immigrant named Ramin, was behind the counter. Ramin was *always* behind the counter. Near as Marlin could tell, Ramin and his wife both worked about ninety hours a week. The place was always clean and well stocked.

"John Marlin," Ramin said, grinning. "Hello." Ramin was one of the friendliest people in town.

"How you doing, Ramin?" Marlin said. He held up the photo of Shelby Roach. "A question for you. Any chance you've seen this guy in the past few days?"

Ramin studied the photo for several seconds, then shook his head. "Sorry, no."

"Have you seen an old Ranchero?" Marlin could tell that Ramin didn't understand what a Ranchero was, so he said, "It's like a cross between a truck and a car. It has an open bed in back, but it—"

"Like this," Lauren said, holding up her phone, which was playing the video clip from the other convenience store, where someone had filled the vehicle with gas.

Ramin was already nodding. "Yes, yes. There was one just here. But the man in your photograph was not driving it."

"Who was driving?" Lauren asked.

"A man about that age, but a different man. He bought two hot dogs."

"What color was the Ranchero?" she said.

"Same as that one!" he said, gesturing toward Lauren's phone.

Ramin was picking up on the excitement in Lauren's voice.

"How long ago?" Lauren said.

"Just one minute before you arrive!" Ramin said.

"Literally a minute?" Lauren said.

"Yes! He left and then you arrived!"

"Which way did he go?"

"That way!" Ramin said, pointing toward the west, away from town. He probably thought this conversation was like something out of a western—the civic-minded citizen telling the lawman which way the desperado had fled.

"We'll be back," Marlin said, hustling out the door, right behind Lauren. "Thanks, Ramin!"

"Have I completely lost my mind," Red said, "or is that Ranchero behind us again?"

They were going west on Highway 290, just leaving Johnson City. After getting rejected by that crazy old bat, they'd decided to give it a shot at the library in Fredericksburg, 30 minutes away. Farther than Blanco, but they could stop for some Wiener schnitzel afterward at that great little restaurant on Main Street.

"Maybe," Billy Don said, looking through the rear window. "Hard to tell. Too far back."

Red eased off the gas, but the vehicle far back in the distance got no closer. Red floored the gas pedal, and his big, heavy truck—which was prone to bogging down on occasion—responded beautifully this time. He picked up speed quickly, and it wasn't long before the vehicle in question was just a dot in Red's rearview mirror.

Then it began to close the gap. Slowly.

Red floored the gas again.

Lauren whipped the truck to the right, out of the convenience store parking lot, and gunned it west on Highway 290.

"There are dozens of side roads for the next few miles," Marlin said, buckling up. "He could've already turned down any of them."

"Then I guess the smartest choice is to stay on the highway and hope he did, too. Agreed?"

"Yeah."

She already had the truck up to eighty, leaving the city limits behind.

"We don't have a reason to stop him," Marlin said.

"Yeah, but at least we can see who's driving."

Now she had it up to ninety. The truck was unmarked, except for the red-and-blue strobe lights tucked behind the grill, which she had activated. They passed several trucks and a motorcycle, then hit a wide-open stretch of highway with no vehicles on it. They passed Towhead Valley Road on the right, then Country Air Drive on the left, and now Marlin could see a vehicle on the horizon. Just a dot. Then it disappeared seconds later as the highway ahead curved slightly to the left. Lauren kept the truck steady at just under one hundred miles per hour, but she reached down and turned the grill lights off.

Marlin studied her face. She appeared totally focused—and content. Special rangers primarily investigated crimes after the fact, which meant they didn't often engage in a vehicle pursuit. Lauren was obviously enjoying the chase.

They topped a rise and the view opened up for at least two miles ahead. Marlin could see the vehicle again, with less of a lead now. He couldn't determine if it was a Ranchero, but it was plainly beige or off-white.

Lauren eased off the gas a little.

Thirty seconds later, even closer now, she said, "Sure looks like a Ranchero to me."

"Yup, it is. No question."

When she was about fifty yards behind the vehicle, she slowed even more and settled in at about eighty. The gap between the two vehicles remained constant. Lauren was pacing the Ranchero.

"He's speeding," she said.

"Perfect," Marlin said.

Pacing wasn't the most accurate way of gauging a vehicle's speed, but it gave them a legal reason to pull the Ranchero over. Lauren goosed the gas until she was fifty feet behind the vehicle, then she hit the grill lights again to initiate the stop.

"Cops're pulling 'em over," Billy Don said, still turned backward in the seat.

Red could see the faint flashing of red and blue lights in his mirror, nearly a quarter-mile back now. "That's what they get for speeding," he said.

Red slowed to seventy miles per hour.

"Ain't you gonna turn around?" Billy Don said.

"What for?"

"Then you can drive by and see if it's Shelby."

Red couldn't believe he hadn't thought of that. So obvious.

"Well, yeah," Red said. "I thought you meant for some reason on top of that one."

"That don't even make sense."

"Maybe not to you," Red said.

The Ranchero began to slow and ease to the shoulder.

"That's Shelby Roach's vehicle for sure," Lauren said. "That's the plate number."

After both vehicles had come to a stop, the driver of the Ranchero did something that was likely to make a cop uneasy during a traffic stop. He stepped from the vehicle without being asked. He was about six-two, slender, with shoulder-length blond hair and a ragged goatee. A cigarette dangled from his lips.

"Knox Thornton," Lauren said. "This'll be interesting."

Marlin and Lauren both stepped from the truck.

"What a pleasant surprise," Knox Thornton called out. His jeans were riddled with holes, but they were the type that came from wear, not because it was fashionable to sell them that way in the store. The leather of his Red Wing work boots was scuffed and scarred. "Long way from home, ain't ya?"

"Back in the vehicle, Knox," Lauren said. "You know how this works."

"Say please."

"It's not a request," Lauren said. "Back in the vehicle, and roll down the passenger-side window."

Traffic was light, but Thornton was standing just a few feet from the outside lane of the highway, and Lauren had every right to order him back into his vehicle for his own safety. Refusal would constitute failure to obey a lawful order—an arrestable offense.

Thornton took his time about it, but he got back into the Ranchero. Lauren approached from the passenger side. Marlin remained a few steps back, listening and watching.

"License and proof of insurance, please," Lauren said.

"Seriously?"

"Yes, sir."

"Gonna tell me what the problem is?"

"You were speeding," Lauren said. "License and proof of insurance."

"Are you fucking kidding me? You're running traffic nowadays? And you just happen to pull *me* over?"

Marlin had a good view through the rear glass into the cab, and he could see that Thornton was opening his wallet to retrieve his ID, which he handed to Lauren. She took it and said, "Insurance."

"I got no idea about insurance," Thornton said. "Ain't my truck."

"Yeah, I know," Lauren said. "It's Shelby's. But you're driving it, so you're on the hook for insurance."

Thornton grunted with impatience and began to search for the slip of paper proving the Ranchero was insured. He checked the visor first, then opened the glove box, revealing a small box of sandwich baggies, and beneath that, a compact digital scale. Thornton quickly slapped the glove box closed, but it was too late.

"Well, *now* you can step out of the vehicle," Lauren said, opening the passenger-side door.

"Ah, man. That's not my stuff and you know it."

"Slide out this way."

"This is bullshit," Thornton said.

"That's it," Billy Don said. "That Shelby's Ranchero. No question about it."

Red agreed. It *was* Shelby's vehicle.

"But that ain't Shelby," Billy Don said when they got closer.

Red agreed with that, too.

They were driving east, back toward Johnson City. It wasn't a regular deputy's car or highway patrol cruiser that had the Ranchero pulled over. Instead it was a truck with flashing lights hidden behind the grill. Three people were standing on the far side of the Ranchero: a tall woman in jeans and a white shirt, the county game warden, and some guy who wasn't Shelby. Red couldn't see the man's face—he was turned the other way—but it definitely wasn't Shelby. This guy was taller, with longer arms and legs. Gangly. But not skinny. Lean and hard. The kind of guy who might surprise you in a bar fight.

Red went another mile down the road, then turned around. On the second pass, he still didn't get a good look at the man who'd been driving Shelby's Ranchero.

"Weird," Billy Don said.

"Yup."

"Where's Shelby?"

"Got no idea."

"Maybe he sold his vehicle," Billy Don said.

Red thought about that idea as he drove. He supposed it was possible, considering how broke Shelby had been. Did it really matter what the explanation was? It was obviously a coincidence that the Ranchero had been following behind him on two separate occasions. What other explanation was there?

"Forget about it," Red said. "Got some dude trying to kill me. Don't need to get sidetracked by my stupid cousin's bullshit."

"I'm sorry about your sister, Knox," Lauren said. "She was a sweet gal."

The three of them were standing far off the shoulder, along the passenger side of Lauren's truck. Thornton gave a slight nod. He knew Lauren was only softening the blow to come.

"There's drug paraphernalia in the glove box," Lauren said. "So we're going to search the vehicle."

There was nothing illegal about possessing a scale and baggies, but those items did give them probable cause to search—without asking for consent or getting a warrant.

"Oh, come on," Thornton said. "You know that ain't my shit. I wouldn't be that stupid. Why would I open the glove compartment if I knew what was in there?"

"Maybe you forgot," Lauren said. "Besides, you know it doesn't matter whose it is. You're driving, so it's on you, plus whatever else we might find, thanks to Shelby. Think he might've left some drugs in there? Now's the time to speak up."

"Man, I don't know. All I did was borrow his vehicle."

"Is Shelby a dealer now?"

Marlin had positioned himself where he could keep an eye on Thornton while also watching for highway traffic.

"I got no idea."

"Why would he have a scale?" Lauren said. "That shouts dealer to me."

"Maybe he's on Weight Watchers."

Thornton took a drag on the cigarette in his left hand, and as he did, his eyes met Marlin's for a moment, holding the gaze long enough to convey that he wasn't intimidated. That sort of thing was important to men like Thornton, and they tried to show it in their attitude and their body language. When Thornton did look away, he spat lightly, as if he had a stray shred of tobacco on his tongue. He stood with his right thumb hooked in the pocket of his grimy jeans. He had a significant, healing gash on the knuckles of that hand. Scabbed over. Probably anywhere from a couple days to a week old.

"I don't need the attitude, Knox," Lauren said. "We're not trying to screw you over."

"Right."

"But we have to search."

Thornton sighed, then said, "Knock yourself out."

CHAPTER FIFTEEN

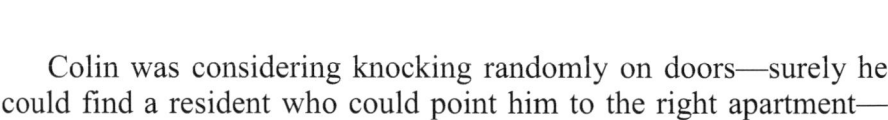

Colin was considering knocking randomly on doors—surely he could find a resident who could point him to the right apartment—when he spotted Derek crossing the parking lot toward his car.

Colin struggled out of his Mini Cooper and timed his approach so that he arrived at the Dodge Charger at the same time as Derek, who was looking down at his phone, preoccupied.

"Hey," Colin said.

Now Derek looked up, plainly startled for a moment, until he realized the humongous person in front of him was somebody he recognized from the pawnshop. "Oh, hey, uh…"

"It's Colin."

"Right, Colin. Didn't expect to see you here."

Derek didn't necessarily have a guilty or fearful expression on his face, but maybe he was a good actor.

"Yeah, I bet you didn't," Colin said.

"Pardon?"

"Cut the shit, Derek."

Colin had decided on an aggressive approach, with no pussyfooting around. He stepped closer, and now he was looming over the much smaller man, who was trapped in an empty parking spot, with cars in all the neighboring spots. Derek had nowhere to go.

"What are you talking about?" he said, still appearing calm.

"Dude, you know exactly what I'm talking about. Don't deny what you did. I'm giving you a chance to fix it and walk away unharmed."

Derek didn't respond at first, except to slowly slip his phone into the front pocket of his jeans. Then he said, "Seriously, I'm really confused."

Colin poked Derek in the chest with great force. "The cash, fuckface. I want the cash back. Now. All of it."

Colin stared at Derek, and Derek stared back. Finally Derek said, "It's obvious you're very upset, but I have absolutely no idea what's happening here."

Colin let out a groan of frustration and reached to grab Derek by the shirtfront—the same intimidating move that had been so effective with Bobo—but his hands never touched fabric. Derek did something quick with his hands and deflected Colin's arms. That made Colin angry. Extremely angry. The kind of anger that clouded his vision and muffled his hearing. Colin had been experiencing that kind of anger more and more in the past few months.

Colin lunged at Derek, intending to wrap the little guy up and just squeeze him into submission, but Derek ducked out of the way before Colin's arms closed.

"Take it easy, man," Derek said. "You've got the wrong guy."

Derek was holding his hands up in front of him, as if could placate Colin. Good luck with that.

"You had your chance," Colin said.

He made another grab, but Derek was too quick. So Colin drew his right fist back, preparing to give Derek the first of many well-deserved blows to the face, but suddenly Colin's face stung. What the fuck? Derek had just popped him in the mouth with an amazingly quick left jab. Colin threw a jab of his own, but Derek slipped under it and popped Colin in the face again. Now he could taste blood.

"Little fucker," Colin said, wiping his lip. "Think you can hurt me? You're only gonna—"

Whap!—another jab—and *bam!*—Derek smashed him in the cheekbone with a right cross.

"Son of a bitch!" Colin said. His knees were a little wobbly. Who knew a guy Derek's size could hit that hard?

"We can stop anytime you want," Derek said, not even a little out of breath. "And you can tell me what this is all about."

"You know what this is about," Colin said, trying to get close enough to make a grab and tackle Derek to the pavement. Then he could smash his head. But Derek kept dancing, left and right, just out of reach. The little bastard had had some training. Boxing? Mixed martial arts?

"I don't want to hurt you," Derek said, still squaring off, with his fists raised.

"You couldn't if you tried," Colin said. If only he could get hold of the smug cocksucker.

"You already have a gash on your face. You'll need stitches."

"Fuck that. You'll need a goddamn ambulance."

"I'm serious, Colin. I've been taking it easy so far. But if you don't—"

Colin opened both arms wide and rushed forward, confident that his sheer mass and momentum would carry him through any jab Derek might throw, and then he could finally get his arms around the smaller man.

Derek swiveled smoothly out of the way and drilled Colin on the side of the head with a punishing left hook as he passed. Colin took the blow on his right ear, which suddenly felt like it was on fire. But he had bigger problems coming.

The punch made him lose his balance, and as he began to fall forward, he realized his head was about to slam into the front bumper of Derek's Charger.

The search turned up nothing illegal, but there was an unloaded handgun in a soft-sided carrying case under the driver's seat.

"Is that your thirty-eight?" Lauren asked. "Or Shelby's?"

"Mine. I can travel with it, even without a carry permit. It wasn't in plain view."

"That's true," Lauren said. "But why do you need it?"

"Don't need a reason. I'd like to get back on the road. You gonna write me a ticket or what? You got radar in that truck? Bet you don't."

"Forget about that for a second," Lauren said. "Right now, we're trying to locate Shelby. We'd like you to follow us back to the sheriff's office and have a chat."

"That sounds fun, but I'll pass."

"That's discouraging, Knox. We're trying to figure out what happened to April. Somebody was with her on Saturday night, we know that much. You're not willing to help?"

"Didn't say that, but I'm not going anywhere to do it."

"Okay, that's fine. We'll talk here. Where's Shelby?"

"No idea. Haven't seen him lately."

Thornton dropped the butt of the cigarette on the ground and crushed it with the heel of his boot.

"But you're driving his Ranchero."

"He loaned it to me."

"When was this?"

"Couple of days ago," Thornton said.

"Two days?"

"Three or four days ago. Can't remember for sure."

"Today is Wednesday. Was it Sunday? Saturday?"

"I told you, I can't remember. I don't keep track of time real good."

"Was it before or after April died?"

"I honestly don't remember."

That's a lie, Marlin thought. When you lose a loved one, every moment in the days and weeks afterward is saturated with grief and pain. The emotion of your loss is woven into every thought and conversation. You remember what came before and what came after.

"When you borrowed the vehicle," Marlin said, "did you and Shelby talk about April passing away?"

"No," Thornton said.

"Well, wouldn't the subject have come up if you'd seen Shelby *after* April died?"

"Not if it was Sunday," Thornton said, "and neither of us had heard the news yet."

That was a valid point.

"So you definitely borrowed it before you heard about April?" Marlin said.

"Yeah."

"So it was either on Saturday, or on Sunday before you heard. Correct?" Lauren said.

"Sounds right."

"Where were you when you borrowed it?" she said.

"Back home."

"At your house, or do you mean San Saba in general?"

"My house."

"What happened to your truck?"

"Transmission's slipping. Need to work on it."

"And you haven't seen or talked to Shelby since then?"

"Nope."

"Nobody seems to know where he went," Lauren said, "and he won't return calls. Any idea why that is?"

Marlin was impressed with Lauren's interrogative skills. She was doing an excellent job, asking quick, varied questions to keep Thornton from having much time to think about his answers.

"Probably in mourning somewhere," Thornton said. "Doesn't want to be disturbed."

"Is that a joke, Knox?"

"No, ma'am. Wouldn't joke about that. He loved my sister. She loved him. They talked about getting married."

"You got a cell phone?"

"You know I do. You've called me on it before."

Marlin figured Lauren had asked that question to see if Thornton would lie. Always give a guy like Thornton a chance to lie. Then, later, you could use the contradiction to your advantage—to apply pressure and eventually arrive at the truth, if you were lucky.

"Have you tried calling him?"

"Of course. No answer."

"And he hasn't called you?"

"Obviously."

"You got your phone on you?"

"I do."

"May I see it? Just want to make sure your memory is accurate."

That was an aggressive question. Lauren was implying that she didn't believe Knox's answers.

"Nope," Thornton said. "May I see yours?"

The conversation was put on pause for a moment as an eighteen-wheeler rumbled past.

"How many phones do you have, Knox?"

"As many as I need. They're very convenient. Technology is a wonderful thing."

"It's very important for us to figure out whether you borrowed the vehicle on Saturday or Sunday," Lauren said.

"If you forced me to guess," Thornton said, "I'd say it was Saturday. I'm fairly sure it was Saturday."

Thornton had a good reason to claim it was on Saturday. He wouldn't want the cops to know he'd seen Shelby after receiving the news about April's death. Otherwise, they'd think he'd gotten angry and harmed Shelby.

"Here's the problem with that," Lauren said. "We know the Ranchero was in Johnson City on Saturday night. That means Shelby and April were down here together, and then he loaned it to you on Sunday. Agreed?"

She was lying, and it was a great lie to tell. She was trying to force Knox to commit to a firm answer regarding the timeline of events. Didn't mean he'd take the bait.

"Man, I don't know," Thornton said. "I can't remember what I had for lunch yesterday."

"Had to have been Sunday," Lauren said, "which means Shelby knew what happened to April when you saw him, but he didn't tell you. Or he did tell you, but you're reluctant to share that with us."

Thornton was shaking his head. "Now you're sayin' I did something to him?"

"No, I wasn't, but did you?"

"Shit," Thornton said. "I think y'all need to use a little more imagination."

"What does that mean?"

"Who was it that supposedly saw the Ranchero?"

"Can't tell you that."

"Well, what if they're wrong and it wasn't Shelby's?"

He wasn't taking the bait. It would be better for him if it remained unclear when he borrowed the vehicle.

"Seems unlikely," Lauren said. "Not many Rancheros on the road."

Thornton made a dismissive snort. "People get confused about all kinds of shit." He turned toward Marlin. "How many calls do you get from people claiming they saw a mountain lion?"

"Let's just focus on the subject at hand," Marlin said.

"A bunch, huh?" Thornton said. "And none of them saw shit, right? Or they saw a house cat or a coyote. Point is, just because somebody said it was a Ranchero, that don't mean shit. You know how unreliable witnesses are."

"Who was it that broke the news to you about April?" Lauren said.

"My daddy, after the sheriff called him."

"Where were you at the time?"

There was a slight pause. Thornton was fully aware that any of his answers could bite him in the butt later.

"At home."

"Did you go anywhere later that afternoon or that evening?"

"Nope."

If he'd said yes, Lauren would've asked him what he was driving at the time. But Thornton had skirted that issue.

"How is Shelby getting around without his vehicle?" she asked.

"Christ, how the hell should I know? My sister died and you people won't give me any peace. Your questions aren't real important to me right now. Besides, the sheriff already asked a bunch of this same bullshit. Isn't that enough?"

Marlin didn't like Thornton's brusque demeanor, but he remained quiet for the moment. They were walking a fine line—still pretending this was only an interview and that they were seeking Knox's help, versus outright accusing him of withholding valuable information or being involved in a crime.

"Thanks for mentioning the sheriff," Lauren said, "because that reminds me of something. When he called you on Sunday afternoon, you said you hadn't seen Shelby in several days. But we know you borrowed Shelby's vehicle on Saturday or Sunday. Why would you tell the sheriff you hadn't seen Shelby in several days, when you had actually seen him on that very day, or the day before?"

Oops.

Marlin hadn't remembered that detail himself. Lauren was damned good at slowly picking Thornton apart, and Marlin was regretting that this interview wasn't being recorded. He watched Thornton's reaction, but there wasn't much to see. Just a shrug. Cool customer. Caught in a lie, but you wouldn't know it from looking at him.

"Maybe I borrowed it on Friday," Thornton said.

Lauren gave him a long skeptical look, but with a smile. Like she was saying, *You really expect me to believe that?*

He stared right back.

Lauren said, "You never told the sheriff you were in possession of Shelby's vehicle."

"Look, I don't know how many times I have to repeat myself. My memory is for shit. Always has been. Then you throw in a dead sister and maybe you can understand why my answers aren't to your complete satisfaction."

Lauren persisted, saying, "How long have you been in Blanco County?"

Thornton reached into the pocket of his T-shirt for another cigarette and lit up, delaying his answer. This was a stalling tactic. Marlin would have asked him to hold off on the smoke until they were done, but Lauren was leading the interview, and she was doing great, so he let it go.

"Couple of days," Thornton said.

Lauren laughed. "Here we go again. 'Couple of days.' You can't remember for sure?"

"No, and I don't give a shit. What does it matter? This is why people don't like talking to the cops."

"Okay," Lauren said, sensing that Thornton was about to stop answering questions. "All right. Couple of days, then. That's fine. But why are you in Blanco County?"

"Huh?"

"Why exactly are you hanging around in this area, Knox?"

CHAPTER SIXTEEN

Colin realized he had been staring at a wall for quite some time, but he wasn't sure how long it had been. Ten feet in front of him were a dozen framed black-and-white photographs. People. Landscapes. Animals. Colin was no expert on photography, but he could tell this was good stuff. Somebody who knew how to use a camera. Beneath the photographs was a small entertainment center, on top of which sat a small flat-screen TV.

He was sitting on a leather sofa. His head ached. Not unbearable, but insistent.

"Colin?"

He turned to his left, sending a twinge of pain through his neck. Derek was sitting there, on the other end of the sofa, half turned toward him, with one leg propped up on the cushions.

"What the fuck?" Colin said.

"You okay?"

"I'll kick your ass," Colin said, but he was weak and felt as if he might throw up.

"You remember what happened?" Derek said.

Colin thought about it. The parking lot. Derek punching him several times in the face. Oh, right. The car bumper. He raised a hand to his forehead and found a large, tender knot. But no blood. That was a good thing. The question was, how did this skinny little fuck get the best of Colin?

"Where am I?" Colin asked. He noticed he wasn't sitting directly on the couch, but was instead sitting on a Mexican blanket—like this guy had put the blanket down to protect the leather.

"My apartment," Derek said.

"You carried me?"

"No, you walked. Sort of. You were pretty woozy. I tried to take you to the emergency room, but you wouldn't go."

"Asshole," Colin said.

"Gee, thanks."

Colin tried to stand, but his legs were jelly.

"You should just stay put for a while," Derek said. "You might fall again. You probably have a concussion. You want an ice pack?"

"Don't need one," Colin said. "What the fuck was that?"

"What was what?"

"That shit you did out there. Some kind of kung fu?"

"No, I used to box."

No wonder. "Pro?"

Derek laughed. "Hell, no. I'm not that dumb. Or that good."

"I need that cash," Colin said. He was fully aware that his thinking wasn't as sharp as it normally was.

"Last time I'm going to say this," Derek said. "I have no idea what you're talking about. I don't know about any cash."

"It was in the suitcases."

"The suitcases you brought into the shop?"

"Yeah. I went to get 'em yesterday and the cash was gone."

"How much cash?" Derek said.

"Forty-six thousand dollars," Colin said.

"Holy moly," Derek said.

"It's not mine."

"Whose is it?"

"Bobo said you must've took it."

"That's bullshit, but it would explain why he fired me this morning. He said he couldn't afford to pay me anymore."

Colin was so tired. He began to stretch out on the sofa, but Derek put a hand out and stopped him. "You shouldn't sleep," Derek said. "Not if you have a concussion."

"Fuck."

"Sorry."

"What am I gonna do?"

"See a doctor. That's what I recommend."

"No, I mean about the cash," Colin said. "If I don't find it, I'm fucked. Beyond fucked. I'm a dead man."

"Why?"

Colin had an idea. This guy Derek seemed to know how to handle himself. And he seemed pretty smart.

"I need some help, man," Colin said. "I'm in big trouble. I don't know what to do. Can you help me?"

"You kidding? A minute ago, you were trying to kick my ass."

"Sorry. I really am. I thought you took the cash, but now I know you didn't. And now I know you're the only person who can help me."

"Why me?"

"Because Bobo has to be lying, right? If you didn't take that cash, that only leaves him. He took it. He has the cash, but he blamed you."

"Assuming the cash was really in the suitcases to begin with."

Colin hadn't even thought about that possibility. "Oh, fuck," he said. Maybe Charmaine was lying. Maybe she stole the cash and was setting Colin up.

"You need to start at the beginning," Derek said. "Tell me where the cash came from and why you're in danger."

"And then you'll help me?" Colin said.

"I just wanted to see the place where April died," Knox Thornton said. "That's all. It just didn't feel real until I did that."

"You went out to Rodney's place?" Lauren asked.

Thornton said, "Yeah. I hopped the fence and walked around. Should've gotten permission, I guess, but I didn't."

"When?"

"Guess it was Monday morning. Or yesterday morning."

Nothing Thornton was saying was adding up.

"So why are you still here?" Marlin said. "Why not go back to San Saba?"

Thornton shrugged. "Truth is, I'm too sad to go home. I'll just sit around and think about April."

That didn't ring true to Marlin at all. Thornton had to have some other reason for remaining in Blanco County, but what was it?

"Why did you try to use Shelby's credit card for gas yesterday morning?" Marlin said.

Thornton paused long enough that it was obvious he was formulating an answer.

"Ain't been thinking straight, obviously," he said. "I ran off and left all my cash at home. I don't have a credit card, so I was screwed."

"How about a debit card?" Marlin asked.

"Nope. I always deal in cash."

Not surprising, for an alleged meth dealer.

"So how did you end up with Shelby's credit card?"

"Found it clipped to the visor. Not a real safe place for Shelby to store it, but nobody's ever accused him of being a genius."

"And you had no choice but to use it, because you had no cash?"

"I knew Shelby wouldn't mind. Well, he wouldn't have minded, if the card had worked. But it got declined. Guess you already know that."

Marlin decided to move on to some more difficult questions. When interviewing a subject like Thornton, there were always a handful of questions that might cause him to clam up or end the interview. It was better to ask those questions last, after getting as much information as possible. Now was the time.

Marlin said, "Were you mad at Shelby when you heard what happened to your sister?"

"Mad at Shelby?" Thornton said. "We don't even know if he was there."

"Who else would it have been?"

"You asked me that already. Isn't that what you're supposed to be finding out? Besides, aren't y'all saying it was an accident? I'm sad, yeah, but why would I be mad at anybody? Accidents happen."

"Here's what we suspect," Marlin said, and Thornton shifted impatiently on his feet. "We think Shelby was out there to steal some cattle, and your sister was just tagging along. You ever hear Shelby talk about cattle rustling?"

Thornton gave him a smirk. "I'm no snitch."

"What happened to your hand?" Marlin said.

Thornton tipped his head backward in frustration, a gesture meant to convey, *Oh, here we go again. I knew it would come to this.*

"You're grasping, dude," he said. "I smashed it when I tried to fix my transmission."

"When was this?"

Thornton smirked. "Couple days ago."

"How'd you smash it? What happened exactly?" Marlin said.

"Doesn't matter. You won't believe me."

"So you won't tell me?"

"Nope."

"I'd like to take a picture of the injury. You mind?"

"I do, yeah."

"Would you mind removing your wallet and showing us the contents?"

Thornton frowned. "What the fuck for?"

"I'd like to see the contents of your wallet. You mind?"

"Hell, yeah, I mind," Thornton said. "I already let you search the vehicle and you didn't find shit. Waste of time. Now you're just hassling me."

"When you pulled your wallet out a few minutes ago to get your ID, I could see the edges of a lot of bills inside. But earlier, you said you didn't have any cash."

Thornton didn't miss a beat. "I didn't have any cash when I got to town, but I sold my wristwatch to a guy in the Dairy Queen parking lot. Seventy-five bucks. Watch was worth three hundred, but I needed the money. That's how I bought gas."

Another lie.

"Who was the guy?"

"No idea. Just some guy."

"Look at your arms," Marlin said. "You've got a tan, but I don't see a ring on either wrist where you wore your watch."

"I always carried it in my pocket," Thornton said. "Don't like wearing a watch or jewelry or any of that shit."

He was a fast thinker, Marlin had to give him that.

So Marlin said, "If you have Shelby's vehicle, what is he driving?"

"I don't know and I don't care. He's got a motorcycle. Maybe he's riding that. Maybe he's hitchhiking."

"How did he get home from your place?"

"I dropped him off. That was the last time I seen him and I haven't talked to him since. Now I'm done talking. If you want to write me up, go right ahead."

Marlin couldn't think of anything else to ask.

Lauren handed him his driver's license. "Thanks for your help, Knox. If you see Shelby, please give the sheriff's office a call."

As Thornton pulled back onto the highway, Marlin said what both of them were thinking. "Doesn't look good for Shelby, does it?"

"Nope," Lauren said. "You up for a drive?"

"Where to?"

CHAPTER SEVENTEEN

Derek wasn't sure what to make of this oily, sweaty, acne-pocked ogre on his couch. Sure, he'd dealt with him at the pawnshop, but he'd never really paid much attention to him. They'd never had a lengthy discussion. But now, Derek could see that Colin Kelly was basically a freakishly muscled adult with the mind of an adolescent. An angry, maladjusted, self-centered adolescent.

"I got a girlfriend named Charmaine," Colin said, starting at the beginning, as Derek had requested. "We've been together, off an on, since high school back home. We moved down here and lived together until late last week. Then I caught her cheating on me and locked her out of the apartment."

She cheated on you? Derek thought. *A fine catch such as yourself? Who would've expected that?*

"She kept calling me and shit," Colin said, "trying to get back together, but I said screw that. I was so damn mad. So then I decided to pay her back by pawning her stuff."

Derek said, "So all that merchandise you brought in last week wasn't yours?"

"Well, technically, no. Some of it was ours, but most of it was hers. Her clothes and shoes and all that crap. I was just trying to make life difficult for her. Make her pay to get her stuff back."

Derek didn't bother pointing out that what Colin had done was illegal.

"So those suitcases were hers," Derek said.

Colin nodded. "I didn't know the smallest one was stuffed with cash. But Charmaine knew. I figure that's the real reason she was so desperate to get back together. She needed to get that cash back. Unless she's lying. She could be setting me up."

"Where on earth did she get that much money?" Derek said. "What does she do for a living?"

"Cocktail waitress," Colin said. "Yeah, I know, that don't explain the cash. She earns good tips and all, but nowhere near that kind of money, even if she saved up for years. That's where the cheating comes in. See, it's not *her* money. It belongs to one of the guys she was cheating with—another guy from back home. I used to hang with him. His name is Knox Thornton."

Colin paused there, as if he expected Derek to recognize the name and react accordingly. Derek could only shake his head, meaning he didn't know the man.

Colin said, "I'm telling you, Knox will fuck me up bad if he thinks I took his money."

Derek stood up from the couch. He didn't know why, but he needed to stand. He always seemed to think better when he was standing. "You want a Coke or something?"

"Got a beer?" Colin said.

"In your condition, you really shouldn't have…ah, screw it. Be right back."

He returned with two opened bottles of Miller and handed one to Colin. The bodybuilder drank half of it in one long swallow.

Derek took a sip of his own, then said, "Tell me exactly what your girlfriend said."

"Okay, well, she totally freaked when I told her I'd pawned all her stuff, and to be honest, I started to feel bad about it, so I offered to get it back. That's when she said the problem wasn't just her stuff, it was the suitcase was loaded with cash. I said what in the hell are you talking about, and that's when she told me she'd been seeing Knox Thornton. Until then, I didn't know who she was cheating with, I just knew she'd been cheating. What happened was, she ran into him on a trip home. She used to go home almost every weekend because her grandma was sick. It's like an hour away from Leander."

Colin paused for a moment to guzzle the rest of his beer.

Then he said, "So about a month ago, Knox asked Charmaine if she'd hold onto some suitcases for him. She was like, okay, whatever, but she thought it was a little weird, and after she brought the suitcases home, she peeked inside and saw all that cash. She knew better than to ask him about it. She was smart enough to know

Knox wasn't earning all that money as a welder, and he didn't actually have a job, anyway. You want to know what Knox really does?"

"I guess so," Derek said.

"Deals meth. Sells it in bulk to a bunch of other dealers, and all of these people would stab you in the throat if they thought you were a snitch."

"How do you know all this?" Derek asked.

"Like I said, I used to hang with him."

"So he's a friend of yours?"

"Yeah, kinda. Was."

"Did you work for him? Is that what 'kinda' means?"

Colin started to say something, but then he changed his mind and said, "We speaking confidentially here?"

Derek nodded.

"Yeah, I worked for him," Colin said. "For a little while. Then me and Charmaine moved here. I wanted to get away from all that shit. People think living in the country is all peaceful and quiet, but you got all kinds of crazies living out there."

Derek was tempted to wash his hands of this mess. Just tell Colin to hit the road and solve his own problems. But the big guy seemed so helpless. And dumb. It was obvious his intelligence was limited. Or maybe it was the blow to his head, or even a side effect of the steroids he abused. But instead of deserting this fucked-up guy in his time of need, Derek simply suggested the obvious, sensible solution.

"You need to call the sheriff's department," Derek said, "and tell them everything you told me. Let them sort everything out."

"Oh, man," Colin said. "I wish it was that easy. But think about it. What can the cops actually do about it?"

"They'll talk to this Knox guy and he won't bother you after that."

"Are you friggin' nuts? The cops'd know the money in the suitcase is dirty, and Knox would consider that the same as snitching. Besides, he ain't scared of the cops. Never has been. In fact it's the other way around. Most of the cops in San Saba County are scared of him."

"What makes him so scary?" Derek said. "I don't get it. He's just one guy."

"Yeah, but there's almost nothing he won't do, and he gets away with it."

"Like what? What will he do?"

"How about kill a guy?" Colin said. "He killed a guy last year, but he never got charged with it."

"No way."

"Way."

"Who? When?"

"A witness who was gonna testify against him," Colin said.

"Why didn't they charge him for that? How do you know he really did it?"

It was obvious Colin knew something, but he was reluctant to share it. "We still talking confidentially?" he said.

"Sure," Derek said.

"You promise? Because I'm about to tell you something only three people on the planet know, and Knox is one of them. And if you ever tell anybody, I'll deny it. Forever. And I'll come looking for you. I promise you don't want that."

Derek should've ended the conversation right then and there—but he was just too damn curious. "I promise," he said.

Colin leaned forward. "I know Knox did it, because I saw it happen."

The first photograph revealed that the trespasser behind Red's trailer had shoulder-length blond hair and a goatee. Skinny dude, wearing jeans and a black T-shirt with something printed on the front, like the name of a band or something. But Red couldn't make out what it said. Too blurry. The man was probably in his late twenties or early thirties, but it was hard to tell for sure, because he wasn't facing the camera head-on. It was more of a profile shot. Plus, it was a nighttime photograph using an infrared flash, and that made the photo look weird. Even the deer in the earlier photos looked odd, with glowing green eyes.

"Recognize him?" Red whispered.

He was leery of drawing the attention of the librarian, who was a man, of all things. Who knew there were male librarians? The male librarian had been nicer than the old lady in Johnson City, but it was obvious he was equally protective of his library and everything in it. He'd agreed to let them use a computer only after Red had left his driver's license at the front desk and they'd promised not to access any "adult content." The male librarian hadn't raised any stink about Red's license being expired, or maybe he hadn't noticed.

"Don't think so," Billy Don said quietly.

"Looks like a scumbag, don't he?" Red said.

"Going for the Kid Rock look," Billy Don said.

He wasn't being as contrary now that it appeared Red had been right about everything.

"I *told* you I heard somebody sneaking around back there," Red said.

He couldn't resist rubbing it in, even though he had already rubbed it in quite extensively an hour earlier, back at the trailer.

Billy Don remained quiet.

"And you said it was probably a pig," Red said. "Remember that, Billy Don? Remember when you said it was probably a pig?"

"I remember what I said. But just 'cause you got some guy trespassing on your place, that don't mean he's the one who fired the shot through the window."

"Oh, are you shittin' me?" Red said, louder than he meant to.

Billy Don flinched and they both looked toward the front desk, where the male librarian was giving them a *Ssshhh* gesture. Red gave a little wave.

"I've known mules less stubborn than you are," he whispered to Billy Don.

"Whatever," Billy Don said. "Got a right to my opinion."

Red shook his head and clicked forward to the second shot. The camera had taken a total of four photos of the man—two as he passed by the first time, and two more as he was leaving, which was after Red had shined the spotlight toward the rear of the property.

"That don't help any," Billy Don said, and he was right.

The second photo was almost identical to the first, except that the man had advanced forward by about three feet. So Red clicked to the third shot. The biggest difference here was that the man was now striding from left to right and he was facing the camera full on, which gave them a great view of his face.

Also, there was a revolver dangling from the man's right hand.

Case closed. Slam dunk.

Red leaned back in his chair and looked at Billy Don, who was still looking at the photograph.

"Dang," Billy Don said.

"Believe me now?" Red said.

"Sure do, but that's not why I said dang. You're gonna think I'm nuts, but don't he kinda look like the guy we just saw driving Shelby's Ranchero?"

"What? No. That don't even make sense."

"But look at him."

"I'm looking at him. Not the same guy."

"You sure?"

"Yeah.

"But they *look* alike, don't they?"

"Maybe a little," Red said.

"It's the stringy hair."

"Lots of guys have stringy hair," Red said. "Especially the kind of guy that drives an old Ranchero. The hair and that wimpy goatee. Makes 'em look like Lynyrd Skynyrd rejects. But you're getting us sidetracked again. The important thing to remember is that this dude wants to kill me. You agree?"

"Can't believe I'm saying this, but that seems like the only explanation."

"Unless he's plotting to steal our cash," Red said.

"Could be that, too."

Red said, "Let's think about this for a second. He shot at me through the window, and then he came sneaking around at night with a gun, probably wanting a second crack at it. But if he was after the cash, why do it that way? Why not break in while we weren't home?"

Both men sat in silence, thinking. Amazing how peaceful it was here in the library. Red could get used to it, as long as he wasn't expected to read. Perfect place to kick back and take a nap—except the male librarian up front probably had a policy against napping. No porn and no napping. Those two policies right there probably explained why the library was empty.

Billy Don said, "Maybe he already snuck in, saw the safe, tried to open it, but couldn't—so then he came up with a different plan. He wanted to shoot you, yeah, but just in the leg or the shoulder. Then he was gonna torture the snot out of you until you opened the safe. Maybe he was gonna strip an electrical cord down to the bare wire and clamp 'em to your nipples. Something like that."

Red turned to look at Billy Don.

Billy Don said, "What?"

"That's just weird. Where did that come from?"

"If he's after the cash, he wouldn't kill you outright, would he? What good would that do? He'd want to wing you, and then force you to open the safe."

Red couldn't disagree. "But who is he?"

"Don't know."

"Maybe he was listening in when you were blabbing to

somebody about our Vegas trip," Red said.

The day before, Red had forced Billy Don to make a list of everybody he'd told about their upcoming gambling excursion. Red hadn't seen anybody on that list who concerned him too much. Just a bunch of locals who wouldn't have enough brains or ambition to rip someone off.

"You know I wouldn't talk about that kind of stuff with some stranger hanging around," Billy Don said. Then, a moment later, he added, "Unless I'd been drinking, of course."

"Of course," Red said. "The question is, what're we gonna do about it?"

"Go to the cops," Billy Don said. "Right?"

"Sometimes it's like you don't even know me at all," Red said.

CHAPTER EIGHTEEN

"Now you're bullshitting me," Derek said.

"Hell if I am," Colin said. "Why would I lie?"

To earn empathy, Derek thought. *So I'll help you.*

But was Colin really clever enough to manipulate anyone like that? And would he tell such an outlandish lie? If a man named Knox Thornton from San Saba was suspected in a murder, surely there would be something online about it. Derek would check on that later.

"You witnessed an actual murder?" Derek said.

"Yep."

"That's crazy."

"No shit."

"Who did he kill?" Derek said. "When? Where?"

"I'm not getting into all that."

"Why not?"

"Not a good idea," Colin said. "Can I have another beer?"

"Why isn't it a good idea?"

"Because the more you know, the more the cops can badger out of you. If you don't know it, you can't spill it. Believe me, the less I tell you, the better."

"Does that mean you didn't tell the cops what you saw?"

"Man, don't you get it? Knox Thornton is a dangerous man. Hell, no, I didn't tell the cops. I know what Knox is capable of. I saw him shoot a—" Colin clapped a hand over his mouth, his eyes bugging. He had just let a crucial detail slip. He pointed a thick index finger at Derek and said, "Fuck. You forget what I just said, you hear me? Forget that part."

"Yeah, I will," Derek said, beginning to realize just how much of a quagmire he was in.

"Can I have another beer?" Colin said.

"Let me ask you something. Would your girlfriend take the money and blame it on you?"

"Absolutely," Colin said. "Would your boss take the money and blame it on you?"

"Absolutely," Derek said.

Colin blinked his eyes several times, as if he were trying to clear his vision. "Can I have another beer?"

Derek turned and went back into the kitchen.

Eunice Roach, Shelby's mother, lived on a small ranch she and her now-deceased husband had bought in the 1960s. Shelby had moved back home and was staying in a small cabin fifty yards from the house. Lauren had suggested that they make the hour's drive to ask Eunice Roach some questions, but they'd decided to call first, so the drive wouldn't be wasted. They'd gotten voicemail on the first attempt, but the mother—Eunice Roach—answered on the second.

Lauren explained who they were, why they were calling, and said, "Can we stop by and talk for a minute?"

"That would be fine, except I'm in Lake Charles right now."

Lauren had it on speakerphone, and Eunice Roach's voice sounded like she'd been smoking two packs a day since the advent of modern tobacco farming. Marlin could hear the musical jingling and jangling of slot machines in the background.

"Okay, well, we're looking for Shelby," Lauren said.

"Yes, ma'am, I know. A deputy called me the other day, but I didn't know where Shelby was then, and I still don't."

"When did you see him last?" Marlin asked.

"Three or four days ago. He comes and goes at all hours. His cabin is separate from the house, you understand?"

"Have you called him?"

"Several times. Left messages."

"Mrs. Roach, would you give us permission to enter Shelby's cabin?" Lauren asked.

"What exactly for?"

"To see if we can find anything that might tell us his whereabouts."

She didn't answer.

"Mrs. Roach?"

"I think I'd better say no. I love my boy, but he don't always make the smartest choices. I wouldn't want you finding something in there that could get him in trouble."

"I'm going to be frank," Marlin said. "Considering the way Shelby's girlfriend died on Saturday night, and that Shelby hasn't been seen since then, we're concerned for his welfare. If you'd grant us access to the cabin, that might help us determine whether or not he's okay."

"Oh, Shelby's fine," she said. "Trying to steer clear of the cops, is all. But I'll tell you what. When I get back home tomorrow afternoon, I'll check the cabin myself."

They thanked her for her time and hung up.

Lauren had to interview a witness in a horse-theft case later that afternoon in Lampasas, so she and Marlin split up after agreeing to meet at eleven o'clock the following morning. Marlin, in the meantime, would attempt to obtain a search warrant for Knox Thornton's cell phone records—at least the one phone they knew he owned. It would be helpful to confirm whether or not he'd had contact with Shelby Roach after Bobby Garza told the Thornton family about April's death.

Marlin was driving back to the sheriff's department to write a probable-cause affidavit when he remembered Phil Colby's text from earlier in the day. He dialed and Colby answered on the second ring.

"About damn time," Colby said. "It's almost like you've got a job or something."

"Busy day. What's up?"

"Not a lot. I wanted to tell you about something. Or someone. Lauren Wilcox."

Wilcox was Lauren's maiden name.

"Yeah, she's been in town the past few days," Marlin said. "We're working a case together. She's a—"

"Special ranger," Colby said. "Right. I saw her outside Ronnie's and we talked."

"Hasn't changed much, has she?" Marlin said.

"God, no. I recognized her right off the bat, although it took me a minute to place the face. It's been a long time."

"Since San Marcos days," Marlin said.

"Exactly," Colby said. "I hadn't thought of her since then. Had you?"

Something was strange about Phil's tone. Like he was nervous.

"Not in a long time," Marlin said.

"That's what I figured," Colby said. "Anyway, like I said, I ran into her outside Ronnie's last night and we started talking. I'd just walked out with five pounds of food, so I invited her over to my place to eat supper."

"Oh, yeah?"

"Yeah, and, well, that's why I wanted to talk to you. I know it's been years since either of us have even seen her, but considering that y'all used to—"

"Phil?"

"Yeah?"

"I got an idea what's coming. You want to just spit it out?"

Phil laughed. "Okay, here's the deal. We really hit it off. We kept talking and talking, and we had some wine, and before you know it, it was past eleven. And, so, she ended up spending the night."

Derek handed Colin a fresh bottle of Miller and said, "You know, I understand that you're in a bad position, but I don't see how there's anything I can do about it."

In other words, *Goodbye and good luck with that murderer friend of yours. Take care, now. You can show yourself out.*

Colin didn't react. Instead, he said, "I still don't think you're getting it, dude. Bobo told me you probably took the money, and I believed him."

"No offense, but so what?"

"Knox will wonder about that, too."

Oh, shit.

"But I didn't take the money," Derek said.

"Neither did I, but that don't matter. Knox won't believe any of us. He'll figure it was Bobo or me or you or even Charmaine. We all had a chance to steal it. He'll come looking for us, one by one, until he finds the money."

"And what exactly will he do to us?" Derek said. He was having a hard time believing anyone, even a suspected killer, would be so brazen as to "come looking" for four people.

"Whatever it takes," Colin said. "Anything."

"Anything?" Derek asked.

"*Anything.*" Colin tipped his bottle up and drank half.

"We have to go to the cops," Derek said.

"Fuck, no, man. It'll be like that Mongo dude in that old movie. It will only make him mad."

"You're saying he'll come after us even if we tell the cops what's going on?"

"Yep," Colin said. "See, what'll happen—if he thinks you took the money—is that one day you'll just disappear. Nobody will know where you went."

"Because Knox will have grabbed me?"

"Yeah, and he'll try to make you tell him where the money is. Of course, you won't be able to tell him anything, but by then, what's he gonna do? Let you go? Think the cops can protect you from a guy like that? Even if they could—which they can't—how long would they keep doing it? A month? A year?"

"Fuck," Derek said, sitting down on the far end of the couch. Suddenly he felt trapped. Claustrophobic.

"Only good news," Colin said, "is that Knox doesn't know the money is missing yet. Well, according to Charmaine. That's 'cause his sister died on Saturday in some kind of freak accident with a bull, and he's been tied up with that. But it's only a matter of time."

"Fuck," Derek said again. "Why did he give her that money in the first place?"

"The cops have been trying to serve a warrant on him for years. He probably heard a rumor he was about to get raided."

Derek didn't know what to do or say.

"Something just came to me," Colin said. "Knox is gonna figure Charmaine eventually looked in the suitcases, so the first thing he's gonna think is that she took the money. We should do everything we can to make him believe that's what happened."

"Wait, what?"

"We should blame it on Charmaine. I could tell Knox that she *told* me she took the money."

"You basically want to sacrifice your ex-girlfriend?"

"It's not a sacrifice if she *did* take the money, is it? Besides, you just *know* she's gonna blame it on me. But she'll also tell him I pawned the luggage, so it might've been one of the scumbags at the pawnshop. That's what she'll say. She'll want as many people to blame as possible."

"If Knox thinks she did it, what will he do to her?"

"Nothing good," Colin said. "That's for sure. Best case, she has the money and she gives it back. Then Knox would probably just slap her around a little and be done with it."

"And if not...?"

"Don't know, but I was wrong about needing your help. Truth is, I think you need my help as much as I need yours. We're both fucked."

CHAPTER NINETEEN

"Huh," Marlin said. So Lauren had spent the night with Phil.

"It's just, you know—I felt I should tell you," Phil said. "Should I have kept my mouth shut?"

"Hey, it's really none of my business," Marlin said. "But if you felt obligated to share it with me, that's fine. Lauren didn't say a word about it today."

He realized he actually took a small bit of pleasure in telling Phil that Lauren hadn't said anything—almost as if it hadn't been important enough to her to mention it.

"Yeah, we both agreed it should come from me," Phil said.

"What, you're suddenly like a couple or something?" Marlin said. "Making decisions together?"

"Nah, nothing like that. But I am hoping to see her again."

Marlin didn't know what to say. Did this situation bother him? Honestly, yes, it did, but why? It was ridiculous. Prior to Monday, he hadn't seen Lauren in decades, and it wasn't like they'd been all that serious when they'd dated.

"You there?" Phil said.

"Yeah."

"If you'd rather I didn't see her…" Phil said.

Too late for that, isn't it? Marlin thought.

"That's silly," he said. "It's no business of mine."

"I don't want to piss you off or anything."

"Phil, seriously, don't worry about it."

"You sure?"

"Yep."

"I appreciate that." They were both silent for a moment. Then Phil said, "Okay, I might as well tell you that Lauren and I got together once before. Long time ago."

"Really? You never mentioned that."

"I know."

"When was it?"

"About two months after y'all broke up."

Marlin was just entering the edge of Johnson City. He pulled over and stopped in the parking lot of a fried chicken restaurant called Big Daddy's.

"How many times did you go out?"

"Maybe three or four."

Did you sleep together? He left that one unasked. He already knew the answer. If they hadn't slept together, Phil wouldn't have kept it to himself all these years.

"Well," Marlin said.

"Now you're pissed," Phil said.

"I'm not pissed, but it is kind of weird that you never said anything."

"I started to at the time, but it was over as quickly as it started, and after that, I didn't see the point. I figured it wasn't like we were sneaking around behind your back, because you were the one who broke up with her, remember? And now, well, I never expected to see her again, but here she is, and we had fun together last night, so I decided it was time to tell you everything. Better late than never, right?"

"I guess."

"Think I should feel guilty about it?"

"No, but the fact that you never told me sort of answers that question, doesn't it?"

Witness Disappears in Drug Case.

That was the headline for the first hit that popped up when Derek Googled "knox thornton," which he did just minutes after Colin had walked out his front door. After all, Derek wanted to confirm that Colin wasn't spinning some crazy tale.

He most definitely was not.

The headline was from an article in the *Austin American-Statesman* dated in the fall of the previous year. The paywall prevented Derek from seeing beyond the first few paragraphs, but what he saw was enough to make him become even more nervous about his situation.

> *A key witness in a case against a suspected San Saba County methamphetamine dealer has gone missing, according to the county attorney's office. Grant Bender was scheduled to testify in the felony trial of Knox Thornton, originally to begin on Monday.*
>
> *"He hasn't been seen for more than a week," said Craig Lyons, assistant county attorney. "Obviously, we don't know why he's missing, but we are concerned for his welfare. The sheriff has been investigating, but as far as we can tell, Mr. Bender has vanished without a trace. At this point, we haven't decided whether we will present our case without his testimony."*

"I think you need my help as much as I need yours."

That's what Colin had said earlier, before he left, and it gave Derek no comfort to realize it was true. Now, more than three hours later, Derek was still weighing his options.

Option one: Work together, as Colin had suggested.

Option two: Have nothing more to do with Colin and hope Knox Thornton found his money before he came looking for Derek.

Option three: Talk to the cops. That one, of course, made the most sense, despite what Colin had said. Just call the police and tell them everything, from start to finish—not just about the missing money, but everything Colin had said about the murder of Grant Bender. Better yet, drive down there and ask to see a detective. They'd protect him, right? They couldn't just let him get killed. Right?

Derek grabbed his cell phone and dialed. "My gut tells me it was Bobo," he said when Colin answered. "Had to be Bobo."

"What about Charmaine?" Colin asked.

"No, Bobo fired me out of the blue, and I know it wasn't because he couldn't afford to pay me. He wanted to put the blame on me. That's the only explanation. Oh, hang on a second."

"What?" Colin asked.

"I just realized something."

"What?"

"I think I know how we can prove Bobo did it."

"How's your case going?" Nicole asked after dinner.

She was reading a Helen Haught Fanick novel while Marlin was watching Texas play Baylor in the Big 12 baseball tournament. He was having trouble concentrating on the game.

"Fine," Marlin said. "Slow, but steady."

"Working with Lauren okay?" Nicole asked.

"Sure," he said. "She's a good investigator."

Oh, and she also slept with my best friend—not just last night, but during college, too.

He'd been telling himself he shouldn't be bothered by Phil's revelation, but he couldn't stop thinking about it. And he was having a difficult time figuring out what was bothering him more—Phil and Lauren getting together now, or Phil and Lauren getting together back in college.

"How so?" Nicole said.

"Huh?"

"How is she a good investigator?"

"Very logical and organized. Seems to remember every detail about the case. Just really sharp."

"Why did she make the switch from deputy to special ranger?"

"I don't know."

Marlin wondered how it would go tomorrow. At a minimum, it would be awkward seeing her now. Obviously, Lauren would know everything Phil and Marlin had discussed during their phone conversation, and Phil would have told her that Marlin got a little testy. He would just as soon not even address the issue with Lauren, but there was no getting around it. Knowing her, she would probably bring it up in the first minute, so they could deal with it and move on.

There was no denying that Marlin felt some resentment toward her now, after learning what had happened between her and Phil. Why had she hooked up with Phil, of all people? Had she felt some attraction to him while she'd been dating Marlin? If so, had Phil felt the same way about her? Marlin should have asked him more questions earlier.

"Oh, that was a nice one," Nicole said.

"What?"

"They just turned a double play. You sure seem distracted."

CHAPTER TWENTY

"Got a plan yet?" Billy Don asked the moment Red came out of his bedroom the next morning. The big man was practicing blackjack on the couch, dealing five hands onto the coffee table—one hand for himself, one for the dealer, and three for imaginary players. Red had been pleasantly surprised over the preceding months at Billy Don's level of dedication. He practiced all the time.

"Ughr," Red said, because he wasn't ready to talk until he'd had some coffee. He went into the kitchen, poured himself a mug, then went back into the living room.

"At least we didn't get murdered in our sleep," Billy Don said. "Shotgun to the head or something like that."

"Jesus Christ," Red said. "You gotta say that kind of stuff?"

They'd left floodlights on all night, front and back, and Red had slept with his Colt revolver on his nightstand. He was even starting to wonder where he could get a guard dog. Might be wise to have a big, mean dog around. But then the dog would run all the wildlife off, so that wouldn't work. Plus the cost of dog food, and vet bills, and on and on. Shit always got so complicated.

Billy Don said, "Just sayin'." He dealt himself another card and busted his hand.

The truth was, Red hadn't slept much. Not just because he was worried about the man in the photos, but because he was trying to decide how to deal with the threat. He hadn't come up with anything new or useful.

Assuming having cash on hand was the problem, he could break down and get a safe-deposit box at the bank, except he didn't trust banks. You just never knew when the economy was going to collapse, and when it did, Red figured it would happen quick. One minute, the talking heads on TV would be saying everything is fine and dandy, the next minute, the world would be in a panic and investors would be jumping off buildings. Bank doors would be chained shut.

He could also break down and tell the cops what was going on, except he didn't trust cops, either. They'd want to know why anyone might be after Red, which would mean telling them about the cash, and the next thing you know, they'd be serving a warrant on his trailer for some trumped-up charge, and the cash would disappear. *What cash?* they'd say. *We didn't see any cash.* Plus, Red had to admit that calling the cops would make him feel like a wimp. What sort of man calls the cops just because his life is in danger? Would Rick Perry call the cops? Or Ted Nugent? Well, those were probably bad examples. But how about John Wayne or Arnold Schwarzenegger? Would they call the cops? Hell, no, they wouldn't. They'd take care of business themselves. They were real men, same as Red. So calling the cops wasn't an option.

The only other idea he'd had was one they'd already discussed—take the cash and head for Vegas, whether they went by train, truck, bus, or overpriced plane ticket. But there was something cowardly about that, too, so it didn't sit right with Red. He'd never run from trouble before, except on those occasions when it was the best option.

"So did ya?" Billy Don said.

"Did I what?"

"Come up with a plan?"

"Not yet."

Billy Don shuffled the deck and began to deal another round. "I got an idea," he said, "but I don't know if it's any good or not."

Red eased down onto his recliner in the corner and sat quietly for a moment. Billy Don was waiting for him to ask about the idea. Red drank some coffee. Then he leaned to his left, pushed a curtain aside, and peered out a window. Nothing. Just caliche and cedar trees.

"I already checked the camera," Billy Don said. "No new pictures of him."

Red gave another grunt. He was relieved to hear that, but he made sure not to show it. Billy Don slapped more cards on the table, still waiting for Red to ask about the idea. Red stretched and yawned.

"What we should do is turn the tables on him," Billy Don said.

"Hell, we know he's out there, but *he* don't know *we* know. So we should use that to our advantage."

"Yeah, and how do we do that?"

"Set a trap," Billy Don said. "Catch him. If we can get ahold of him, we can give him a real strong incentive to stop doing what he's been doing. We can even find out why he's been doing it."

Red always hated to admit when Billy Don came up with a good idea, but in this case, he was eager to accept a solution from any source. The idea did happen to take advantage of the one skill Red and Billy Don had by the truckload—lying in wait.

"What sort of trap?" Red said.

"Well, that part of the plan is still a little murky," Billy Don said, slapping a queen down on the table in front of him. "But I bet we can come up with something."

A few seconds later, Billy Don dealt himself an ace. Blackjack. Red took that as a good sign.

On Thursday morning, a freelance writer named Ursula Hernstrom took her fourteen-year-old nephew fishing on Brady Creek Reservoir, 50 minutes west of San Saba, Texas. The nephew, Dean, had bad skin, baggy pants, and a sullen, sarcastic demeanor—but Ursula wasn't going to let that stop her from having a good time. It had been two solid months since she'd had a chance to get out on the water.

They launched the boat at sunrise, but it quickly became apparent that Dean had no interest in aquatic life or bass boats or anything, really, except the cell phone that was all but glued to his left palm. He began tapping away on the damn thing the moment they hit the water. Ursula couldn't understand the fascination. Why would you want to text with some other kid when you could be enjoying a beautiful day on a magnificent body of water? Okay, the fish weren't biting, which made things a little slow, but that was beside the point.

Finally, the phone lost its signal, and Dean had no choice but to interact with his aunt. The first thing he said was, "How much longer are we staying out?"

"Really, Dean?" Ursula said. "That's your idea of conversation?"

He began to pout.

"How's school?" she asked.

"That's your idea of conversation?" he said.

"Touché," she said. A moment later she added, "Are you really not having any fun?"

Dean shrugged. "I'm bored."

"Hey, you want to work the fishfinder? I'll show you how." Ursula had recently installed a Lowrance HDS-12, one of the best sonars money could buy. It had a high-definition color display and depth penetration up to 3,000 feet.

"Why bother?" Dean asked. "My dad says this lake is fished out."

Ursula didn't think much of Dean's dad, or his knowledge about fishing, but she kept that to herself. They settled into silence for fifteen minutes. Ursula was ready to call it a day when one of the rods dipped in its holder. "Hey, there we go! Grab that, will you?"

"You grab it."

So she did, and she promptly felt a lot of weight on the line. Big fish. Really big fish.

"Seriously, Dean, you should take this one." She gave him no choice and forced the rod into his hands.

"What do I do?"

"Take it slow or the line'll break," she said. "Let him run a little. Wear him out. Probably a black bass, or maybe a big ol' cat."

"How big, you think?"

"Long as your arm."

"Really?"

"Hey, you never know. Take your time. Give him some line if you need to."

Dean nodded, and he actually appeared excited about the prospect of landing a big fish.

"That's it," said Ursula. "You got the hang of it."

Dean kept reeling. And then the line suddenly snapped.

"Aw, crud," Ursula said. "That sucks."

"This is a dumb sport," Dean said, handing the rod back to her.

"We'll get another one," Ursula said.

"Whatever."

She was wrong. Two hours later, they'd caught nothing, so Ursula decided it was time to give up. They were on the way back to the boat launch when Dean spotted the dead body floating among a clump of tall reeds. As Ursula called the sheriff, the kid finally appeared to be having a genuinely good time.

CHAPTER TWENTY-ONE

"Mornin'," Lauren said, stopping in Marlin's office doorway at eleven o'clock.

He'd decided that he wasn't going to let this moment turn into anything ugly or regrettable. He had questions, but they would remain unanswered. It really wasn't worth the drama, was it?

"Hey," he said. "How's it going?"

"I'm gonna grab some coffee," she said, aiming a thumb over her shoulder. "Need anything?"

"I'm good, but thanks."

She hesitated. "Can we talk for a second?"

"Sure. About what?"

"Well, you know. About Phil."

"We really don't—"

"I know you talked to him yesterday, and I just want to explain why I didn't—"

"Lauren, seriously," he was shaking his head. "It's not necessary. Let's just leave it alone, okay? That's what I'd rather do."

She remained in the doorway. "You're not upset?"

"Nope. It's all good. Just took me by surprise, that's all."

"Phil said you got a little snippy on the phone."

Marlin let out a small sigh. "Phil has a way of testing my patience occasionally, but he's my best friend, and he always will be. Besides, this thing between you two is none of my business."

She appeared unconvinced. So he said, "Go get your coffee. I have something interesting to share."

He raised a sheaf of papers and tried to put an intriguing

expression on his face.

She laughed. "You never could raise just one eyebrow," she said. "But I'll bite. What ya got?"

"Get your coffee and we'll talk. Then we're supposed to give Bobby an update in 30 minutes."

"Is it Knox Thornton's phone records?" she said.

"Maybe."

"Oh, goody. Be right back."

She returned two minutes later and took a seat across the desk from him. "So spill it," she said.

Marlin glanced down at the papers and said, "Knox Thornton called a number at about four o'clock on Saturday afternoon, about ten hours before April died. I called the number and the greeting says, 'Hey, you know who it is. Leave a message.' I want you to hear it. Hang on."

He dialed the number again and played it on speakerphone.

Lauren immediately said, "That's Shelby Roach."

"You sure?"

"Absolutely. No question at all."

"So Bobby was right. He's using a burner phone that can't be traced to him."

"Doesn't surprise me at all," Lauren said. "Bet Knox has one, too. Probably has a burner for business and a different phone for personal calls. I've seen 'em do it that way."

"Glad he didn't use a burner to make this particular call to Shelby," Marlin said. "Even better, the call lasted a little more than three minutes, so they definitely talked, despite what Knox has been saying."

"Or he was leaving a very long voicemail," Lauren said.

"That's probably what he'd say, huh? Anyway, we already suspected he was lying, but I'd say this confirms it. He called that number again at one in the morning, about an hour before April died. The call lasted 16 seconds, so that one probably was actually voicemail. Then he immediately called April's phone and that one was eleven seconds. We already knew that from pulling April's phone records on Monday."

"Did you get location information for these calls?" Lauren asked.

"Yeah. All of the calls we're talking about pinged off the tower closest to Knox's house in San Saba County."

"So he wasn't with April that night," Lauren said. "At least he told the truth about that. What next?"

"He called both phones—Shelby's and April's—at 3:17 a.m., and those didn't connect, either."

"April was dead by then," Lauren said.

"Yep. And if our theory is right, Shelby was freaking out, trying to decide what to do next. The last thing he wanted to do was tell Knox what had happened."

"Can't blame him," Lauren said.

Marlin checked the papers again. "Later that morning, between eight and eleven, Knox called both phones several more times and never got an answer."

"I'm guessing Knox knew exactly what Shelby and April were doing that night. He was probably just being protective—worried that his sister was gonna get busted or shot, because she wasn't experienced with that sort of thing—so Knox kept checking in to make sure nothing went wrong. Sound reasonable?"

"It does, yeah," Marlin said. "He finally gave up and there was no more activity on Thornton's phone until Sunday afternoon at 4:24. That's about 10 or 15 minutes after Bobby spoke to Chuck Thornton and told him about April. Chuck Thornton then called Knox, which makes sense. Here's the good part, though. If Knox was hearing the news about April for the first time from his father, wouldn't you think he would immediately call Shelby?"

"Definitely."

"Well, he didn't. I figure that means he already knew what happened, because Shelby had already told him. Think that's a reasonable conclusion?"

"I do, yeah."

She took a long sip of her coffee. Marlin noticed that she appeared a bit tired, and he found himself wondering: *Did she spend the night with Phil again last night?* He did his best to push that thought aside.

"And it appears Shelby didn't tell him over the phone," Marlin said, "so it must've been in person."

"And nobody has seen Shelby since," Lauren said.

Did she drive home last night and drive back here this morning? Did she stay at a motel?

"Shelby probably went back to San Saba on Sunday morning or early afternoon and met with Knox," Marlin said. "What happened after that is anyone's guess."

"Yeah," Lauren said, "and it all fits, but I wish we could confirm without a doubt that Shelby and April were together on Saturday night. And even if we can do that, as things stand, if we assume

Shelby went home on Sunday and told Knox what happened to April, that doesn't mean Knox did anything to Shelby. Maybe Shelby is alive and well and hiding out somewhere."

"Understood," Marlin said, "but in that case, why would Knox lie about having contact with him? He lied to Bobby and then he lied to us. If Shelby is okay, why would Knox lie?"

"Maybe he's covering for Shelby. He knows Shelby hauled ass, but he doesn't want us to know he knows."

"Gotta say I'm skeptical about that," Marlin said. "Would Knox cover for Shelby if Shelby got April killed, even if it was an accident? Seems like Knox would tell us everything he knew so we could grab Shelby as quickly as possible. He'd want Shelby charged for something in connection with April's death. Right?"

Lauren shifted in her chair, thinking. After a moment, she said, "The only thing I can think of is that Knox might cover for Shelby if Shelby can give solid info on Knox's meth operation. He wouldn't want Shelby in our hands, because then Shelby might want to trade information for a lesser charge."

"True, and in that case, it would be better for Knox if Shelby was dead."

Lauren laughed. "Isn't it weird to try to put yourself in these scumbags' heads and figure out what they'd do?"

"Always is, but I'd say we're doing pretty well."

"Agreed." She took out her notepad. "So let's list the likely scenarios, as we see it. One: Knox is telling the truth about not seeing Shelby since April died. Two: He saw Shelby and killed him. Three: He saw Shelby and let him go, which doesn't seem likely."

"Yep."

"Have to say I'm leaning toward scenario number two—he killed Shelby—because that fits with Knox having possession of Shelby's vehicle."

"It does, but I still don't understand why he's driving it around. Would he really be dumb enough to kill a man and then get caught in his vehicle?"

"He's relying on the claim that he borrowed the Ranchero on Saturday, or even Friday."

They sat quietly for a solid minute, simply thinking.

Then Lauren said, "I don't want to muddy the picture even further—"

"We're just brainstorming," Marlin said. "Let's hear it."

"Okay, I think we have to consider the possibility, however slight, that Shelby was not with April in Rodney's pasture. I'm assuming he was, but what if he wasn't? What if she was out there with somebody else? Or, another angle—what if she was there with Shelby, but they weren't driving the Ranchero? Maybe Shelby borrowed someone else's vehicle because Knox had his."

It was irritating to have to consider so many different possibilities, but it was something that had to be done. Assumptions had no place in an investigation without a solid foundation. You wanted to consider all the possibilities, then use facts and sound reasoning to rule them out, one by one.

"What if there were three people out there?" Marlin said. "April, Shelby, and somebody else? They could've been in that third person's vehicle."

"Interesting," Lauren said. "Now, here's an idea, springboarding from that. Let's say there *were* three of them out there. April died and the other two—Shelby and someone else—took off. Then Shelby manned up and told Knox that April was dead, and Knox totally lost it and killed him on the spot."

"And now," Marlin said, sitting up straighter in his chair, "Knox is looking for the other person. He wants to kill them, too. That's where you were going?"

"Exactly," Lauren said. "And maybe that other person lives in Blanco County. That's why Knox is down here. If the third person lives here, they'd know what's worth stealing in the area. They could've scoped out Rodney's cattle beforehand. I can picture Shelby shooting the breeze with a friend of his, telling him about all the things he's stolen, and the friend says, 'Hey, I got an idea.'"

They sat silently again for another few moments. Marlin realized he was enjoying working with Lauren quite a bit. She had a quick, intuitive mind. They seemed to operate on the same wavelength.

"It's pretty much wild-ass speculation," she said.

"Yeah," Marlin said. "But it makes sense. I can't think of any other reason Knox would still be in the area. That bit about wanting to see where April died, and being too sad to go home? I didn't buy that at all. Did you?"

"Nope. So who would it be? That third person?"

"No idea," Marlin said, "and nothing we've uncovered so far points toward anyone else. Interviews, phone records, all that. Of course, if we talked to the person who was out there with them—assuming there was someone—they'd have a good reason to lie. Whether April's death was an accident or not, they were committing a crime. Technically, we could charge them with a felony for killing that bull, not to mention all the other charges—deadly conduct, trespassing, failure to report a death, and whatever else we could come up with."

"Shelby is the key in all this," Lauren said. "I just know it. There's no way he isn't involved. Think we can get a warrant for his throwaway phone?"

"I'd say it's a long shot," Marlin said.

He didn't need to explain why.

When he had written the affidavit for Knox Thornton's phone, he made the case that Thornton had provided false information during an investigation—that he was hiding something—so the judge had approved it. But with Shelby Roach, they had nothing but speculation as to his involvement in April Thornton's death. They couldn't access a person's phone records based on speculation, even if the speculation made logical sense. They needed evidence and demonstrable facts. They had neither.

Lauren was shaking her head. "I don't remember Shelby ever talking about Blanco County, or mentioning any friends down here."

"Doesn't have to be a friend," Marlin said. "Maybe—"

Bobby Garza appeared in Marlin's doorway, behind Lauren.

"Is it eleven-thirty already?" Marlin said.

"Forget about that," Garza said. "I just got a call from the sheriff over in McCulloch County. An hour ago they pulled a body out of Brady Creek Reservoir."

CHAPTER TWENTY-TWO

Derek walked through the door of the pawnshop a little before noon, and right behind him was Colin Kelly, looking larger and more menacing than he had the day before. Bobo was prepared for this—he had expected it to happen—but that didn't mean he had any great strategy for handling the situation. He found himself wishing at least one customer was browsing in the store to serve as a witness, but the place was empty.

"Gentleman," he called firmly from behind the jewelry case, "you need to turn around and hit the road before I call the cops."

"Go ahead," Derek said striding straight to the counter. "Call 'em. Wanna borrow my phone?"

Colin stood beside Derek looking like an angry dog that was just about to bite. "Do it," Colin said. "Call 'em. You can borrow his phone." Not the most creative addition to the conversation, but Colin obviously had his limitations.

"I'm not bluffing," Bobo said. "You're both trespassing."

"You're an asshole, Bobo," Derek said.

"Maggot," Colin said.

"Bottom feeder," Derek said.

"Bet you like kiddie porn," Colin said.

Despite his nerves, Bobo was actually starting to get angry, or at least indignant, because he only liked porn in which the women were in the 18 to 20 range. "Fuck you both! Get out!"

They ignored him. Bobo was wishing he had a gun in the shop. Well, he did have a gun—lots of them, for sale—but none of them were loaded. He didn't like guns. He didn't keep one for protection. He'd rather be robbed than shoot somebody. Insurance would cover any losses.

"Colin needs that cash," Derek said. "Now, before you start pretending you don't know what I'm talking about, just save it, okay? You found the cash in that suitcase, and you stole it, and then you blamed it on me. That makes you a fucking thief, Bobo. Not to mention a lying traitor."

"Douchebag," Colin said.

"Grade-A asshole," Derek said.

"Dickwad," Colin growled, looking like he was on the verge of smashing Bobo's head through the glass countertop.

Bobo decided to focus his efforts on Colin. He was the weak link. "He's playing you," Bobo said, nodding toward Derek. "He took your cash, and now he's trying to blame me. And you're falling for it. I thought you were smarter than that."

"Lying sack of shit," Derek said, and now he was coming around the end of the counter, heading for the back office.

"Hey!" Bobo yelled, starting after him, and then he felt Colin's big hand grab the scruff of his shirt.

The security cameras.

That was the brilliant idea Derek had had last night on the phone with Bobo. That's how they could prove that Bobo took the cash. There were two cameras in the showroom, one in the storage room, and one here, in the office, aimed directly at the safe.

Derek's heart was racing as he sat down at the desk and woke the computer up. Meanwhile, Bobo stood silently nearby, with Colin holding him by the arm.

Derek opened the application that allowed him to view the security video. He selected the office camera, and now he could see the live shot from that camera, showing the three of them in the office. Beneath the video feed was a blue horizontal timeline, with hourly hash marks, like the bottom line on a graph. A vertical red line on the blue timeline indicated the current time. Derek could review stored video simply by clicking backward anywhere on the timeline—an hour earlier, a day earlier, or up to a week earlier.

"Wasting your time," Bobo said.

"Shut up," Colin said, giving his arm a shake.

"I ain't got your money. Never did."

"Shut up."

Another cool feature was that the security cameras sensed motion and would insert a marker in the timeline when there was activity in front of the camera. There wasn't much activity back here, in the office, so it wouldn't take Derek long to find what he was looking for.

"He's a hell of an actor, I give him that," Bobo said.

"I told you to shut up."

Today was Thursday. Bobo had fired Derek yesterday. Derek figured Bobo had found the money on Tuesday, or Monday at the earliest. And the cameras would have seen it all. When Bobo went into the storage room, found the suitcases, and opened them up, it would be on video.

Derek began to scroll backward, to last night, and then further back still, to yesterday afternoon, and then to Wednesday morning—and he noticed something that made his heart drop. He scrolled further back, to Tuesday night, and Tuesday afternoon, and then into Monday.

He stopped scrolling and looked at Bobo, who had an obvious smirk on his face.

"You erased the video," Derek said.

"The fuck're you talking about?" Bobo said. "I don't even know how to use that shit. You installed that system."

Which was true. A year earlier, Derek had convinced Bobo to do away with his old DVR-based cameras and install these newer cameras, which recorded to the cloud. Only problem was, the user could go in and erase the stored video.

"You figured it out," Derek said. "Even *you* could figure out how to do that. You erased everything prior to yesterday morning."

"Yesterday morning, huh?" Bobo said. "Just so happens you had a chance to erase it yourself before I shitcanned you." He didn't sound scared at all. He sounded confident. Derek realized Bobo had planned everything just right, and it was working. Bobo turned his head toward Colin. "See, he's jerking us both around. Trying to pin it on me, so you won't blame him. He erased the video yesterday morning."

Colin looked at Derek, and it was obvious the bodybuilder was beginning to have some doubts. Derek knew Bobo was lying, and Bobo knew that Derek knew—but that didn't matter. What mattered was what Colin believed, and later, what Knox Thornton would believe, when he learned that his money was missing.

There was one last straw for Derek to grasp.

Derek rose quickly from the desk. "Open the safe."

"What? Fuck you. Nobody gets in there but me."

"Open the damn safe, Bobo."

Bobo had never given Derek the combination. There was a slot that allowed Derek to drop cash into it, but he had no way of taking cash out.

"Hell, no," Bobo said.

"This is not optional, Bobo," Derek said. "You're gonna open it, one way or the other."

"You guys will rip me off," Bobo said. "You'll take the cash that's in there and say it was the cash from the suitcase."

"You and I both know you go to the bank when the cash gets much higher than five grand," Derek said. "But you wouldn't do that with stolen cash. So if there's more than four or five thousand in there—say, oh, fifty thousand—we'll know where it came from."

Bobo heaved out a sigh. "You fucking people. I don't know why I should—"

Colin shoved him roughly toward the safe. "Open it. Now."

"Okay, you assholes," Bobo said. "Fine. But if you rip me off—"

"Christ, Bobo, I already said, we won't rip you off," Derek said.

"I work hard for my money," Bobo said.

"Yeah, right. Open it."

Bobo turned toward the wall safe and cupped one hand around the electronic keypad, to shield Derek and Colin from seeing the numbers he punched. "Don't get any ideas," he said. "I'm gonna reset these numbers right after you leave."

"Just. Fucking. Open. It." Derek was losing his patience.

Bobo entered the code and swung the heavy door open.

"It *is* your business, you know," Lauren said.

"What is?"

"This thing—as you called it—between Phil and me."

They had taken Marlin's truck this time, and now they were driving northwest on U.S. Highway 71. They had just passed through Llano, known, for good reason, as the Deer Capital of Texas, and they had another 45 minutes to go before they'd reach Brady Creek Reservoir. They'd agreed it was worth the drive to see if Lauren could identify the body, and to see what they could learn from the deputies working the case. The McCulloch County sheriff had told Bobby Garza that he had no missing-persons cases, but he'd heard about Shelby Roach, who was a person of interest in Blanco County. The general physical description matched, but the corpse wasn't in great shape.

"I don't see how it's my business," Marlin said, but he was beginning to suspect they'd need to have a discussion, if only to clear the air. Like a thorn that needed to be removed.

"Just let me get this out, okay?" Lauren said. "You don't even have to respond."

She waited until he nodded. Then she said, "I don't know how good your memory is, but when you and I were dating, Phil and I became close. I mean like friends—that kind of close. After you and I broke up, I ran into Phil a few times—mostly out clubbing—and we always talked and laughed for hours. He and Terri had split up for a while, so we went out a few times, and one of those times it became more than just friends. Just for that one night. He's such a great guy, and I liked him, and it just happened. I wasn't ashamed of it then, and I'm not ashamed of it now. In Phil's defense, you were already seeing somebody else, so there was no reason he and I couldn't spend some time together. Despite all that, I remember him calling me the next day—after that one night—and worrying that you would be mad at him. At us. It was tearing him up. I understood, so I told him there was no reason you ever had to know. That part was my idea, not his. I basically had to talk him into it, and it took some doing."

Marlin was uneasy with the conversation. It seemed odd to be discussing such personal matters with a woman he hadn't seen in so many years, despite the relationship they'd had back then.

They'd been riding in silence for at least a mile when she said, "I just wanted you to know, because I don't want you to be angry at Phil."

"I understand."

"Do you wish I hadn't said anything?"

"No, it's okay."

Another mile passed before she said, "What about now?"

"What do you mean?"

"Will it bother you if Phil and I see each other?"

"Not at all," he said, and he could feel her looking at him again, to see if he was telling the truth.

The medical examiner had the body strapped to a gurney, ready for transport, when Marlin and Lauren parked in the gravel lot serving the boat ramp. If the fishermen who had spotted the body had parked here, they were gone now, leaving only four vehicles—the ambulance, two deputies' units, and the medical examiner's sedan. There wasn't a boat to be seen anywhere on the reservoir, which wasn't unusual for a weekday in May.

Lauren knew everyone on the scene, so she quickly introduced Marlin.

"What's the story?" she asked the medical examiner, a tall, slender man in his forties.

"He's been in the water for at least a couple of days. Hoping I can narrow that down. He's in pretty bad shape, as you would expect. Would've been worse in the summer, but the water temperature is still pretty low."

"Any idea how he died?"

Under normal circumstances, with a body in a lake, Marlin would suspect drowning, or possibly trauma from a boating accident.

"Couldn't see any obvious fatal injuries at first," the medical examiner said, "but just before you drove up, I found what appears to be two small-caliber gunshots to the back of his head, hidden by his hair. Can't confirm that yet, though. No exit wounds. And there are some ligature marks around the ankles."

"Meaning the body was weighted down and sunk?"

"Possibly. I'll need to take a closer look."

"Either of y'all know Shelby Roach?" Lauren asked the two deputies, both men in their early thirties. There was a good chance they might, considering that McCulloch County was adjacent to San Saba County, to the east. But neither of them did.

"Okay, well," Lauren said, "might as well have a look."

She and Marlin stepped closer to the gurney, and the medical examiner pulled back a sheet covering the head and torso. Marlin had seen his share of bodies that had been submerged in water for extended periods, but it was never enough to steel him completely to the gruesome sight. The torso and arms were bloated significantly. The skin was colorless—nearly translucent. The eyes bulged and the lips were plump. Small, ragged wounds marked where turtles and fish had gnawed on the flesh. The stench was nearly unbearable. Marlin began to breathe through his mouth.

Lauren was hardly fazed, except that her eyes widened in surprise.

"Whoa," she said. "That isn't Shelby Roach. I'm pretty sure that's Grant Bender."

CHAPTER TWENTY-THREE

Shelby Roach was glad he had taken Spanish for four years in high school. Students were only required to take two years, but he'd liked the subject—and in fact it was the only class in which he'd ever made A's. Of course, living in Texas, he used the language frequently, and by now he was fluent. That would come in handy.

His bus pulled into Saltillo just before noon. The city was much larger than he had realized, and it wasn't particularly pretty, but compared to Monterrey, which they had passed through an hour earlier, it wasn't so bad. Not that he intended to stay here. He didn't yet know where he was going, but this wasn't it. He figured if he was going to be a fugitive, he should do it in some little oceanside town. Get a job. Get a tan. Start to blend in. Wouldn't take long before the locals no longer thought of him as a gringo. A new life. It was kind of exciting, in spite of the circumstances.

"*Te vas a ir de aquí?*" the man seated next to Shelby asked. Are you getting off here?

He was a nice guy. Name was Vicente. About Shelby's age. They'd had a few friendly conversations during the trip. Earlier, Shelby had made up a pretty good story. He'd said that he loved Mexico—the land and the culture—and that every few years, he'd travel around the country with no agenda at all. Just explore. Pick his next destination on a whim.

"*Tal vez por la tarde,*" Shelby said. Maybe for the afternoon.

"*Has venido aquí antes?*" Vicente asked. Have you been here before?

"No."

"*Linda ciudad. Deberías conocerla por un día o dos.*" Nice city. You should check it out for a day or two.

"*Quizás. Pero la verdad es que me gusta el océano.*" I might. But I really like the ocean.

"*No es de mi incumbencia, pero creo que quieres privacidad?*" Vicente was assuming Shelby wanted privacy. There was an insinuation there—wasn't there? He had gathered that Shelby wasn't just some rambling tourist. Maybe it was the two black eyes that had given Shelby away. But Vicente hadn't been nosy enough to ask how Shelby had gotten them, or the cut on his lip.

"*Claro, me gusta la privacidad,*" Shelby said.

"*Barra de Potosí,*" Vicente said. "*No tan lejos de Ixtapa.*" He was recommending a small fishing village not far from Ixtapa. "*Mi hermano vive allí. Él podría ayudarte a instalarte allí,*" he added. He was saying his brother lived there, and the brother could help Shelby get settled in. Then Vicente wrote his brother's phone number on a scrap of paper and gave it to Shelby.

"*Eres muy amable. Gracias,*" Shelby said. His hand rested on the right, front pocket of his jeans, which held a tight roll of bills, mostly hundreds and fifties. All his money. Enough to hold him until he found a source of income.

"*De nada,*" Vicente said.

The cash was not in the safe. Sure, there was some cash—roughly three thousand dollars—but nowhere near the amount that was missing from the Delsey suitcases.

"Fuck," Colin said. "Son of a bitch."

Derek was overcome with despair. The quick, easy solution was off the table. He wanted to go home and curl into a ball. How had he ended up in this mess?

Bobo stood to one side of the safe, still looking smug. Then he slammed the door shut. "See?" he said to Colin. "He's jerking you around. He deleted the video, and he knew the cash wouldn't be in the safe. He's got it stashed somewhere."

"That's a lie," Derek said, but he couldn't muster any real outrage. He was too scared and tired.

"He figured he could blame it all on me," Bobo said.

"Liar," Derek said.

"Okay, whatever," Bobo said. "At this point, I couldn't give a rat's ass. All I know is, it ain't my problem. Now get the fuck out of my shop. Both of you."

Red had passed through Dripping Springs, and he continued east on Highway 290 toward Austin. "Can't believe this is the best plan we can come up with," he said.

"It'll work," Billy Don said. "Why wouldn't it work?"

"Why *would* it work?" Red said. He checked the rearview mirror. Nervous habit lately. He didn't see anybody tailing him. Then again, traffic was heavy today, and if there was someone tailing him, would he know it? Maybe that person would be smart enough to drive past him, then wait somewhere up ahead. Then fall in behind him again. Then repeat as necessary. If the killer drove some sort of plain-vanilla sedan, it would be hard to spot him.

"Because it's so simple," Billy Don said.

"Just like you," Red said, grinning at his quick-witted insult.

"You didn't come up with nothin' better," Billy Don said. "Besides, I'm just trying to help. It'd be a lot easier for me to keep my distance until this dude blows your head off. A lot of guys wouldn't even want to ride in the same truck as you. This vehicle could explode at any minute."

Red didn't want to think about that. There were probably thousands of ways to kill a person.

"What street are we looking for?" he said, changing the subject.

Billy Don looked at a scrap of paper on which he had scribbled some directions. "Circle Drive. Just past Fitzhugh."

"On the left?"

"Right."

"On the right?"

"No, the left."

"Make up your mind."

"On. The. Left." Billy Don's temper was starting to flare. Sometimes he couldn't take a joke.

On the other hand, it was true that Billy Don had come up with the only practical idea for catching the man who was trying to kill Red. It wasn't a complicated or elaborate plan, but it would require a particular item they would've had a hard time finding in Blanco County. But Billy Don—yes, again, it was Billy Don—suggested that they should search for the item on Craigslist. Red had no idea why Billy Don was familiar with Craigslist, but did it matter?

The bottom line was, they'd used Red's phone to search Craigslist and damned if it didn't work. In fact, they'd had more than a dozen listings to choose from. Then they'd called one of them and gotten ahold of a woman just west of Austin who used to design costumes for plays or musicals or musical plays or something, but she'd just retired and blah-blah-blah, and so she was selling a lot of her crap. Who knew it would be so easy to buy a mannequin?

"There are only a couple of possibilities," Lauren said, keeping her voice low, so other customers in the restaurant wouldn't overhear. "Either Grant Bender was alive until recently, which seems highly implausible. Or...you ever see the movie *Bernie*?"

"Body in the freezer."

"Exactly."

"The autopsy will tell us if that happened," Marlin said.

The deputies in charge of the investigation had had very little information to share. The body was found. They pulled it from the lake. They planned to bring in a couple of scuba divers to search for the weight that had been used to sink the body. Maybe that would give them a piece of evidence that might lead somewhere. That was pretty much all they had.

"If Bender was alive this entire time..." Lauren said, but she trailed off. Then she said, "What if the abrasions on his ankles were ropes or cables or something else used to keep him tied up somewhere?"

"Remind me again... How long has he been missing?" Marlin asked.

"Seven months."

The idea that somebody could have kept Bender in captivity for that long seemed to be a stretch. Then again, it had happened for much longer periods and with more captives—like the three young women in Cleveland who had been held prisoner by the same man for time spans ranging from nine to thirteen years. That boggled the mind.

"What would be the point?" Marlin asked. "Why hold him and then kill him later?"

Lauren shook her head. "Don't know, but if that's not what happened and instead he's been dead since last fall, why keep him in a freezer since then? Why not dispose of him immediately?"

They'd stopped for lunch at Cooper's Barbecue in Llano. The

place, as usual, was packed. Marlin was picking away at a brisket plate, while Lauren was tearing into a beef rib with both hands.

"I don't have an answer for that," Marlin said. "Makes no sense at all."

"When I was a deputy, we found a body in a freezer once. The man killed his neighbor and stuck her in there for nearly a year. He wasn't a suspect—never even showed up on our radar—so he figured leaving the body in the freezer was smarter than dumping it somewhere."

"How'd you nail him?"

"I wish I could say it was brilliant investigative work, but the man got drunk and made some dumb comments to a friend, implying that he knew something about the murder. When we showed up at his door, man, he totally cratered. Gave a full confession within five minutes. Not quite as rewarding as using razor-sharp questions to slowly pull the truth out of him, but I couldn't complain."

"That's what we need right now," Marlin said. "Somebody with loose lips. To be honest, I have no idea what we should do next."

Lauren placed the bare rib bone on her plate and wiped her mouth with a napkin.

"We'll think of something," she said. "Give it time."

"Hope so," Marlin said.

"Oh, we will," she said. "So far, I'd say we make a hell of a team."

Forty minutes later, when they were halfway back to Johnson City, she said, "Okay, I just thought of something we can try."

CHAPTER TWENTY-FOUR

"He's lying," Derek said. "In case you were wondering. Bobo is a fucking liar."

They were in Derek's apartment again, seated on the couch, each with a bottle of beer in hand. They'd had a lot of beers so far. Derek wasn't even keeping count at this point. Derek didn't usually drink in the daytime, but he couldn't think of a good reason to refrain right now.

"Yeah, I know," Colin said. "I believe you."

His oily thighs and arms were going to leave stains on the fabric, but Derek figured that was the least of his concerns at the moment.

"Thanks."

"Unless you are a really fucking good liar," Colin said, with a small laugh. It was obvious he didn't think that was outside the realm of possibility. "Somebody's lying—Bobo or Charmaine or you." Colin was slurring just a little.

"If I stole forty-six thousand dollars," Derek said, "Bobo wouldn't have to fire me. I'd quit. Hell, I wouldn't even bother telling him. I just wouldn't show up the next morning. And then I'd probably hit the road for at least a week or two, in case somebody came looking for me."

"Somebody like me," Colin said.

"Exactly."

"Or Knox Thornton," Colin said.

"Yeah. Especially him."

"Where would you go?" Colin said.

"No idea," Derek said. "San Antonio, maybe. Dallas."

Colin laughed again. "Dude, that's really fucked up. You're saying if you had that much money, you'd hide out in Dallas? Now I *know* you aren't lying, because if you'd thought about it for more than ten seconds, you'd pick someplace like Vegas or Europe."

"What can I say?" Derek said. "I'm frugal."

They sat in silence for a few minutes, occasionally gulping from their bottles. Derek was getting sleepy. The alcohol was settling his nerves. He wasn't quite as on edge. Not that he was dismissive of his predicament, but it didn't seem quite so hopeless as it had a few hours ago.

Colin's phone chimed with an incoming text. He read it and began shaking his head. "No fucking way."

"What?"

"This is crazy."

"What?"

"Friend of mine says they found Grant Bender's body."

Grant Bender. That name was familiar, but Derek couldn't place it. He must've had a puzzled expression on his face, because Colin said, "The witness I told you about yesterday. The one that disappeared."

"Because Knox—"

"Yeah."

"But wasn't that, like, last October?"

"Yeah."

"Where'd they find him?"

"Hold on." Colin texted the person back, then said, "It's frigging crazy."

"How would they even know it's him so quickly? After all this time, there would only be bones left."

Colin's phone chimed. "In a lake. That's where they found him."

"Is this, like, confirmed or just a rumor?"

"Pretty sure."

"Who's your friend?" Derek said.

Colin shook his head, meaning he wasn't telling. He began to return the text.

"You won't tell me?" Derek said. "How do I know your friend isn't full of bullshit?"

"He knows," Colin said. "Believe me, he knows."

"Well, I'm not buying it based on some random friend's text."

Colin lowered his phone and looked at Derek. "Okay, fuck. We still talking confidential?"

"From now on, just assume everything we discuss is confidential, okay?"

"Deal. Okay. My friend is a county deputy. Actually, not just a friend. He's my uncle."

"For real?" Derek said.

"Yep."

Derek wanted to point out that it was pretty damn stupid for Colin's uncle to share information about a murder investigation, but why bother? Instead, he said, "So you never knew what Knox did with Grant Bender's body until now?"

Colin, typing again on his phone, didn't hear the question, or he was ignoring it. Then he gulped the last four ounces in his beer bottle and held the empty toward Derek. "Another one," he said.

"I'm not a goddamn bartender," Derek said.

"I'm busy here," Colin said. "Another one. *Please.*"

Derek reluctantly rose from the couch, went into the kitchen for two more beers, and returned to the living room.

Colin, checking his phone, said, "Two shots to the head, but I already knew that." Then he realized what he'd said and clapped his hand over his mouth, just as he'd done the day before.

"Yeah, I know," Derek said. "I'm supposed to forget you ever said that. Here you go." He passed Colin a bottle. "What we need to do is sit here and brainstorm until we come up with an idea. Okay?"

"We came up with an idea on the drive back from Brady," Marlin said.

"Yeah?" Nicole said.

"A welfare check."

They were seated at a small table in the beer garden behind Nutty Brown Café on Highway 290, a few miles east of Dripping Springs. Nicole was wearing her hair pinned back and looked stunning in the early-evening sunlight. Marlin had noticed that the young waiter seemed to be visiting their table more often than he really needed to. Nicole had been watching a large, colorful parrot named Cheeto who lived in an enclosure nearby, but now she returned her attention to Marlin.

"But that'd be iffy," he admitted.

"Sounds like it's not even iffy," Nicole said.

A welfare check—also called a wellness check—allowed a law enforcement officer to enter a residence without a warrant if the officer had a reasonable belief that someone inside was in need of emergency aid—but the search couldn't be motivated by the possibility that it might help solve a crime. The welfare check had to be conducted as part of a cop's daily "community caretaking functions," as one court ruling had called it.

"Yeah, it would probably be pushing it," Marlin said. Nicole gave him a skeptical look. "What?" he said.

"'Probably?'" she said. "You know better than that."

"Hey, it's entirely possible Shelby Roach is inside his cabin, needing some kind of assistance. He hasn't been seen in days. And we have reason to think Knox Thornton might've harmed him. We talked to Shelby's mother yesterday, but she wasn't there to check on him for us. She was out of town."

"Did you ask for permission to go inside his cabin?"

"Yeah."

"What'd she say?"

The waiter brought a small garden salad for each of them, giving Nicole a big smile in the process.

When he left, Marlin said, "My hair could be on fire and he wouldn't notice. Too distracted."

Nicole smiled, then repeated her previous question.

"She said no," Marlin said.

Nicole picked up her fork and stabbed a cherry tomato. "I'm guessing this wasn't your idea, was it?"

"The welfare check? What does it matter whose idea it was?"

"Well," she said, "you've never been opposed to creative solutions, but in this case…it crosses the line. The property owner said no, and that pretty much settles it, doesn't it?"

"I don't see it that clearly. I think we have some latitude."

"Okay, then how come nobody has entered the cabin before now? And what reason do you have to think he might be in there, as opposed to somewhere else?"

Marlin didn't answer. He wasn't all that hungry, either.

Nicole said, "I'm not trying to sound critical, but what you're describing goes against the intent of welfare checks. Y'all want to look inside that cabin on the chance you might see or find something that will push your investigation forward. True? Or are you really claiming you suddenly have a pressing need to see if Roach is in there, clinging to life, just waiting for you to show up and save him?"

"How's the salad?" the waiter asked, suddenly appearing beside their table.

"It's fine. Everything's fine," Marlin said, more briskly than he intended.

"I'll have your entrées right out."

Marlin took a swallow of the draft beer in front of him.

"You sort of snapped at him," Nicole said.

"Yeah, I know. And at you, too. I'm sorry. I'll leave a big tip."

"I'm going to offer my unsolicited advice," Nicole said. "From what you've told me so far, Lauren is a great investigator and you're working well together. I think that's fantastic. Seriously. But don't let her lead you down a path that could get everything thrown out in court later. You've always had a good head for the law. You know a welfare check isn't a smart choice."

Marlin was irritated, but he also knew she was right.

It was a good night for drinking, except they'd run out of beer. Fortunately, Derek had a bottle of bourbon on hand. He had no reason to leave the apartment, so he wasn't going to—maybe not for several days. Colin showed no signs of leaving either, and Derek was okay with that. The oily bastard could crash on the couch. Maybe it was a false sense of security, but Derek felt safer with someone else around. The television was on, but Derek hadn't been paying attention to the program for quite some time. He couldn't concentrate. He couldn't stop thinking about the predicament he was in.

An important question suddenly popped into his head. "Hey, will Charlize give you a heads-up when Knox asks for the suitcases?"

"You asked that earlier," Colin said. "Are you hammered?"

"I was distracted. What did you say?"

"Yeah, I think so. And it's Charmaine, not Charlize."

"But you're not positive?" Derek said.

"Of course I'm positive. Her name is Charmaine."

"No, I mean about her warning you."

"If she has the chance," Colin said.

"Jesus, man, don't say stuff like that."

"Just being realistic. If she tells Knox the money is gone, and then she points the finger at you, me, and Bobo, he won't give her the chance to warn us. He'll drag her along with him. Or do something else to her."

"Like what?"

"I don't know. Tie her up, maybe."

"So Knox could be on his way over here right now," Derek said, looking at the front door. The liquor had settled his nerves, but now he could feel his anxiety rising again.

"Well, it's possible. And as you've probably gathered, me and Charmaine aren't on the best of terms. She might not warn me even if she has the chance, especially if she thinks she can take the heat off herself by saying I did it."

"We can't just sit here and wait for him to show up," Derek said.

"We're not just sitting. We're drinking, too." Colin raised his glass to illustrate his point and a small amount of bourbon spilled over the lip and landed on the couch. Derek really didn't care anymore.

He said, "We're supposed to be coming up with ideas—some way out of this mess. So...think."

Derek flipped through the channels and came to rest on one of the local news reports. He was hoping to learn something about the discovery of Grant Bender's body, but he was too late. They were in the middle of the weather report. A thunderstorm was rumbling through the Hill Country west of town and would reach the Austin area in the next few hours.

"I have an idea," Colin said.

"Already?"

"Yep."

"What is it?" Derek said.

"Truth is, I had it earlier today, but, man, I haven't had the guts to say it out loud. It's pretty extreme."

"What is it?"

"You agree that we're seriously up shit creek, right?" Colin said.

"Well, yeah."

"And that Knox might even kill us if he can't find the cash. Right?"

"According to you."

"You don't believe me?"

"No, I believe you."

"And you're serious about everything being confidential?"

"Of course I am," Derek said.

"Then there's one way for sure we can stop that from happening. It's crazy, but it will work."

"For fuck's sake," Derek said. "Just spit it out."

"Okay, here goes. We should go see him and tell him the truth. Tell him everything that's happened so far, but explain how none of it's our fault. Tell him he needs to be talking to Bobo or Charmaine, because one of them has the cash, not us. And then, if he doesn't believe us—if he thinks we're lying or says anything threatening—then we kill him before he tries to kill us."

CHAPTER TWENTY-FIVE

It was a good night for drinking, so Shelby was doing just that, in a small bar in Saltillo.

"My advice to you," the bartender said in Spanish, "is to be very careful. You blend in well, but you are still an American. Who is this man Vicente you met on the bus? Why would he help you? Why would his brother want to help a stranger?"

Shelby Roach had spent a good portion of the day just rambling around Saltillo—the Catedral de Santiago was kind of cool, if you were into old churches—and trying to decide his next move. He'd come to the conclusion that Barra de Potosi, the little fishing village more than a thousand miles away, sounded perfect. Then he'd spotted this dive—a locals-only kind of joint—and decided to toast this new phase of his life with a shot of tequila. After that, he'd renewed the toast nine or ten more times, sometimes with tequila, sometimes with beer. In another hour or so, he'd find a cheap motel, crash hard, then board another bus in the morning. Sleep all the way to paradise.

"No reason *not* to trust him," Shelby said in response to the bartender's questions. Over the course of the past three hours, he had slowly told the bartender, Luis, his story. Not all of it, but enough to make it plain that Shelby was on the run. Wait. Was that accurate? On the run? Technically, he didn't know if the cops were looking for him. He only assumed they were. Being on the run from Knox was something else entirely. That didn't make him a fugitive. Just a pussy. Wise, but still a pussy.

"You need to be cautious," Luis said. "Bad things can happen."

Luis was about sixty or sixty-five, and it appeared he'd endured a bad thing or two himself. He had a purple scar running horizontally across his forehead.

"Just like back home," Shelby said. "Shit can happen anywhere—even in a small town in Texas."

Luis laughed while he washed a glass. "Good point, my friend. And that is why you are here."

The bar was a long, narrow room, with the actual wooden bar running the length of the left-hand side. Against the opposite wall were half a dozen two-seat tables, empty except for one table occupied by two young working-class men. They were behind Shelby, but he could watch them in the mirror behind the bar. They didn't seem to speak much, but they were quietly putting a large dent in a bottle of liquor Shelby couldn't identify. Too dark for tequila, gin, or vodka. Bourbon? Scotch?

"I screwed a guy around pretty bad before I left home," Shelby said.

"Yes?" Luis said. "How so?"

"Oh, I blamed something on him," Shelby said.

"Is he the one who injured your face?" Luis asked.

Shelby had almost forgotten about his black eyes. "No, that was somebody else."

"You lead a colorful life," Luis said.

"Tomorrow, or maybe later tonight, I'm going to set things right."

Shelby had realized there was no reason he couldn't call Knox and tell him he'd lied about his cousin Red. Knox couldn't do anything to Shelby at this point, so why not protect Red? It was the right thing to do. Shelby accepted that he had his shortcomings, but being a traitor wasn't one of them.

"Good for you," Luis said. "Smart. What goes around, comes around."

"You think Vicente's brother doesn't exist?" Shelby said, circling back to the other line of conversation, because he wasn't sure what Luis had been implying earlier. "I've got his phone number."

Luis shrugged. "I don't mean to worry you. It's possible Vicente has a heart of gold and his brother is a saint. I tend to be a skeptic. A cynic. My wife teases me about it. I say it comes from serving drinks for forty years."

"Speaking of which," Shelby said, and he shook his empty beer bottle.

An hour later, when he was ready to leave, he paid the tab with a fifty and left the change for Luis.

From outside Red's trailer, looking through the open window with the curtains slightly parted, after dark, from behind, with a wig on, and a baseball cap over the wig, the mannequin looked fairly realistic.

"Not bad, huh?" Billy Don said, obviously proud of the scheme he'd concocted.

Red said, "Yeah, well, we don't know if it will work, so you might want to stop patting yourself on the back."

The woman who'd sold them the mannequin had also provided the men's wig, which wasn't exactly like Red's hair, but it was close enough. Billy Don had made the mistake of asking the woman the difference between a wig and a toupee, and that was a full five minutes of Red's life he'd never get back.

"I think it looks perfect," Billy Don said.

Red could hear rumbling to the west. A thunderstorm coming.

"Good enough, I guess," Red said.

The mannequin was what the woman had called a "full body," meaning from head to toe, which was what they'd needed. They'd put the mannequin in Red's recliner and tilted it backwards toward the window. It still looked a little staged, so they'd draped a light blanket over the mannequin from the shoulders down. Better. Did it look like Red had fallen asleep while watching TV? Pretty damn close. And the top of the mannequin's head was an easy target. Somebody could sneak up to the window and shoot right through the baseball cap. Boom. Dead mannequin.

"We should get into place," Billy Don said.

Red was wondering if it was going to be a waste of time because of the coming storm. Even a killer wouldn't want to be caught out in the rain, right? But what if he did show up and they weren't prepared?

"Yeah, let's do it," Red said.

They turned and walked toward Red's truck, which was parked in its regular spot, about thirty yards away. But Red had backed the truck into the space this time, so they could watch the trailer through the windshield. They climbed inside and quietly closed the doors. Nice and dark in here. The porch light didn't reach this far.

They had all the equipment they'd need for the night. A fully charged Q-beam spotlight was resting on the dashboard, ready for action. Red's Colt Anaconda, a big old .45, was tucked under the seat, also ready for action. Billy Don had a 12-gauge pistol-grip shotgun filled with three rounds of double-aught buckshot, which could do some serious damage in a hurry. And, of course, Red had placed a small ice chest full of beer on the middle of the bench seat. After all, it was a good night to drink. What night wasn't?

Derek's first inclination was to say, "Are you fucking nuts?" But his dire circumstances—or perhaps the alcohol—stopped him.

Was it really nuts? Seriously, when you thought about it, was it nuts? What other choice did they have? This guy Knox Thornton had them backed into a corner. Well, he *would* back them into a corner once he knew the money was missing. Derek had no doubt about that. Thornton was a killer. Nothing would stop him. Derek would end up submerged in a lake with two bullets in his head.

Derek was taking too long to respond, so Colin said, "It was just a joke, dude."

"No, it wasn't," Derek said. "We both know it wasn't. You don't have to pretend. Remember, everything is confidential. Right now, as far as I'm concerned, we're just brainstorming. We are in danger, and every option is on the table."

Where had he heard that before? *Every option is on the table.* Something a politician said about a threat from an enemy.

"So you'd do it?" Colin said.

"I don't know about that, but let's keep talking and see what else we come up with."

"It would totally be self-defense," Colin said. "We'd be within our rights."

"Only if he actually pulled a gun right then and tried to kill us," Derek said.

"Yeah, okay, maybe," Colin said. "Or we could *say* that's what happened—the two of us telling the same story, backing each other up."

"So we'd try to lie to the cops? Forget that. I couldn't do it. They'd know I was lying. We'd have to do it without anyone knowing it was us."

Colin shrugged, like *Whatever you want*. He went to take a drink, but his bourbon was all gone. He went into the kitchen for more ice, then came back and filled his glass nearly to the top. The man could drink some serious liquor. He held the bottle toward Derek, who nodded. Colin topped his glass off. What the fuck, right? He'd feel it tomorrow, but tomorrow was a long time away.

"What if we give him a warning?" Derek said. "Tell him that if anything happens to us, we have a friend who will take him out."

"Take him out?"

"Kill him."

"Who's this friend?" Colin asked.

"He's just, you know, imaginary," Derek said. It sounded lame. Very lame.

"Not for one second will Knox worry about any of your friends or my friends, real or made up," Colin said. "I'm telling you, man, in San Saba County, he rules the place, because he's willing to follow through on the things he says he'll do. If he says you're fucked, you are fucked. But most of the time, he won't even tell you. Just something bad will happen. One time during high school—"

"I'm not sure I want to hear anymore about Knox's exploits," Derek said. "Not good for my morale."

"He had this feud with a guy on the football team. Big tight end named Bruce. Anyway, Bruce had wood shop in the same class as Knox, and one day he was using the table saw—"

"Oh, shit," Derek said.

"And suddenly Bruce is yelling and there's blood everywhere. His hand is just, like, spewing like a friggin' geyser or whatever, and he's screaming that Knox came up behind him and pushed him. Knox is saying, like, bullshit, there's water on the floor and I slipped into him. And there *was* water on the floor, and everybody thinks Knox put it there on purpose. Bottom line, Bruce lost two fingers. We're talking about a guy who coulda had a scholarship with UT or Oklahoma. Fucked him up good."

Derek was feeling queasy. He wasn't fond of blood. Back when he boxed, he always hoped he wouldn't bloody his opponent's nose, or have his own nose bloodied.

"That's the kind of dude we're dealing with," Colin said. "Just so's you know."

The first raindrop hit the truck windshield just before midnight.

Red and Billy Don had been sitting in silence for quite some time. Red wasn't sure how long they'd been waiting, but it was three beers' worth. Pretty soon he would need to quietly open his door and take a major leak. Red had seen no intruders, except for one solo possum that ambled by an hour earlier, apparently on the hunt for June bugs.

Billy Don's breathing had become deep and regular, and Red figured he might be asleep. Hard to tell in the dark. But if he was, that was okay. Red could wake him in an hour or two and then take a nap of his own. That's how cops or spies on surveillance did it—take shifts.

Another raindrop hit, and then another, and then the rain came down with a quick and sudden intensity, followed by a nearby lightning strike and thunder so deep and loud it shook the truck.

"Fuck is it?" Billy Don said, stirring abruptly.

Red wanted to use his Korean cell phone to check the weather radar, but he didn't want to risk allowing even that small amount of light to expose them to anyone who might be lurking in the nearby trees. Didn't seem likely that the killer would show now, but maybe the rain would pass.

"Gotta piss like a scalded hound," Billy Don announced.

If Red was alone on this stakeout, he'd relieve himself into an empty milk jug or Gatorade bottle. But here in these close quarters with Billy Don, Red wasn't comfortable with either of them using that tactic.

"Crack your door and take a leak," Red said. "That's what I'm gonna do. Then it'll be your turn to keep watch."

"If I open my door, a lotta rain's gonna get inside," Billy Don said. "Then again, you haven't cleaned this truck in so long, it'll be an improvement."

Shelby went eastward from the bar, just as Luis the bartender had instructed him to do, and then he took a right four blocks down. Then he stopped.

He was supposed to see a cheap motel half a block down on the left. Nineteen dollars for the night, Luis had said. Shelby figured it was probably even cheaper than that for locals, but Shelby wasn't a local, and nineteen bucks was a bargain.

Problem was, he didn't see any motel. Just an isolated street with darkened buildings and warehouses on either side.

Wait. Had Luis told him to go west from the bar? Or maybe he had said east, but Shelby was supposed to take a left four blocks down.

He turned to go back in the opposite direction and almost bumped face first into one of the young men from the bar. His friend—shorter and stockier—was right beside him.

"Whoa," Shelby said, in English. "You spooked me. Didn't hear ya."

Both of the men were smiling. Everything seemed fine. Then Shelby noticed that the man closest to him was aiming a small revolver at his stomach.

"*Su dinero*," the man said, using his free hand to point toward the right front pocket of Shelby's jeans. The man had seen the roll of money when Shelby had paid his bar tab just a few minutes earlier. And maybe Luis was in on it. Maybe Luis had intentionally sent Shelby to this quiet street, where there would be no witnesses.

"Seriously?" Shelby said.

The man said something else, but his accent was too thick for Shelby to understand.

"Guys," Shelby said, switching to Spanish now, "you don't want to do this. This is a mistake."

"Hand it over," the man with the gun said.

Shelby wasn't normally a courageous man, and he wasn't feeling courageous now. But he was full of booze, for one thing, and he knew if he lost his bankroll, he was totally screwed. What would he do then?

"No way," he said. "I can't. All I've got is—"

The short, stocky man stepped forward and tried to grab Shelby's arm, but Shelby twisted it away and then came around with his other elbow and slammed the man in the chin. To Shelby's amazement, the man fell to the concrete sidewalk as if he had been shot through the brain stem.

Where the hell did that move come from? Instinct?

Now the armed man raised the revolver higher, aimed it straight at Shelby's head, and pulled the trigger.

Click.

A dud. Or an empty chamber.

Shelby immediately jumped on the man, trying to stop him from pulling the trigger again, and they crashed to the ground together.

The barrel of the gun was just inches from Shelby's head when it roared. No dud this time.

CHAPTER TWENTY-SIX

When Red woke, the rain had stopped, he had to piss again, Billy Don was snoring, and a man had just walked past the truck, on the passenger side.

Red's eyes popped wide open, but he didn't startle or let out a sound. Years of hunting had steeled his nerves against sudden unexpected surprises—like a hawk suddenly landing on a branch right next to your head, or a mouse scurrying up your leg.

The man, dressed in dark clothes, was moving slowly and deliberately, making his way toward the trailer. Toward the open window. Toward the mannequin.

Red reached over and jostled Billy Don's left arm. As the big man woke up, Red whispered, "Keep quiet. He's here."

Red could feel Billy Don's arm go rigid as he sat up straighter and peered out the windshield.

The man was now less then ten yards from the trailer. He was picking his steps carefully, to minimize noise—the same way Red would try to sneak up on a deer or pig.

"Get ready," Red said, reaching under the seat for his .45.

"I'm ready," Billy Don said in a low growl, obviously looking forward to the next few minutes.

Red had to admit, Billy Don wasn't the brightest or hardest working man he knew, and his ethics were questionable, and you couldn't count on him to be sober or punctual, but in a situation like this, it would be hard to find a better partner.

The trespasser—the killer—was wearing a lightweight jacket, and now he pulled an object from his pocket and held it low in his right hand.

"Gun," Billy Don said, although Red couldn't see it very well in the dim light. Maybe it was a gun, maybe it wasn't. Maybe it was a flashlight or a cell phone.

"Don't shoot unless you have to," Red said, slipping his hand around the door handle. "But if you do have to shoot, make sure you nail him."

"Roger that," Billy Don said.

They watched as the man crept closer and closer to the window. They'd agreed earlier that they would wait to see if the man fired a shot, because then there would be no doubt about his intentions, and they would clearly be within their rights to hold him at gunpoint or even shoot back, if necessary.

The man took three more steps, and now he was right in front of the window. The scene would look perfectly natural to him. The TV was still on. The mannequin was "asleep" in the recliner. A bottle of Tullamore Dew stood on the small table beside the chair. Sure, the window was open, which was weird considering that a thunderstorm had just passed, but the killer would assume Red had drunk enough whiskey to sleep through it.

Red was holding his breath, muscles tensed, ready to spring from the truck with the spotlight in his left hand and his revolver in his right.

The killer stood at the window for nearly a full minute, just watching. Then he raised the object in his hand—clearly a gun—and fired a shot into the trailer.

Shelby felt a sharp pain inside his head, and he knew he'd been shot. The bullet had busted through his skull and had to be lodged in his brain right now.

But his thinking was still clear. The pain was deep inside his ear, not in his brain.

And now Shelby noticed that the man with the gun wasn't moving. Blood was oozing from a small hole on the underside of his chin.

Shelby quickly rose off the ground and stood trembling, unsure what to do next. Two men were lying prone on the sidewalk—one unconscious and one probably dead. Shelby looked left and right. There was nobody to be seen anywhere up and down the street—not even the distant headlights of a car. Now what?

Go back to the bar? Tell Luis what happened? But he wasn't sure he could trust Luis. Should he try to call the cops? He had his cell phone. They probably didn't use a 9-1-1 system down here, but surely he could figure it out.

Jesus, he was drunk. How could he even consider calling the cops? Why would they believe a gringo? He'd wind up in a Mexican prison for sure. That left one option.

He turned and ran.

Red immediately triggered the spotlight and aimed the blinding beam straight into the eyes of the killer, who had spun around after hearing them exit the truck.

"Don't you fuckin' move!" Billy Don shouted.

The man remained still.

"Drop your gun!" Billy Don yelled.

The man did not drop his gun.

"Drop it!" Billy Don yelled.

"Turn off that damn light," the man said.

It was the same guy who was in the photos from the trail camera—a total stranger, as far as Red could tell.

"Who are you?" Red called.

"Turn off that light and let's talk. I can't see a fucking thing."

"Hey, asshole," Billy Don said, "we ain't doing shit until you drop that gun. You got about ten seconds."

"And then what?" the man said. "You're gonna shoot me?"

"Five seconds," Billy Don said.

"He ain't kidding," Red said. "Believe me."

The man didn't move. The cocky look on his face was annoying. This was a guy who didn't take orders.

"Five," Billy Don said. "Four. Three."

"Here we go," Red said.

"Two," Billy Don said.

"Fuck y'all," the man said, obviously thinking it was a bluff.

"One," Billy Don said.

The man said, "Y'all don't know who—"

Billy Don's shotgun boomed and the man finally dropped his gun.

"Assuming we're still just speaking theoretically," Derek said, "and that we haven't decided one way or the other what we might or might not do, why do we need to talk to him in person? Why not over the phone?"

"Because if he flips out and thinks we took the money, we'll want to do something about it right then and there. If we tell him over the phone, man, that's no bueno. We wouldn't have control of the situation. He could come after us later and we wouldn't know when or where. So we need to talk to him face to face."

Surprisingly, that made sense.

"How would we actually do it?" Derek said.

"I don't know," Colin said, "but it ain't gonna be easy. Knox is smart. The good news is, he has about a million enemies, so the cops won't even know where to start."

"But, like, do we try to cover it up, or do we just kill him and leave the body where it is?" Derek said. "If we dispose of the body, how would we do it? Is it possible to make sure it will never be found? Bury it? Burn it? Dissolve it in acid?"

"You're asking me?"

"Well, yeah, because this was your idea!"

"I figured we'd just shoot him and be done with it. Why get fancy with it?"

"Because shooting somebody means they're going to bleed all over the place. Other methods aren't as messy. But none of that matters if we aren't going to try to hide what happened. So that's the first question we need to answer."

"What's the question?" Colin said. "You lost me."

"Would we or would we not try to cover it up?" Derek said, getting a little impatient. "Would we leave the body for somebody to find, or would we try to dispose of it? Either way, once we figure that out, there are more things to decide. Like when and where. We'd need to have a plan, and then stick to it."

"I don't get why we'd cover it up," Colin said.

"I'm not saying we'd have to go that way," Derek said. "But if we just kill him and leave the body, that has risks associated with it."

"Like what?"

"Well, say we decide to shoot him. Do you have a gun, by the way?"

Colin laughed. "Seriously?"

"What?"

"Do I have a gun? That's what you asked?"

"So you do have a gun?"

"About a dozen. All kinds. You don't own a gun?"

"No," Derek said.

"That's so weird. How do you not own at least one gun? This is fucking *Texas*, dude."

"Never needed one, but that is so unimportant right now. Focus, okay?"

"Yeah."

"If we decide to shoot him and leave him there, we've got ballistic evidence to worry about. They can match a bullet or a shell to the gun we use."

"Then we toss it in a lake when we're done."

"Somebody could still find it," Derek said. "Haven't you ever watched any of those crime shows? They could find it and trace it back to you."

"Okay, so we pour acid down the barrel, then stick it in a bucket of cement, and then toss *that* in a lake. Hell of a lot easier than disposing of the body. Besides, like I said, there are about fifty different people that would want to kill Knox. That's no exaggeration. So I say we just shoot him and haul ass out of there. They'll never be able to pin it on us."

Derek took another sip of bourbon.

"One of us would just walk up and shoot him?" Derek said. It sounded downright evil. "Which, uh, which one of us would do it?"

"I'll do it," Colin said without any hesitation.

"You'd shoot him?"

"Hell, yeah," Colin said. "Truth is, he's had this coming for a long time. Besides, he banged my girlfriend. Payback's a bitch."

Red could still remember the time, several years back, when he and Billy Don had kept a United States marshal tied up in the trailer for the better part of two days. Long story, but they hadn't believed he was really a marshal. So they'd ended up using some very interesting tactics—like playing a video clip of a *Hee Haw* song over and over, thousands of times—to make the guy tell the truth. Boy, was Red embarrassed when it turned out the man *was* telling the truth, which was bad news, because treating a marshal that way had to violate about a dozen different federal laws. Fortunately, as luck would have it, the marshal had reasons of his own to keep their little encounter to himself. Red and Billy Don had really dodged a bullet on that one.

The killer outside the trailer hadn't been so lucky. He had dodged every piece of buckshot except one, which had caught him squarely in the thigh of his right leg. Billy Don had claimed that he had aimed low, so they could take the guy alive, but Red figured it was just a bad shot. How do you miss a guy with that much buckshot?

Regardless, there had been a lot of moaning and cussing on the killer's part, but Red didn't say much until they had the guy securely duct-taped to one of the chairs in the kitchen. Now they could get to the bottom of this mess. Red was standing on one side of the man, Billy Don on the other. Make him feel surrounded.

"First question," Red said. "Who are you?"

"You motherfuckers are dead," the man said through clenched teeth. There had to be a considerable amount of pain from the wound to his leg, but there wasn't much bleeding at this point, so Red figured the man would be okay in the long run. He probably wouldn't need surgery or anything like that.

"Let me remind you," Red said, "that you're strapped to a chair and we ain't."

"I'm gonna kill you both," the man said.

"So far," Billy Don said, "the only thing you've been able to kill is a mannequin. Impressive as hell. And it only took one shot. You must be some kind of marksman."

"Who are you?" Red asked again, leaning in closer.

They had checked the man's pockets, but he wasn't carrying a wallet. No identification of any kind. Just a cheap cell phone, but the screen was locked and Red couldn't access it without a passcode.

"Best thing you can do right now," the man said, "is let me go and hope to God I never come back."

Billy Don moved around and stood directly in front of the man, then leaned down and placed one of his big palms on each side of the man's head, gripping it like a basketball.

Then he said, "Listen up, you little Lynyrd Skynyrd piece of shit. Seems like you got the idea we oughta be scared of you. Thing is, it's the other way around. That man right there ain't much, but he's my best friend, and a couple times now you've tried to kill him. He wants to know why, 'cause as far as we can tell, he ain't done nothin' to you. So what you're gonna do, sooner or later, is tell us why. And if you don't, believe me when I say I'll cut you into pieces and drop you down an old dead well on the ranch next door. That ain't no bullshit. Nobody'll know where you went."

It was plain from the man's expression that he believed what Billy Don was saying. That, or Billy Don was putting quite a bit of pressure on the man's skull. His big hands had the strength of a vise. The skin of the man's cheeks was getting pushed forward, so it was bunching in front, giving him duck lips. Red wanted to laugh, but that wouldn't set the right mood for an interrogation, so he tried to scowl instead.

"Think I'm bluffing?" Billy Don said. "I bet nobody knows you're here, right? That means nobody will know where you went."

"Plus," Red said, "you shot at me first. Twice. So I got every right to defend myself. In fact, we could take you out front right now and pop one in your head, then say you wouldn't drop your damn gun. That's pretty close to what happened, anyway."

Red noticed that Billy Don's face was getting crimson, either from anger or from clenching the man's head.

"Okay," the man said through his duck lips. "Jesus, stop squeezing."

CHAPTER TWENTY-SEVEN

When Marlin stepped onto his front porch at seven the next morning, Phil Colby was waiting in his white Chevy truck, parked behind Marlin's green Dodge Ram. Marlin hadn't heard him pull in, and Geist hadn't even barked. Colby gave him a wave through the windshield but didn't get out.

Great.

Marlin hadn't wanted to deal with this right now, but it was as good a time as any. He descended the wooden stairs and walked over to the passenger side of Colby's truck, where the window was already down.

"Hey," Colby said.

Marlin could smell coffee. A convenience-store cup was nestled between Colby's thighs.

"How long you been out here?" Marlin said.

"Oh, maybe half an hour," Colby said.

Which explained why Marlin hadn't heard anything. Thirty minutes earlier, he and Nicole had been in the shower together. They had stayed in there long enough to run out of hot water, making up after the sharp words from last night.

"What, you needed to spend some quality time parked in my driveway?" Marlin said.

"You haven't returned my texts, so I needed to make sure the metal plate in your head wasn't interfering with your cell reception."

Marlin had to grin. "Sorry about that. Been a busy couple of days."

"That's the issue? Not ducking me?"

That was something Colby had in common with Lauren. He

wouldn't dance around a subject. If he had something to say, he'd address it head on.

"Maybe a little," Marlin said.

"So what's the deal?"

"You know what the deal is," Marlin said.

"Yeah, what I meant was, what're we gonna do about it?"

"Nothing," Marlin said. "There's nothing we need to do."

"You sure?"

He could remember what Lauren had told him the day before—that she had been the one who'd wanted to keep her fling with Phil private.

"It took me by surprise, that's all," Marlin said. "And I didn't know the full story."

"So we're good?"

"Yep. Always were."

"Okay, cool. Because there's something else I need to tell you about Lauren."

Marlin laughed, and then he realized Phil wasn't joking. "What now?"

"It has nothing to do with me and her, or with you and her, but brace yourself."

Red had tossed and turned all night, pondering the situation, and now he lay in bed thinking some more. He didn't do that often, and it made him feel uncomfortable. So he got up, got dressed, and went into the living room, where the would-be assassin was still taped to the chair. Billy Don was seated at the table, practicing blackjack. Good to know he hadn't forgotten about their upcoming trip to Vegas. Not just a trip, a mission.

"I let him take a leak a couple of hours ago," Billy Don said without looking up. "Then I taped him up again."

Red nodded, then he sat in the chair across from Billy Don—but he turned it so he was facing the would-be assassin.

"Morning, Dave," Red said. "How're you doing on this fine day, sir?" He was pretending to be cheerful to throw the guy off.

"I need out of this fucking chair, that's how I'm doing."

"Understandable," Red said. "Can't be real comfortable, but we can't turn you loose just yet."

"That was the deal we made last night. You said you'd let me go in the morning."

"No, I said I'd ask a few more questions, and if you answered them to my satisfaction, then we *might* let you go." He turned toward Billy Don. "Isn't that what I said?"

"Yup."

"We got any coffee?"

"Yup."

"I mean already brewed."

"Nope. Make some for me while you're at it."

Red rose and walked over to the pantry.

"I need to get to a doctor," the man in the chair said. "My leg is getting stiff. I think an infection is setting in."

"That's rough," Red said. "But you have a bigger problem than that."

"What?"

"I've been thinking things through," Red said, "and I'm pretty sure everything you told us last night is a crock of shit."

"Aw, man," the man said, shaking his head. "Here we go again."

The man—Dave, if he'd given his real name—had told a wild and unexpected story. He'd said that he was in a beer joint in Fredericksburg a few weeks earlier when a man offered him five thousand bucks to kill a Blanco County poacher named Red O'Brien. According to the man in the bar—who was a rancher type in his sixties—Red had shot one of his most valuable trophy bucks behind an eight-foot deer-proof fence. That part sounded plausible enough, because that was the type of thing Red and Billy Don were known to do on occasion. But as Red had lain in bed mulling over the details, he started to doubt the story. Now he was going to use his shrewd questioning skills to pick it apart.

"The rancher you mentioned last night—what was his name?" Red said.

"I already told you, he didn't give a name."

"So y'all didn't even know each other, but he just out of the blue said, 'Hey, you wanna kill a guy for me?' That don't even make sense."

"We were drinking and talking about all kinds of shit. That's where it ended up."

"You got his phone number?"

"Nope."

"What's he look like?"

"Grayish hair. Maybe five-ten. Beer belly."

"That describes nearly every damn rancher in the state."

"Don't know what to tell you," Dave said. "Why would I make all this shit up?"

"Good question," Red said. "Why *would* you make it all up?"

Dave sat silently.

"Ever killed a man before?" Red said.

"Yeah. Have you?" It was a challenge.

Billy Don snorted.

Red said, "Actually, yeah."

The man sighed deeply—a show of impatience—but didn't reply.

"Where do you live?" Red said.

"Mills County." But he hadn't answered right away.

"Which part?"

"Not telling you that. I don't want you coming 'round looking for me. You won't see me again, and I'd just as soon not see you."

"Name a street in Goldthwaite," Red said.

"Hanna Valley Road."

"What's your last name?"

"Nope."

"Where is your car parked right now?" Red said.

Dave opened his mouth, but no words came. Red figured it was because he couldn't think of a good lie. Red didn't believe a word he had said so far. It wouldn't have taken much for Dave to come up with the rancher story. He had probably seen the bumper sticker on Red's truck that read: IT AIN'T POACHING IF YOU DON'T GET CAUGHT. That, and the deer mounts hanging on the wall in the living room. Any half-wit could take that information and run with it. Red knew, because he had done that sort of thing himself, when necessary. Lying convincingly was easy, once you had enough practice.

Red was about to ask another question when he heard a sound.

Mike Tyson once said, "Everybody has a plan until they get punched in the mouth."

Knox Thornton had always found that to be true, meaning your average loudmouth or thug wannabe could talk a good game until something went wrong. The punch in the mouth—real or just a figure of speech—would usually make an aspiring bad-ass decide he wasn't quite as tough as he thought he was.

These two rednecks were different.

Knox could tell that they could handle a punch in the mouth, shake it off, and come looking for more. He knew this because even though they had known Knox was gunning for one of them, they hadn't wimped out and called the cops. Instead, they'd handled it themselves. Which was why, for the first time in a very long while, Knox Thornton was nervous. And why he couldn't tell them the truth. If he did, these hicks wouldn't hesitate to find a backwoods solution to their problem. If they knew Knox had learned that this guy Red was out in the pasture when April died, and that Knox was seeking revenge because of it, they would know that turning him loose wasn't an option. He'd come back later and try to kill both of them. So they'd eliminate the threat in the easiest and most permanent manner possible. Just like Knox would do it himself.

So he had to convince them that the rancher story was the truth. It wasn't a bad story, made up on the fly, but it couldn't withstand too many questions. Like the question about where his car was parked. He couldn't answer that, because they'd find Shelby's Ranchero and that would be a tipoff.

Knox was trying to think of an answer that would work, but right then, he heard a sound—the worst sound possible under these circumstances. His phone was ringing.

Dave's phone—which was on the kitchen table—was ringing. Red would be able to answer it without entering the passcode.

He looked at Dave and grinned. "Oh, this is perfect," he said. "Now I can find out how much bullshit you've been spreading."

Red grabbed the phone and stepped into the living room. Then—doing his best to sound like the captive in the kitchen—he answered it by simply saying, "Yeah?"

"Knox, hey, it's Colin."

Yep, "Dave" was a liar. Not his real name. But...*Knocks?* What kind of weird name was that? Oh, wait. Knox. Had to be Knox. Red kept his answer short, just more than a grunt. "What's up?"

"Man, I just wanted to tell you how sorry I am about April. That is just fucking devastating, you know? I couldn't believe what happened. I only heard a little while ago, but I wanted to call and, you know, give you my sympathies and all that. How're you holding up?"

"I'm all right," Red said. Who was April? What happened to her?

"Honestly," Colin said, "you sound a little out of it. Sure you're okay?"

"Yeah, I'm fine. It's been rough, that's all," Red said. Then he added, "Plus, I got a head cold."

"Oh, that explains it. Hey, I was thinking we should get together soon. You up for that? Let me take you out to dinner or something. Seriously, dude, you need, like, friends around you right now. For support and all that shit. I know we haven't stayed in touch much lately, and I'm sorry about that, but let's meet up, okay? It'll lift your spirits."

Red wasn't sure how to respond. This guy Colin could probably tell Red everything he needed to know about Knox, but how could Red get that information without blowing his cover?

Before Red came up with a good answer, Colin said, "Okay, truth is, I need to talk to you about something else. Listen, man, I know about you and Charmaine. But that's totally cool, okay? I don't blame you for hitting that. Everybody else was. It's not like I'm in love with her or anything. But have you talked to her lately?"

"Nope," Red said. He coughed a few times to bolster his head cold story.

"So she hasn't talked to you about the cash in the suitcase?"

Suddenly, with that one sentence, this situation had just become a lot more interesting. Cash in a suitcase? How much cash? Obviously enough that this guy Colin was concerned about it. Red couldn't decide how to answer, so he said, "What do *you* think?"

Colin took a breath so deep it was audible through the receiver. Then he said, "Okay, that's what I figured. You already know what's up. She's probably blaming it all on me, right?"

"Of course she is," Red said, totally winging it now. He was doing his best to keep his cool, but now that they were talking about cash in a suitcase, there was a lot more on the line.

"Well, the bitch is lying, but what do you expect from a slut like her?" Colin said.

"Watch your mouth," Red said, because he didn't think Colin should talk about a woman that way.

"Okay, you're right. I'm sorry. I wanna tell you what happened, but I don't wanna do it over the phone. I can explain everything."

Again, Red waited. He didn't want to say the wrong thing and blow it.

"Can we get together?" Colin said. "Today?"

What should he say? He made up his mind in a split second.

"Yeah," Red said. "Where are you right now?"

"Same old, same old. Hanging in Leander."

"I'm in Blanco County," Red said. "At a friend's place. Meet me out here."

This time, Colin paused. "Uh, no offense, but who's your friend? Seems like we should keep this between us."

"He's up in Dallas for a few days," Red said. "I'm all alone. You need to get over here and tell me what's going on. Stop fucking around."

"I will, Knox," Colin said. "I promise. Just give me directions and I'll leave right now."

"Got a pencil?" Red said.

CHAPTER TWENTY-EIGHT

"What changed your mind?" Lauren said.

They were having coffee at a restaurant in Round Mountain, and Marlin had just told her that he no longer thought a welfare check on Shelby Roach's cabin was a good idea.

"Actually," he said, "Nicole and I talked about it last night."

"Oh, yeah?"

"Yeah."

"And what did the two of you decide?"

"It's shaky ground," Marlin said. "I think we both knew that already, didn't we? I mean, when it boils down to it, why do we want inside that cabin?"

Lauren didn't say anything, because she knew it was a rhetorical question, and she knew what the answer was.

It was an awkward moment—or at least it was for Marlin. Nicole had basically scuttled Lauren's idea, and Marlin had decided before this conversation that he wasn't going to paint it as something else. He could have said he had weighed the pros and cons all by himself last night. Or he could've even called the county attorney, who almost certainly would have advised against a welfare check. But that's not what had happened. It had been Nicole who had caused Marlin to rethink the idea, and there was no reason for Marlin to present it as something else.

To Marlin's relief, Lauren said, "Okay, I can buy that, but I still say there's a chance Shelby is dead or injured inside that cabin. Nobody has been in there since he disappeared. But you're right—a welfare check would be pushing it. So…you got a plan B for the day?"

Marlin had also prepared for that question.

"Re-interview the people living near Rodney's place, and then widen the net further, if we have to. If we can find someone who saw the Ranchero that night—or some other vehicle they didn't recognize—that would be a big help. Don't you think?"

The truth was, Marlin wasn't hopeful about this approach. The sheriff's deputies had already spoken to the majority of the residents in the area. Chances were slim that anything new would emerge. Lauren knew it was something they'd do simply because they couldn't think of anything that might be more productive.

"That's fine," she said. "We can do that."

Ten minutes later, riding in Lauren's truck, Marlin said, "I talked to Phil this morning. He came out to the house." He couldn't help himself.

Lauren looked over at him for a few seconds. "Everything cool?"

"Yeah, but he told me something very interesting."

She took a right off the highway and crossed a cattle guard onto a narrow county road. She hadn't responded to Marlin's last remark with anything other than an enigmatic smile, so he said, "You really want to be a deputy again?"

"Well, I hadn't really thought about it much, to be honest, until I heard about the opening down here. That, combined with the work we've been doing. I miss it. I really do. Don't get me wrong, I love being a special ranger—and being the first female special ranger—but it's a little more...predictable...than being a deputy."

He could understand that. He was fortunate enough that he had the best of both worlds. He loved being a game warden, but he truly enjoyed helping Garza and his deputies in larger investigations from time to time. It was one of the perks of being a warden in a sparsely populated county, where the sheriff's department was occasionally stretched thin.

"Have you brought it up with Bobby?" Marlin asked.

"Nope. Still thinking about it. Please don't say anything to him, okay?"

"Sure."

After the thunderstorm the night before, the skies had cleared and the sun was just cresting the trees, shining through the windshield with a fierce intensity. Lauren dropped her sun visor and reduced her speed.

"One thing for sure," Lauren said. "What I'm talking about is replacing Bill Tatum as chief deputy. I've got the years and the experience."

As far as Marlin knew, there had never been a female chief deputy—or a sheriff, for that matter—in Blanco County. But Marlin was all for hiring the best candidate for the job, regardless of gender, race, sexual orientation, age, and all those other characteristics that played no part in a person's qualifications. He knew Bobby felt the same way.

"I think you'd be great," Marlin said, "but you'd definitely face some competition. I know Ernie Turpin will expect a shot at it, and I'd say he has a case."

"Good deputy?" Lauren asked.

"Excellent. And he'd make a good leader. Five or six years ago, I might not have said that, but he's really matured."

Of course, Marlin couldn't help wondering what it would be like to have Lauren working at the sheriff's department. Bill Tatum's office—which would be Lauren's office—was just two doors down the hallway from Marlin's office. Would that be weird, or would they get used to it? How would Nicole feel about it?

"In case you're curious," Lauren said, "this has nothing to do with Phil."

"Last time I'll say this," Marlin said with a lighthearted tone in his voice. "Not my business."

"Okay, cool," Lauren said.

"You mind if I put a window down?" Marlin asked. It was a beautiful spring day, with low humidity and a temperature in the mid-seventies. They were less than a mile from the entrance to Rodney Bauer's ranch.

"Not at all," Lauren said. "Jesus, these wildflowers are gorgeous."

Marlin lowered the glass and enjoyed the fresh air coming in. On the left side of the road was an open pasture thick with bluebonnets and Indian blankets that were still unusually vibrant this late in May. On the right, a thick wall of cedar trees edged to within ten feet of the county road. Then there was a narrow break in the brush line for a row of utility poles running perpendicular to the road, and as Marlin glanced down the cleared right-of-way, he spotted something that caught his eye. Just a quick glint of reflected sunlight and a flash of white or beige. Too quick to tell for sure.

"Hang on," he said. "Stop for a sec."

"What's up?" Lauren was gently applying the brakes.

"I think there was a vehicle parked in that right-of-way. Maybe a service truck, but let's take a look. There isn't supposed to be anyone else down there. It's posted."

Lauren had come to a stop, and now she checked the rearview mirror. There was no traffic coming from behind, so she dropped it into reverse and began to back up. She started to slow as they reached the break in the tree line, and then she brought the truck to a stop when they had a clear view down the long strip of open land.

"Good eye," Lauren said. "What the hell is that doing down there?"

About fifty yards down the gravel right-of-way, parked under the electric lines, was Shelby Roach's Ranchero.

"Shit, Red, really?" Billy Don said. "You told him to come over here?"

Red had taken Billy Don outside the trailer to explain the situation to him. He didn't want the guy named Knox to hear any of it.

"Hang on," Red said. "There's more."

He did his best to recount the entire phone conversation—putting the emphasis on the cash in the suitcase, of course.

"How much cash?" Billy Don said, suddenly not as judgmental.

"He didn't say, but if it's in a suitcase, you gotta figure it's a pretty big stash, right? Nobody's gonna stick a few hundred dollars in a suitcase, or even a few thousand."

Billy Don turned and looked down the caliche driveway, as if expecting Colin to show up at any minute. "But what does that money have to do with us?" he asked.

"Well," Red said. "I'm still figuring that part out. But think about it. What we've got in there is a man who tried to kill me. Twice. We can prove it, too, if we decide to call the cops. We've got the photos of him sneaking around the back of the property, plus the fact that he shot at me two times, and both of us can swear to that in court. That means he's at our mercy. You seeing where I'm going?"

"Nope."

"That cash," Red said slowly and carefully, "could be ours."

Billy Don looked at the trailer, then back at Red. "But it isn't ours."

"Yeah, but it could be. In fact, it *should* be."

"How ya figure?"

"Don't you think this guy Knox should pay some sort of penalty for trying to kill me?" Red said.

"Sure. I could take him out back and beat him into hog slop. How's that for a penalty?"

"That's one way to go about it," Red said. "And I appreciate the offer. But I'd rather take the cash from him. Wouldn't you?"

"Why couldn't we just do both?"

Red had to laugh. "Good question. I guess we could."

They both stood for a moment and thought it through.

Billy Don said, "You think the guy coming out—"

"Colin."

"Yeah, Colin. You think he has the cash with him? Or he knows where to get it?"

"Probably. Maybe. I don't know. Guess we'll find out, though. That's what I'm betting on."

The Ranchero was empty and locked. No sign of Knox Thornton, Shelby Roach, or anybody else.

"Weird," Lauren said. She looked farther down the right-of-way, to the east, away from the county road. "Anything in that direction?"

"Not much," Marlin said. "Follow it for about half a mile and it hits another county road that runs parallel to this one. Sometimes we get kids on ATVs cutting through, but it gets too rough for a truck to cross all the way."

Lauren walked a complete circle around the vehicle. "The caliche doesn't hold any footprints," she said. "No tire tracks, either, even after the rain. Not that that would have told us much."

"I'm going to assume Knox Thornton still had possession of the vehicle," Marlin said. "And he was the one who left it here. You agree?"

"Yeah."

"And he left it here because it's close to Rodney's place."

"Probably," Lauren said, "but why? So he could go over there again?"

"Don't know. Only thing I can think of."

"If he was telling the truth about going to Rodney's on Monday or Tuesday morning, why would he feel the need to go over there again? And if he's not over at Rodney's, where is he and what is he doing?"

Red figured they had about an hour before Colin would arrive from Leander, which was a suburb on the northwest side of Austin. So now he was back in the kitchen, trying to decide the best strategy for questioning his captive. Red wanted to appear to know more than he really did, so Knox would feel obligated to answer his questions and fill in the blanks. It was like those TV shows when a cop knows part of the story, but he wants the suspect to think he knows all of it. Red had experienced the same sort of treatment many times at the hands of parents, teachers, ministers, deputies, highway patrol officers, game wardens, mall cops, parking attendants, and security guards. Tricky bastards. But that wealth of experience would now work in Red's favor.

While Billy Don stood near a window, keeping an eye out, Red swung a chair around and sat just inches away from the longhaired punk, getting right in his face. Intimidation could be a powerful tool.

"So, how's it going, *Knox*?" Red said.

If Knox was impressed that Red knew his real name, he didn't show it. He only sneered and shook his head.

"I learned a lot just now," Red said, holding up Knox's phone. "You've been telling me a shitload of lies."

Knox looked away, pretending he was a cool guy instead of some loser taped to a chair in the kitchen of an aging mobile home.

"Don't believe me?" Red said.

"Don't really care."

"Wanna know who called?"

"Nope."

"Do you know what's at stake here?" Red said. "You probably don't. So I'll tell you. It's the cash in the suitcase."

He'd decided he might as well be aggressive as hell, because time was a factor. It looked like he'd chosen the right approach, because Knox's eyes widened a little bit in surprise at the mention of the cash in the suitcase.

"You might never see that cash again," Red said. "And if you want my opinion, you can blame it all on Charmaine. But what do you expect from a slut like her?"

Knox didn't seem to care at all that Red had called Charmaine a slut. Sorry excuse for a man. No surprise there.

"The question," Red said, "is who has the money right now? Charmaine or Colin? Or maybe somebody else?"

Red was hoping Colin had the money, and that Knox would somehow confirm that fact. It would be fantastic if Colin would show up at Red's trailer carrying a suitcase filled with cash. At the same time, Red was hoping his questions wouldn't reveal that he didn't know what the hell he was talking about—although in the long run, what did he have to lose?

"You know where the cash is?" Red asked.

"Don't know anything about any cash," Knox said.

"Well, I know that's not true," Red said. He held the phone up again. "When was the last time you talked to Charmaine?" He figured it was a good question to ask, since Colin had asked it.

Knox just sat there, staring into space, waiting, with his jaw set a certain way. Like he was saying, *Just wait until I'm loose. Then I'm gonna fuck you up.*

"No, you ain't," Red said. "You're not gonna fuck anybody up."

"Who you talking to, Red?" Billy Don said.

CHAPTER TWENTY-NINE

Rodney answered the door, and Mabel appeared behind him, which didn't surprise Marlin at all. Mabel would describe herself, if asked, as "curious" or "inquisitive." Rodney would call her "nosy," but only if she wasn't lingering over his shoulder, listening in. In this case, though, Marlin was glad they were both here.

"Have either of y'all seen any strange vehicles in the area in the past few days?" he asked. Lauren was standing to his right.

Rodney opened his mouth and Mabel said, "Strange how? You mean vehicles we haven't seen before? Or vehicles that are strange in some other sense?"

"Ones you haven't seen before," Marlin said.

Rodney opened his mouth and Mabel said, "I've seen a shiny new Explorer a few times, but I think the neighbor at the old Hempel place is driving that. The man that moved out here last year? I still haven't met him. He's seen me out walking a few times, but he only waves. Never stops to chat." Her tone suggested that the man must be rude, if he didn't stop to chat.

"Anything else?" Marlin asked.

Rodney opened his mouth and Mabel said, "Not that I can think of. Something going on that we should be aware of? Not sure I can stand any more excitement around here."

Marlin said, "Nothing to be concerned about. We're just looking for someone. Have you had any visitors you didn't expect, or seen anyone walking in the area?"

Rodney opened his mouth and Mabel said, "After what happened last weekend, believe me, if we see anyone hanging around, we'll call the sheriff. Obviously, I wouldn't send Rodney out there to deal with it."

"From what I saw in the reports," Lauren said, "Rodney handled everything just right last Saturday night, so good job on that." Before Mabel could interject anything else, Lauren said, "The woman who died—April Thornton—she has a brother named Knox, and he's been in the area lately, driving an old beige Ranchero. He told us the other day that he hopped the fence to your pasture because he wanted to see the place where his sister died. I guess that's understandable, but if you see him or that car, can you do us a favor and call the sheriff's office?"

Mabel opened her mouth and Rodney said, "Sure, we can do that." And he gave Lauren a little thank-you wink.

"Who'd be more likely to screw you over?" Red said. "Charmaine or Colin? You've gotta be wonderin' that right now. I mean, with all that cash at stake, no tellin' what your friends might do."

"He ain't lying," Billy Don said. "For example, I'd slit his throat for a thousand bucks." He nodded in Red's direction. "Hell, there are days I'd do it for free."

"See what I mean?" Red said. "You just never know."

Thirty minutes had passed since Colin's call, and Red was starting to feel a sense of urgency. He hadn't revealed that Colin was on his way out to Red's place, but he was wondering if he should share that information. Would that get Knox to talk? It would be helpful if Red knew more about this guy Colin. What was his association with Knox?

Then there was the question of what Red and Billy Don should do when Colin arrived. String him along somehow, or immediately strap him to a chair, just like Knox? They needed to figure that out real quick.

"Who had the suitcase last?" Red asked.

"What suitcase?" Knox said.

"The one with the cash in it," Red said.

"What cash?" Knox said.

"Is this it?" Colin asked.

"I think so," Derek said, "but your handwriting is horrible."

"Let me see."

Against his better judgment, Derek held the scrap of paper where Colin could see it while he was driving. Colin took a hard right and the tires squealed on the pavement. If the little Mini Cooper swerved off the road and hit a telephone pole or even a small tree, they would surely be maimed. Compared to Derek's Charger, this car felt like a tin can. Plus, the interior of the Mini Cooper smelled strongly of baby oil and the sour stench of body odor. The odor could, of course, be Derek's.

He was terrified.

Back on the county road, after leaving Rodney's place, Lauren said, "What now? Back to plan B? Question the neighbors again?"

She had to slow and pull to the side as a Mini Cooper zipped past them. You didn't see many cars like that on the back roads of Blanco County, and when you did, it was usually someone from Austin exploring the Hill Country for the afternoon. Marlin couldn't imagine owning such a tiny vehicle. Where would you put all your stuff? The car was so small, it could probably fit in the bed of Marlin's truck.

"Let's stop at the Ranchero again for a minute," Marlin said.

She nodded, but didn't ask any questions. She understood that sometimes you simply felt the need to return to a scene for a second look. Maybe you'd see something from a fresh angle.

"You handled Mabel nicely back there," Marlin said.

Lauren grinned. "How on earth does he put up with that? Poor guy."

Marlin's phone vibrated and he read a text from Bobby Garza: *McCulloch County M.E. confirms Bender was in freezer long term.*

"This isn't it," Derek said, as they zipped past a blue double-cab truck. He had been so consumed by anxiety, he'd forgotten that he could simply use his iPhone to navigate. Now he had it in his palm, and he saw that they had taken a wrong turn. "We need to go back.

We turned one road too early."

Colin slowed, pulled his right tires onto the shoulder, and whipped the wheel left for a very fast and aggressive U-turn, with gravel popping in the wheel wells.

CHAPTER THIRTY

Shelby blended in just fine with the crowd at the busy bus depot—same as he had on the bus the day before—but that didn't stop him from feeling conspicuous. If a set of eyes lingered on him for a moment too long, he had to wonder: *Do they recognize me? Was my face all over the news this morning? Was there a video camera in the bar? Do they know I was involved in a shooting?*

Then the eyes would drift away, and Shelby's fear would recede.

He knew he should call Knox and tell him the truth about Red. He hadn't made the call last night because everything had gone crazy, but there was no reason he couldn't call now. His bus wouldn't arrive for another hour, and this being Mexico, it would probably be late.

He slipped his phone from his pocket, and right then, it vibrated with an incoming call. This wasn't his regular phone—which he hadn't bothered bringing, for obvious reasons—but his burner phone. Very few people had the number, also for obvious reasons. Just a few of his customers. And Knox. But it wasn't any of them calling. He didn't recognize the number. In fact, it was a Mexican number, or at least a number from some foreign country. He could tell because it started with a +1. The call was being routed to the United States and then back to Shelby in Mexico, which is why it was showing up as a foreign call.

But who was it?

Policia. Had to be the police. Had Shelby given his phone number to Luis, the bartender? He couldn't remember. If he had, Luis would've given it to the police. And this would be them calling right now. Shelby knew how that conversation would go. *We just have a few questions, Mr. Roach. Where are you right now? Can you spare a few minutes?*

He let it go to voicemail.

A moment later, his phone vibrated again. The caller had left a message.

A well-dressed man with shiny hair sat down in a chair across the aisle. He smiled and nodded. Shelby nodded back.

Cop.

The man said in Spanish, "The bus is going to be late. That's what the clerk just said."

The man carried a newspaper, but no suitcase. Not even a small bag. Same as Shelby. Why no belongings?

"Going to be a long day," Shelby said.

"Guess so," the man said. He unfolded his newspaper and began to read.

A minute later, Shelby worked up the guts to listen to the voicemail, which was also in Spanish.

Hello, Shelby. This is Pedro calling you back. So, uh, I guess call me again. Take care.

Who the fuck was Pedro? Shelby was starting to panic. Was he being conned? He didn't know anyone named Pedro. Then he felt immense relief. Pedro was Vicente's brother in Barra de Potosi. Vicente was the man on the bus yesterday who had been so helpful. Shelby scrolled through his Recent Calls list and saw that he had dialed Pedro's number while at the bar last night. He didn't remember doing that. Damn, he'd been more hammered than he thought. He'd call Pedro again later.

Shelby slipped his phone back into his pocket, and then he noticed the man with the shiny hair gazing at him. The man smiled and nodded again, then looked down at his newspaper.

Just a regular guy. Not a cop. Shelby needed to stop being so paranoid.

Marlin leaned right up to the passenger-side window of the Ranchero and looked inside again, without touching the glass. No key in the ignition. Nothing to indicate who had last been driving the vehicle or why they had parked it here.

"Plenty of fast-food garbage," Lauren said. "Stuff that wasn't here when we searched it two days ago."

That was a good indication that Knox Thornton had remained in

Blanco County, living off Dairy Queen and Sonic.

Marlin gazed in an easterly direction down the right-of-way. "Let's take a walk," he said.

They hiked side by side underneath the utility lines. Marlin wasn't looking for anything in particular. Maybe Knox Thornton was camping out somewhere in the woods nearby. Marlin couldn't imagine why he would do that, but men like Thornton often made decisions that would baffle anyone with a rational mind.

The right-of-way had been cleared and the poles erected more than twenty years earlier, but there was a two-wheel pathway through the grass and weeds, where service trucks came and went to maintain the lines and inspect the equipment. Likewise, ATVs and motorcycles had worn smaller pathways. Kids cutting through or just out joyriding. Marlin also noticed quite a bit of trash. Beer and soft drink cans and bottles, mostly, because they could endure years of weather, whereas potato chip bags and candy wrappers disintegrated more rapidly. None of the refuse appeared particularly fresh.

The right-of-way reached a small crest, then sloped gently to a stream no more than five or six feet across. Without last night's rain, this little gully would likely be dry right now. Marlin easily leapt across and Lauren followed.

And there they both stopped. Just on the other side of that stream, the caliche gave way to a long expanse of mud, and in that mud was a fresh trail of footprints.

"Boots," Lauren said.

Marlin had seen more than his share of tracks from work boots over the years, and he knew Lauren had, too.

"Red Wings," Marlin said. "You agree?"

"Yep."

"And what was Knox Thornton wearing the other day?"

"Red Wings."

"Obviously these prints were left after the rain last night," Lauren said. She looked eastward. "Why would Knox walk through here? Who lives down that way?"

Marlin was puzzled. None of this made sense. Rodney Bauer's ranch was in the opposite direction. And then his thoughts turned to a certain pair of rednecks living in a trailer on the county road at the eastern end of the right-of-way.

"Is this it?" Colin asked, slowing.

"Yes, this is definitely it," Derek said.

They were on a narrow county road, not unlike the narrow county road they had been on earlier. There wasn't much to be seen out here, other than a bunch of oak and cedar trees, and some cows in pastures every now and then, usually right after their tires had rumbled over a cattle guard. Sometimes there would be a barn or small outbuilding in a clearing, or Derek could glimpse a home tucked in the woods, some distance off the road. Like the house he was seeing now. A mobile home. What many people still called a trailer, but technically, it was a mobile home. And it had seen better days.

Colin had come to a complete stop at the turn-in for a caliche driveway that wound through a wooded hillside up to the mobile home. Somebody had hand painted the address on a rusty mailbox, and it matched the address Knox had given Colin on the phone.

"Well," Colin said.

"Okay," Derek said.

Colin shifted into gear.

"I'm not sure I can do this," Derek said.

"Sure you can," Colin said.

Derek did his best to appear doubtful. Maybe he should call this thing off right now.

"Mostly, I'll be doing it," Colin said. "All you really have to do is stay out of the way and try not to let him kill you." He gave the Mini Cooper some gas and started up the hill.

"There's a car down there," Billy Don said, still standing by the window.

"What kind of car?"

"Don't know. Some little red car. Just sitting there."

"Are they—"

"He just turned in. Gotta be him."

"Y'all are idiots," Knox said.

"Shut up," Red said.

He rose from his chair and stepped to the window. He saw a small car for a moment, and then it disappeared behind some trees as it came up the hill. He was holding the handgun Knox had used to shoot the mannequin. Nice piece. Beretta M9. Red figured why use his own weapon? He might have to ditch the gun after today, and he damn sure wasn't willing to part with his Anaconda. It had helped him through too many hard times.

Red turned around and grabbed the roll of duct tape off the table. Without a word, he pulled the free end of the tape and began to make several loops around Knox's mouth. Knox, to his credit, didn't bitch. He sat there and took it, like a man. Red was careful to leave his nostrils free and clear, so the man could breathe.

When Red was done, he said, "Okay, let's do this."

Colin stopped in a patch of dirt in front of the trailer. An ancient red Ford truck was parked some distance away, backed into a spot near some trees.

Derek was so nervous, he was worried he might literally pee in his shorts. He should've taken a leak at the bottom of the driveway, but it was too late now. Where was this guy Knox? Derek had expected him to be waiting outside for them, but he was nowhere to be seen. The place looked deserted, or at least not well maintained.

Colin killed the engine and slowly opened his door, so Derek did the same. As he stood, the weight of the .380—as small as it was—felt like a brick in the front right pocket of his cargo shorts. Colin had given him the handgun back at the apartment, and had shown him how to use it. Derek hadn't fired a gun since he was a kid, plinking at cans with a .22.

"Knox?" Colin called out.

They waited. Nobody appeared.

The condition of this trailer would give other trailers a bad name. The flat roof sagged. Various sheet-metal repairs over the years had given the sides of the trailer a patchwork appearance. The wide front porch leaned to one side, possibly because it was cluttered with a variety of objects large and small, including an old refrigerator, a small-block engine, a stack of cinder blocks, and a large ice chest without a lid.

"Knox?" Colin called again. They both closed their car doors.

Derek noticed that one of the front windows had a cobweb of cracks across it, with a small hole at the center, and someone had used duct tape to effect a sloppy repair job. That hole—was it a bullet hole? What kind of people had windows with bullet holes in them?

"What if this is a trap?" he whispered.

"That's dumb," Colin said back, "because I called him. He didn't call me. We asked for this meeting, not him."

Before Derek could point out that that didn't really matter, the front door opened and two men stepped onto the porch. One was average height, but slender. Was he Knox? He didn't look like a sociopath. More like your garden-variety yokel. The other man was huge—roughly the same size as Colin, though not as ripped. Just big. Not fat. Big.

The smaller man said, "Howdy."

Colin said, "Who the hell are you?"

That was Derek's first indication that this rendezvous wasn't going to go as planned.

CHAPTER THIRTY-ONE

"Your worst nightmare, quite possibly," Red said. "I own this place—I'll tell you that much—which means if anyone's gonna be asking questions, it's me. So which one of y'all is Colin? Let's start with that."

"I am," said the beefy dude who was every bit as large as Billy Don. More muscular, too. And younger. "And like I said, who the hell are you?"

Red ignored the question and said, "You didn't say you was bringing a friend."

Colin shrugged. "What of it?"

"What's his name?" Red said.

"Derek," said the second man, who was named Derek, if he was telling the truth.

"Y'all got the suitcase?" Red said, jumping right to the heart of the matter.

"Are you frigging kidding me?" Colin said. "Where's Knox?"

"He's tied up at the moment," Red said, and Billy Don let out an appreciative snort.

"We need to talk to him," Colin said. "That's why we're here. He told us to come out. He said you were in Dallas."

"Been a little change of plans," Red said. "Knox wants that suitcase—fully loaded—and he asked us to get it from you."

A long silence followed. Colin looked like he wanted to say something or ask a question, but he didn't know what to say or ask. The other guy, Derek, simply waited, but his eyes were darting all over the place, as if he expected something bad to happen at any moment.

Finally Colin said, "You work for Knox or what?"

"We work together," Red said.

"First I've heard of Knox having a partner."

"Didn't say we're partners," Red said. "Said we work together."

"What's the difference?" Colin said.

"Here's a much more important question. Where's the suitcase?"

"We don't have it. That's what we came to talk about. To tell Knox the truth before Charmaine and Bobo spread all kinds of lies."

"Why would they lie?" Red said.

Again, he was totally playing it by ear. What was the alternative? If it became obvious to these clowns that Red was faking everything, well, so be it. Nothing ventured, nothing gained. Fortunately, since Colin and Derek didn't know who he was or how he was connected to Knox, how would they know what Red should or shouldn't already know?

To Derek, something didn't seem quite right—beyond the fact that Knox was nowhere to be seen and, instead, these two rednecks seemed to be running things. Who were they? Derek was keeping one eye on them and one eye on the windows to the trailer, just in case. Was Knox Thornton inside, ready to shoot them both? And why was the huge redneck remaining so close to the open doorway, like he was prepared to duck back inside the trailer?

"Charmaine is just a liar in general," Colin said, "and Knox already knows that because of the way she cheated on me. But I will admit this much: If she told him I pawned her stuff, that's true. I did. But I didn't know what was in there, man! That's the main thing I need to tell Knox. I guess it was kind of my fault, but just by accident."

"Hang on a sec," Derek said, because now he was really wondering whether Colin should be sharing these details with anyone besides Knox. This wasn't part of their plan. In fact, shouldn't they turn around and leave right now? Their plan was shot to hell, wasn't it? Because if Knox was really here, and if he came outside and reacted poorly to Colin's story, what then? The original plan was that Colin would shoot Knox, but now that there were two other men to deal with, well, Derek wasn't prepared to be involved with three killings. And that was assuming he and Colin could pull it off, without getting killed themselves.

But the point was moot for now, because nobody paid any

attention to his interruption. Instead, the skinny redneck said, "And what about Bobo?"

"That's his boss at the pawnshop," Colin said, nodding toward Derek. "Or he was, up until Wednesday morning, when he fired him out of the blue. You wanna know why?"

"Why?"

"See, what I think is, Bobo found the money in the suitcase, so he stole it, and he's trying to blame it on Derek. Charmaine blames me, Bobo blames Derek."

"On the other hand," Skinny Redneck said, "you're blaming Charmaine and Bobo."

"Colin, let's go," Derek said.

"Well, yeah," Colin said, responding to the redneck's remark. "But that's because one of them done it. Had to be one of them, and if you ask me, it was Bobo."

"How come it couldn't be you?" Skinny Redneck said. "You had the suitcase in your possession. So did Derek. Either of y'all could've stolen the money."

"But we didn't," Colin said.

"Prove it."

"How the hell can I do that?"

"This is a waste of time," Derek said.

"I think you're lying," Skinny Redneck said.

"Well, fuck you," Colin said.

"The plan is ruined," Derek said.

"Oh, what plan was that?" Skinny Redneck said, very accusatory. "If you're innocent, why would you need a plan?"

"Let's go," Derek said.

But, crap, it was too late, because Colin was suddenly pawing frantically at the front pocket of his cargo shorts, and at the same time, the huge redneck in the trailer doorway was stepping backwards to grab something just out of view, and Derek figured somebody was just about to die.

"These two guys I'm talking about," Marlin said, "are responsible for about half the problems in Blanco County. Okay, that's an exaggeration, but they always seem to be involved one way or another with every weird or illegal thing that goes on around here."

They were back in Lauren's truck and were making the drive the long way around to the county road on the other end of the right-of-way.

"So you're playing a hunch," Lauren said. "That's what we're down to now? Hunches?"

"It's an educated guess, based on past experiences," Marlin said, enjoying the teasing, because he had a peculiar feeling that his hunch—yes, it was a hunch—was going to pay off. Why else would Knox Thornton have tucked the Ranchero in the right-of-way and walked eastward? There were only so many residents living on that road, and almost all of them were quiet, law-abiding, hardworking, sensible, stay-out-of-trouble types.

Almost all. But not all.

It was a shotgun. A pistol-grip shotgun. That's what the huge redneck had reached for. It must have been leaning against the inside wall or resting on a chair, but all that mattered now was that he was coming around with the barrel, and that's when Derek heard a shot from Colin's handgun.

This can't be happening.

Skinny Redneck was crouching to reach into the lidless ice chest on the porch, and Derek couldn't help thinking, *What on Earth does he need with a cold drink right now?* But, of course, Skinny Redneck's hand emerged not with a can of beer, but with a semi-automatic handgun. The shotgun coughed, followed by a boom from Skinny Redneck's gun.

Derek realized he was standing perfectly still. Paralyzed, really. The little .380 was still in his shorts, and that's where it was going to stay. He knew that with certainty, because he was too terrified to move.

He was vaguely aware that Colin had just turned and run away. Now the big redneck was aiming the shotgun at Derek.

Derek could feel warm fluid streaming down his leg.

Red was tempted to shoot Colin in the back as he ran towards his car, but you could get in trouble for that sort of thing, even in Texas, if some liberal prosecutor got his panties in a wad about some scumbag's rights.

So, instead, Red just watched as the big man squeezed himself into the tiny car, cranked the engine, and reversed as quickly as possible down the hill. Then Red focused his attention on Derek, who was still standing five yards in front of the porch. Good lord, it looked like he had just pissed himself. What a sorry sight.

"What now, Red?" Billy Don asked. He had his shotgun leveled at Derek.

Red lowered the Beretta. No need for it anymore.

"Looks like he bailed on you, Derek," Red said.

"I think I hit him," Billy Don said.

"You think?" Red said.

"Yeah. He sure twitched."

"That shot didn't sound quite right."

"It did sound a little weird."

"From that distance, with buckshot, you shoulda taken his head off."

"Guess I mighta twitched myself," Billy Don said.

Red bent and picked up the ejected shotgun shell. "This one of your hand loads?"

"Yeah. So what?"

"Half the time, you're too drunk to measure the right amount of powder. Next time our lives are in danger, use factory ammo, okay? No more hand loads."

"Well, shit, you missed him entirely, didn't you?" Billy Don said. "So don't be badmouthing me."

Red just shook his head, disappointed that the situation had deteriorated so rapidly. One minute he'd been hoping to get his hands on a suitcase brimming with cash, the next he'd had a shootout with a couple of city boys, one of whom had turned tail and run while the other one had wet himself.

"You," Red said to Derek, "take a seat."

"Pardon?"

"Sit down on the ground."

Derek did as he was told.

"Now take your shoes off."

He did that, too. Red had heard about old timey game wardens using this technique to stop poachers from running away.

"Now toss 'em on the roof of the trailer," Red said.

They landed with a satisfying thump.

"You can put the shotgun down," Red said to Billy Don. "He ain't going nowhere."

Marlin and Lauren had just reached a long straightaway—maybe a mile from Red O'Brien's trailer—when Marlin saw a red dot in the distance. Just seconds later, it was identifiable as a car that was coming this way rapidly. Seriously speeding.

"Yeah, I see him," Lauren said, and she began to slow.

Now the vehicle was roughly eighty yards away.

"I think that car passed us twenty minutes ago on the other road," Marlin said.

Lauren engaged her red-and-blue grill lights and goosed the siren.

The car did not slow.

Lauren eased off the gas even more. They were going to have to pull the car over. It was a distraction from their mission this morning, but they couldn't let this driver continue down the road, presenting a danger to others.

Lauren engaged the siren again as the Mini Cooper zoomed past going at least ninety miles per hour. Marlin could see just one person in the car—a very large man. He was looking in their direction, eyes wide, probably surprised that Lauren's plain-vanilla truck had turned out to be a law-enforcement vehicle. Busted.

"What a dumbass," Lauren muttered as she whipped the wheel hard and began to make a U-turn.

CHAPTER THIRTY-TWO

Colin was freaking out—he couldn't help it—because there was a round of buckshot planted squarely in the center of his forehead, like a third eye.

He'd felt it when it had slammed into him, stinging like a hornet, damn near enough to knock him over, and it was at that moment he'd realized how stupid their plan was. And how stupid he had been for even talking to those two rednecks, instead of turning right around and leaving as soon as somebody other than Knox had come out of that trailer.

Now he had a round of buckshot in his head. He could see it in the rearview mirror—a gray lump, buried deep enough that he couldn't pluck it out with his fat fingers. Had it cracked his skull? Why wasn't it bleeding much? If he did manage to remove it, would blood and brains spew out of the hole? The more he worried about it, the faster he drove, until his tires were squealing around every curve.

And Jesus, fuck, what would happen to Derek?

Colin felt bad for leaving him behind, but why the hell had Derek just stood there, instead of running to the car? Would those two idiots be stupid enough to hurt Derek, knowing that Colin had made a clean getaway and could tell the cops exactly what had happened?

Colin reached a straightaway and really pushed the little Mini Cooper hard.

If those guys were partners with Knox—or if they worked together, whatever—chances were pretty good they were every bit as hard-ass as he was. They wouldn't just let Derek go.

Now Colin could see a vehicle coming in his direction, at the far end of the straightaway. Looked like a truck. He hadn't seen many vehicles on these county roads, and the ones he had seen had almost all been trucks.

The truth of the matter was, he couldn't worry about Derek right now. He had to see about getting the buckshot removed from his forehead so there wouldn't be any lasting damage. Hell, he could be bleeding inside his head right now. Maybe that was why he wasn't bleeding *outside* his head. But weren't emergency-room doctors required to report gunshot wounds to the proper authorities? Then what would happen? Maybe he could come up with a good lie to explain a round of buckshot embedded in his forehead. Or maybe he'd have to do the job himself with a pair of needle-nosed pliers. And some whiskey. He'd need whiskey, for sure.

The truck ahead was hardly moving. Like it was looking for something. Colin was fifty yards from the truck and closing fast.

Derek would be fine. Why would they hurt him? They'd believe what he was saying. He'd tell them about Bobo, who was the most likely thief, and they'd—

Bright red and blue lights suddenly strobed behind the front grille of the truck. He heard a short blast from a siren.

Oh, shit.

It was a cop of some sort. Not a state trooper or a county deputy. But what? Park ranger? Game warden?

Colin blew past them at ninety miles per hour, seeing two people in the truck, and then he glanced in the rearview mirror.

Son of a bitch.

They were coming after him.

Knox Thornton twisted and torqued his arms, trying to break free.

He had no idea what was going on outside. A few minutes earlier, he'd heard the low hum of a small engine climbing the hill to the redneck's trailer. Then he heard voices. Muffled. Couldn't make out what anyone was saying. One of them was Red. The other—was it Colin?

Then—*boom! boom!*—two quick shots. One sounded like a handgun, but the second one—Knox had no idea. Sounded more like the pop of a flare gun. Some of the duct tape around his mouth had also covered his ears, so he wasn't hearing things quite right.

Knox squirmed some more. When the big redneck had cut Knox loose to take a leak earlier that morning, he hadn't taped him up quite as tightly as he'd been taped the night before. But Knox hadn't had a chance—until five minutes ago—to try to get free. One of the rednecks had always been in the room with him. As soon as they'd gone outside, he'd begun to test the tape. There was some slack. But damn, it wasn't going to be easy.

"Derek," Red said. "That your real name?"

"Yes, it is. Uh-huh."

This guy Derek plainly was not the type to be involved in situations like this. He was an innocent bystander. A civilian.

"You worked with this guy Bobo?" Red said.

From somewhere in the near distance came the short chirp of a siren. It was on the county road leading to the highway.

"Right," Derek said. "Yep. He was the owner."

"Where's this pawnshop?"

"Leander. Outside Austin. It's a suburb. Sort of. On the outskirts. The edge of town."

"Settle down. I know where it is," Red said.

Now the siren came on and stayed on. Red listened for a moment. The sound seemed to be moving away from the trailer. Good. Did it have something to do with Colin in the little red car? Surely nobody had called about the gunshots, because there were gunshots out here all the time. Red and Billy Don were responsible for many of them, but plenty of other neighbors hunted or sat around shooting tin cans.

"You think Bobo has the suitcase?" Red said.

Derek had not budged an inch. He was frozen in place, seated on the caliche. Smart.

"Oh, I know he has the suitcase," he said. "But it's empty. The question is, where is the cash?"

Red knew what Derek was thinking—that if he was helpful enough and told the truth, they'd let him go. He was probably right.

"One of y'all had to steal it, right?" Red said. "Charmaine or Bobo or Colin."

"Right."

"Or you."

"Wasn't me. I swear. I wouldn't do that. It wasn't my money.

I'm an honest man. I've never even been arrest—"

"Seriously," Red said, "take it easy. I believe you."

"So do I," Billy Don said. The shotgun was hanging loosely from his big right hand. It looked like a child's toy.

"And I'm pretty sure it wasn't Colin, either," Derek said. "I don't know him very well, but he's too scared of Knox to have done something like that."

"Why's he scared of Knox?"

"Because, you know, he supposedly killed a guy."

"Yeah? When was this?"

"Last fall."

"Supposedly?"

"Yeah, they couldn't prove it."

Red wasn't sure how to feel about that. Was Knox really a killer, or was it bullshit? A guy like Knox would enjoy having that kind of rumor floating around.

"What about Charmaine?" Red said. "Think she stole it?"

"I've never met her personally," Derek said, "so I don't know what she'd do. But Colin said she freaked out pretty bad when she heard he pawned the suitcases, so I'm guessing she didn't do it. Colin doesn't think she did it."

"She was banging Knox behind Colin's back, right?"

"Yeah. And several other men, apparently."

"So Colin might not've been the best judge of what Charmaine might've done," Red said.

"That's true," Derek said.

"What about Bobo?" Red said.

Derek started nodding. "He'd steal it for sure if he could get away with it. He said he didn't know anything about it, but, man, I think it was him. That's why he fired me—so he could blame it on me."

Red could still hear the siren in the distance, but quieter than before. "Any other people work there?"

"Just us two."

"Any chance a customer found the money?" Red said.

"No, the suitcases were in storage. They weren't out front in display. If the cash was in the suitcase when it got to the pawnshop, only two people had access to it—Bobo and me."

Red was thinking, *Maybe there's still hope.*

"If Bobo took the money, what would he have done with it?"

"Stash it somewhere for a long time. He'd be too scared to spend it until he thought he was in the clear."

"Where would he stash it?" Red said.

"Only place I can figure is his house," Derek said. "We checked the safe at work and it was empty, but he erased the security video. I think it would've shown him sticking the money in there for a while, and then moving it later."

Red figured the smart money was on Bobo. Had to be Bobo. Wouldn't be hard to track him down. Red didn't know what else to ask at the moment, but then he remembered another name Colin had mentioned on the phone earlier.

"Who is April?" Red said.

"Knox's sister," Derek said. "She died a couple of days ago, not far from here. She was dating a guy named Shelby."

"Wait, who?" Red said. "Did you say Shelby?"

"Holy whorebag," Billy Don said.

"Shelby Roach?" Red said, but how many Shelbys were out there running around?

"I think so," Derek said.

"Should've fucking known he was involved somehow," Billy Don said.

Lauren's truck had more horsepower, but the Mini Cooper was nimble and quick on the curves. After a full minute, the distance between the two vehicles—about sixty yards—was unchanged. Lauren got on her radio and asked the dispatcher to send any available units to the intersection where the county road met the highway.

Marlin noticed Lauren had a slight grin on her face.

"Second chase in two days," Marlin said.

"Fun," Lauren said.

"It's not usually quite this busy around here."

"I'm afraid to push this truck much harder," Lauren said. "Just keeping up with him for now."

Marlin had no problem with that. No sense in risking a crash for a speeder. Usually, idiots like this gave up after a few minutes. It was only the dumbest among them who turned a case of instinctive fleeing into a prolonged chase. "Once we reach the highway, he won't be able to run for long."

The Mini Cooper crested a hill and dropped from sight over the other side.

"In case you don't remember," Marlin said, "there's a pretty sharp curve to the right after this rise."

"Thanks," Lauren said.

A few seconds later, they crested the hill—just in time to see the driver of the Mini Cooper losing control. He had slowed considerably, but he'd hugged the inside of the curve too tightly at too great of a speed, and the vehicle's passenger-side tires had left the pavement. The sudden difference in speed and traction between the left and right tires caused the center of gravity to shift quickly to the driver's side, tipping it, and suddenly the tiny car was up on two wheels.

For a few tense but entertaining seconds, the Mini Cooper continued down the road like it was being driven by a skilled stunt driver performing a balancing act. The driver should've steered to the left, which would've dropped the right-hand tires back to the road. But that was counter-intuitive. He steered right, and the Mini Cooper slowly tumbled onto the driver's side, and then further onto its roof, where it remained, skidding along the pavement at slow speed. Then it hit the gravel on the left shoulder and came to a grinding halt.

Lauren was already on the radio, requesting an ambulance. As she brought the truck to a stop ten yards from the Mini Cooper, Marlin could see the big man, upside-down, struggling to climb out. Marlin stepped from the truck and proceeded toward the overturned car with caution, one hand on the butt of his gun.

"Show me your hands!"

The big man in the Mini Cooper held both of his hands in the open window for Marlin and Lauren to see.

As Marlin got closer, he saw that the man had some sort of wound to the center of his forehead.

"What's your name?" Marlin said, as he took a knee on the pavement beside the open window.

"Colin Kelly."

"An ambulance is on the way," Marlin said.

"Okay."

Marlin tugged at the door handle, but the door wasn't going to open, and the man inside was simply too large to crawl out easily. He might have to stay where he was until the vehicle could be righted. Lauren was inspecting the car to determine whether there were any flames or fluid leaks that might present an immediate danger.

"How you feeling?" Marlin asked. "Anything hurting or

bleeding that you know about?"

"My leg," the man said. "I think it's broke."

"Is it bleeding?" Marlin said. He couldn't see the leg.

"I don't think so. I can't tell."

"Left or right leg?"

"Right."

"Any idea what happened to your forehead?"

"You need to go back and help Derek," the man said, becoming agitated, and possibly not thinking clearly. "Somebody needs to help Derek."

"Who's Derek?" Marlin asked.

"I left him alone back there. Hurry and help Derek!"

CHAPTER THIRTY-THREE

While Billy Don stayed outside with Derek, Red went back into the trailer, to the kitchen, where Knox waited in the chair.

Red said, "I'll do my best, but this might hurt a little," and he began to remove the duct tape that was wrapped around Knox's head. Again, to his credit, Knox didn't whimper or whine when the tape pulled his hair or tugged at his skin.

When Red had removed enough tape that Knox could talk, Red said, "I just found out you know my cousin Shelby. Right?"

Knox didn't reply.

Red said, "All this time, I been trying to figure out why you wanted to kill me, and suddenly it makes sense. Or at least it's *starting* to make sense. It's gotta have something to do with Shelby. I don't know how good you know him, but you've probably figured out he's generally a lying piece of shit. Agreed?"

Again, Knox said nothing. Red set the Beretta on the table and took a seat in one of the dinette chairs.

"Guy outside just told me about your sister dying late on Saturday night. Said it happened not far from here. Some sort of mishap with a bull, and for that, I offer my deepest symphonies. But here's the thing that seems weird to me. Shelby showed up here on Sunday. Seriously, I hadn't seen him in years, and then he just shows up, out of the blue. You think that was a coincidence?"

Knox obviously wasn't going to answer.

"There's more," Red said. "He had blood on his shirt. A lot of it. Enough that I said, 'Hey, what's the deal with the blood on your shirt?' And you know what he said?"

Knox simply stared at Red.

"He said he'd gotten into a fight with some guy that was supposed to buy a livestock trailer. Said the guy backed out of the deal, they had words, so Shelby busted him one. The guy bled all over him. But Shelby couldn't tell me the guy's last name or even where he lived."

Knox didn't appear interested in the slightest.

"So now," Red said, "knowing what happened to your sister, and knowing that Shelby stopped at my place the next day, and knowing that he made up some big story about getting in a fight, well, it makes me wonder what really happened. What was he was up to the night before? I'd guess he was with your sister."

It was as if Knox couldn't even hear Red talking.

"Something went wrong out there, so Shelby hauled ass, and then he began to look for someone else to blame. That sound about right?"

Red knew he'd get no answer.

"Since I live nearby," Red said, "he thought of me. Or maybe he only came here for help—I gave him some money—and it wasn't until he got home that he decided to blame me. He told you it was all my fault—and you had no reason to think he was lying. Is that pretty close to what happened?"

Finally, Knox spoke, his voice raspy from several hours without water. "Last chance. Cut me loose now and I'll forget this ever happened."

Well, crap. It was obvious Knox didn't believe anything Red had just said. Hard to blame him. If Red *had* been with Shelby and April on the night in question, wouldn't he claim he hadn't been? But what was Red going to do about the situation now? If he couldn't convince Knox that he had no reason to kill Red, that didn't leave Red many alternatives. He couldn't just wait around for the next time Knox decided to—

Red was distracted by the sound of a vehicle down by the road, pulling onto his caliche driveway. Was it Colin returning for Derek? Red rose and moved to the window, and now he saw a blue double-cab Ford truck coming up the hill. Aw, man. It had to be the same truck he'd seen two days earlier—the one that had pulled Knox over in Shelby's Ranchero.

Bottom line: it was a cop.

"Oh, hell."

Then Red saw a deputy's car following behind the truck. This shit was getting out of hand.

Several deputies and an ambulance had arrived at the scene of the crash just moments after Colin Kelly had told Marlin and Lauren what had happened at a nearby trailer just ten minutes earlier. The account was brief and perhaps not entirely accurate, because Kelly seemed to be going into shock. But if what he'd said was true, lives could still be in danger, or there could be more casualties. So Marlin and Lauren had decided to investigate, accompanied by Deputy Ernie Turpin in his patrol unit.

They slowly worked their way up the hill to O'Brien's place, and as they neared the trailer, Marlin spotted an enormous man standing on the porch, close to the open front door.

"That's Billy Don Craddock," Marlin said.

Then he saw another man—seated on the ground below the porch.

"Who's that?" Lauren said.

"Don't recognize him," Marlin said, wondering if it was Derek, and just then another man emerged from the trailer and closed the door behind him. "That's O'Brien," Marlin said. Everything appeared completely normal, but O'Brien and Craddock had had plenty of practice at appearing normal when they'd just committed one crime or another.

"Sure we got the right place?" Lauren asked.

Colin Kelly had told a somewhat disjointed story about getting shot by a couple of men outside a trailer, and based on the physical descriptions, Marlin figured it had to be O'Brien and Craddock. But it was possible it had happened at some other trailer in this area, or that it hadn't happened at all. If there had been a shootout here not long ago, it sure didn't look like it.

"Let's find out," Marlin said.

"You play this right," Red said to Derek on the ground, "and you won't have any trouble from us later. But if you don't…"

"Don't worry about me," Derek said.

"Come on up here," Billy Don said, "and be cool."

Red noticed that Billy Don had stashed his pistol-grip shotgun in the lidless ice chest a few feet away.

Derek stood and wiped his backside free of dirt. "Who is it?" he said. The deputy's vehicle was not yet in view.

"Cops," Red said, trying to appear as calm as possible, despite the fact that his heart was beginning to race. Derek climbed the steps in his bare feet and joined them on the porch.

As the truck pulled past the last clump of cedars and stopped ten yards away, Red saw that the county game warden, John Marlin, was along for the ride—same as when the blue truck had pulled Knox over. But why were they here? Had Colin called the cops?

Red knew that—despite the fact that he hadn't really done anything wrong—he could be in big trouble. Even though Knox had tried to kill him, it wouldn't look good that they'd been holding him captive. Nowadays, people got all uptight about shit like that, worrying about whether some criminal had his rights protected. Silly.

Red had no idea what he should say or how he should act. Pretend everything was okay and see if he could bluff his way through this? Or spill the beans about everything that had happened? If he did that, he might as well kiss the cash in the suitcase goodbye.

He decided to wait and see what the cops had to say, then play it by ear.

Marlin and Lauren stepped from the truck at the same time. Ernie Turpin was just dropping his cruiser into park.

"Howdy!" Red O'Brien called out.

"Morning, Red," Marlin said. "Billy Don. Y'all doing okay?"

He was keeping his eyes on all three men at once. The man who had been sitting on the ground had stood and joined the other two men on the porch.

"You bet," O'Brien said. "Just enjoying the beautiful weather after the rain last night."

"Sir, what is your name?" Marlin said, addressing the shoeless man. Deputy Turpin had exited his cruiser and was now standing behind Marlin and Lauren, and five or six yards to their left.

"Me?" the barefoot man said.

"Yes, sir."

"Derek Callahan."

"Friend of mine," O'Brien said.

"We're just hanging out," Craddock said.

"We was doing some target shooting earlier," O'Brien said.

"Just a little thirty-eight," Craddock said.

"Hope we didn't disturb nobody," O'Brien said.

They weren't acting quite right. Something was definitely going on.

"Just the three of you out here today?" Marlin asked.

"Yes, sir," O'Brien said.

"Nobody else inside?" Marlin asked.

"Just us," Craddock said.

"You know a man named Colin Kelly?" Marlin said to Callahan.

"Me?" Callahan said.

"Yes, sir." Marlin was beginning to lose his patience.

"Colin Kelly?" Derek Callahan said.

"Let's stop screwing around," Lauren said. "Do you know him or not?"

"I do, yeah," Derek Callahan said, now starting to get flustered. "He was here a little while ago."

So Colin Kelly's story was at least partially true.

"I'm going to ask the three of you to come down off the porch," Marlin said, because that would be the next step—separate the three men, pat them down, and ask them questions. See if they contradict each other. Had O'Brien or Craddock shot Colin Kelly? At this point, that seemed plausible, or even likely. Marlin had been fairly certain, back at the crash site, that the object embedded in Kelly's forehead had, in fact, been ammo of some sort, either from a small-caliber weapon or a load of buckshot. Wherever it came from, Colin Kelly was lucky to be alive.

The men were slow to move, so Marlin gestured with his arm and said, "Come on down here for a minute and then we'll be out of your hair."

There was a slight pause. All three men were reluctant to comply.

Marlin was about to give a firmer command, but right then, the door to the trailer slammed open and Knox Thornton emerged with a gun. He swung toward O'Brien, who was already diving over the porch railing as the gun roared.

CHAPTER THIRTY-FOUR

Derek Callahan and Billy Don Craddock scrambled down the porch steps, away from Thornton, as Marlin pulled his .357 and began to raise it. Thornton fired a second time at O'Brien, who hit the ground, rolled, and came up running for the cedar trees.

Marlin would note in his report later that Thornton appeared keenly focused on O'Brien, to the exclusion of everyone else on the scene. He was plainly gunning for O'Brien, rather than shooting indiscriminately.

Thornton was aiming for a third shot when Marlin fired his first round, echoed immediately by shots from both Lauren and Ernie Turpin.

Thornton flinched and ducked back into the trailer.

Total elapsed time: Less than six seconds.

A smart cop knows that once you have an aggressive subject engaged, it's best to keep him engaged until you can neutralize him. You don't want to let him retreat and regroup, and you certainly don't want to give him a chance to hole up inside a structure. For all Marlin knew, there were additional people inside—innocent people who deserved protection.

Operating on instinct, Marlin bounded up the porch steps, into the trailer, less than two seconds behind Thornton.

On the outskirts of Saltillo, while he still had a decent signal, Shelby dialed Knox's number. Here in the back of the bus, Shelby had a row all to himself. There weren't more than twenty people on the bus, spread randomly from front to back. Of course, he had to deal with the odor wafting from the small bathroom, but that was the price he had to pay for privacy.

The call rang four times and went to voicemail, and Shelby had to admit he wasn't disappointed by that. The greeting wasn't Knox, but was instead a generic electronic voice that repeated the phone number and invited Shelby to leave a message, which he did.

"Hey, it's me. Listen, man, you freaked me out pretty bad the other day. I didn't expect you to come at me like that, especially after I told you it was my cousin's fault. Anyway, here's the deal on that... I made that part up... I knew you were gonna be upset, even though it was totally an accident, so I blamed it on him, but he wasn't there and he didn't know anything about it. So I just wanted to clear that up before you do anything. He had nothing to do with it. So you should leave him alone. That's all. Later."

Marlin made it through the doorway in time to see Thornton moving left, out of the living room, down a narrow hallway that ran the length of the trailer. There was a heavy trail of blood droplets marking Thornton's path.

Marlin reached the mouth of the hallway with his revolver raised, ready to shoot, only to glimpse Thornton scrambling to his left into an open doorway. Probably a bedroom. Lauren was right behind Marlin, her service weapon at the ready.

But now they had a quandary. Was it worth the risk to approach and enter that doorway? Thornton had nowhere to go. Ernie Turpin was no doubt positioned on one end of the trailer, where a few steps in either direction would allow him to watch the front and rear. He would be ready for any attempt Thornton might make to climb through a window or exit through a door. That would be his first priority. Rounding up O'Brien, Craddock, and Callahan would have to come later.

Marlin started to call out to Thornton, then changed his mind. Better for it to come from Lauren, who knew him better. He made eye contact, and she knew exactly what he was thinking.

"Hey, Knox," Lauren said, "let's end this thing right now. You're injured. Come on out and let me take you to the hospital."

No reply, but Marlin could hear some heavy breathing and quiet moans of pain. He was aware that he and Lauren had very little protection from the trailer's thin walls. If Thornton decided to blast away in the direction of Lauren's voice, there wouldn't be much to stop the bullet.

"There's no way out, Knox," Lauren said. "You hear me? How about we settle down and sort this out? So far, nobody else has been hurt."

Of course, Marlin and Lauren didn't know if that was true. O'Brien appeared okay, but he could've been hit by one of Thornton's shots.

"Whatever your problem is with those guys out there," Lauren said, "we can work it out."

Nothing.

"You okay, Knox? Where are you hit?"

Marlin heard an identifiable sound—a hand moving the slats on an aluminum blind. Thornton was peering outside to see if he had a chance to escape. He had to realize that going out a window was a losing proposition.

"Knox, you need to slide your gun into the hallway," Lauren said. "You have no other options." She was saying all the right things. Pointing out that the situation was hopeless, without making any threats.

Now Marlin heard movement. Boots shuffling slowly across the linoleum floor, coming toward the doorway. He and Lauren both raised their weapons and aimed at the doorway. The breathing had become even heavier. Labored.

"Okay," Thornton said. "Here comes the gun, okay? Don't shoot me."

His voice was ragged. Wet. Suggestive of a chest wound. He began to cough.

"Slide it out easy, Knox," Lauren said. "Then step into the hallway facing *away* from us, with your hands on top of your head. Do you understand?"

No answer. Just more coughing.

"Knox?"

Marlin was shaking his head, signaling that he didn't believe Thornton was going to comply.

"Do you need medical attention?" Lauren said.

"Yeah, I think so," Thornton said. "I put the gun on the floor, like you said."

"That's not what I—"

"I'm coming out."

"No, Knox! You need to—"

Thornton stepped into the hallway, facing in their direction, gun raised, and Marlin and Lauren began to shoot.

Red was in the cedars, hunkered down, and wondering what in the hell was going on inside his trailer. A full minute had passed.

The wound in his arm burned, but it wasn't anything major. Just a six-inch furrow running along his left forearm, where one of Thornton's bullets had grazed him. Bloody, but not too deep.

He had no idea where Billy Don and Derek were. When the door to the trailer had slammed open, they had all scattered. Then there'd been, what, five or six shots? Thornton had been trying to kill Red again, and the cops had returned fire. Was Thornton hit? When Red had glanced backward, he'd seen John Marlin bounding up the steps into the trailer, followed by the woman who'd been driving the truck. Then nothing.

Red thought about going to look for Billy Don, but it was probably better to stay put and not give the deputy, who was still outside somewhere, any reason to shoot at him.

He jumped as he heard more shots from inside his trailer. Not just a shot or two, but a frigging rapid-fire barrage of shots from multiple weapons that lasted a solid three seconds. Three seconds is a long time when you're pulling the trigger as fast as you can.

Then the shots stopped abruptly, and everything was suddenly quiet.

Marlin's ears were ringing and smoke filled the narrow hallway.

Knox Thornton was down, and if he wasn't dead, he was certainly dying. He'd gotten off one shot, or maybe it was two. Hard to know for sure. Marlin knew he had hit Thornton at least once in the torso, and Lauren must have nailed him, too.

Lauren.

He turned and found her down on one knee, with her left palm placed flat on the floor. Her pistol was in her right hand, but she slipped it back into her holster and used that hand to hold her stomach.

"You hit?" Marlin said.

He knelt beside her and saw that the front of her white shirt was soaked red. Blood was oozing between her fingers. He checked the back of her shirt and saw blood there, too. She muttered something, but he couldn't make it out, because he was temporarily deaf from the gunfire. She slowly eased herself to the floor and laid prone, on her back. Marlin unbuttoned her shirt at her abdomen and saw the gunshot wound, just one, about five inches to the left of her navel. Almost a miss, but not quite.

"You're going to be okay, Lauren," he said, and she nodded.

He began to thumb his microphone, but Ernie Turpin was suddenly behind him, and Marlin could hear enough of what the deputy said to know an ambulance was already on the way.

Marlin reached and held Lauren's hand. Her face was pale. His hand was trembling, but hers was still and cool.

CHAPTER THIRTY-FIVE

Three hours later.

Red was sitting in an interview room. He'd been waiting for a long time. At least an hour, here all by himself. A can of Dr Pepper rested on the table in front of him, but it had been empty for a good while. Luckily, he didn't need to piss yet.

In the crazy scene after the shootout—with at least a dozen deputies and reserve deputies, an EMS team, the medical examiner, and the county forensic technician descending on his trailer—the sheriff had instructed some of the deputies to take Red, Billy Don, and Derek to the station.

Here, starting about two hours ago, Sheriff Bobby Garza and the chief deputy, Bill Tatum, had questioned Red, and Red had cooperated as best he could. He'd told them everything he knew—about Shelby, about Knox, about Colin, Derek, Charmaine, and Bobo, and, yes, even about the cash in the suitcase. He hadn't left out any details or fudged any facts.

To Red's surprise, Garza and Tatum had appeared to believe all of it, possibly because Billy Don was in a different room, telling the exact same story.

So now the big question in Red's mind was, were he and Billy Don going to get charged with anything? After all, they'd basically kept Knox Thornton as a prisoner for half a day, and Red doubted that was legal, regardless of the circumstances.

He knew that if he had refused to answer questions until he'd had a lawyer, he could've reduced the odds of getting in trouble. But he had learned that the special ranger lady had been wounded in the shootout, and if Red hadn't cooperated, the sheriff and the game warden would have been pissed at him for a long time to come. A *long* time. When cops get hurt, shit gets serious real quick. But Red was hoping that by spilling everything he knew, they'd cut him some slack.

Now Red was waiting. He could hear a lot of sound and activity coming from outside the interview room. Random muffled comments from various people, some in other rooms, some passing by the door. He could go for another Dr Pepper, or better yet, a cold beer. Or six. His nerves were rattled for sure. But he had to wait. They'd told him to wait.

One other thing he'd learned from the sheriff was that Knox Thornton was dead. Hallelujah. Good riddance. Red had asked who'd killed him, but the sheriff either didn't know or wouldn't tell him. Fine. Didn't really matter, did it? It was either the game warden or the special ranger lady, because they were the ones who'd gone inside the trailer. Red kind of hoped it was the special ranger lady, since she'd gotten shot herself. It might make her feel better knowing she'd taken out the man who'd shot her.

Red picked up his Dr Pepper can, sucked the last few warm drops out of the bottom, and then Tatum opened the door and said, "You can go now."

"So I'm not arrested?" Red said.

"Not right now," Tatum said.

Lauren required immediate surgery, and Marlin knew it was serious when they brought a medical helicopter to meet the ambulance in Johnson City and fly her to an emergency room in Austin. Marlin had had to return to the sheriff's department and give his statement, and now he and Nicole were halfway between Dripping Springs and Oak Hill, on their way to Austin. Nicole was driving because Marlin's hands were still shaking. At least his hearing had fully come back. Phil Colby was already at the hospital, and he had promised to call with any news.

They had been riding in silence for several minutes when Marlin finally said what was on his mind. "I shouldn't have followed Thornton in."

Nicole immediately began shaking her head. "John, come on."

"We could've waited him out. He was already hit."

"You did what you're supposed to do."

"I wish she hadn't followed me."

"She did what she was supposed to do, too." Nicole placed a hand on his shoulder.

Marlin's phone rang—Bobby Garza calling. Marlin answered. "You're on speaker with me and Nicole."

"Are y'all at the hospital?"

"Not yet."

"Heard anything?"

"She's still in surgery, last I knew. One of the EMS guys said a gunshot wound in that location could be really bad or not so bad. She was bleeding a lot, Bobby."

"Yeah, and she got medical treatment very quickly. When you get there, let me know what's going on, okay?"

"Will do."

Marlin knew Garza well enough to know he had another reason for calling. Marlin could hear something in Garza's voice.

The sheriff said, "We got a warrant for Knox Thornton's phone—that burner phone we found in O'Brien's place—and we just finished listening to some voicemails and reading some texts. Not a lot there as far as his meth operation—he probably deleted everything he got—but there was one voicemail you'll like. It was from Shelby Roach this morning."

Despite his mood, Marlin almost laughed. After all this time, Roach had finally come scurrying out from the woodwork. He was alive.

"What'd he say?" Marlin said.

"First, let me give you a missing piece of the puzzle. Shelby Roach is Red O'Brien's cousin."

"You're kidding me. I didn't know that."

"No reason you would've. O'Brien said he hadn't seen Roach in several years and they weren't close." Garza then gave a brief summary of the remarkably consistent statements from O'Brien, Craddock, and Derek Callahan, including a wild side story about some cash in a pawned suitcase—money that Knox Thornton had hidden with Colin Kelly's girlfriend. "And the message Shelby Roach left for Thornton earlier seems to fit right in," Garza said. "He admitted he lied and blamed O'Brien for April's death, and he was calling to stop Thornton from seeking revenge. It sounds like Thornton went after Roach at one point—probably on Sunday, when Roach went back home—but Roach got away and skipped town."

"Any idea where Roach is now? Did he say?"

"Nope. We're working on that. If he ran because he was scared of Thornton, that threat is gone, obviously."

"You still planning to file on him?" Marlin asked.

"Damn right, for killing Rodney's bull and for leaving April out in the pasture and for trespassing and anything else I can think of. And now that we know he was with April that night, we can get a warrant for his cabin. If we're lucky, we can work with San Saba and build a good drug case against him, depending on what we find. Of course, he won't know any of this because he won't know we heard his voicemail."

"Maybe once he learns Thornton is dead, he'll come back home," Marlin said.

"Oh, that would be good. Now that I've got the number for Roach's burner phone, I'm tempted to call it. He probably wouldn't answer, but I could leave a message. I'd sweet talk him. Make like everything is cool now."

"What're you gonna do with Derek Callahan and Colin Kelly?" Marlin asked.

"I'm going to discuss that with Deborah," Garza said, referencing Deborah Timms, the county attorney, who always brought a reasoned and logical approach to a complicated situation such as this one. "Both of them were carrying without a permit, but technically they were traveling, so they could legally be in possession. Kelly drew his weapon first at O'Brien's place, but O'Brien said he didn't want to pursue any charges. Other than that, they didn't break any laws, and I can't write them up for stupidity. I suspect that Colin Kelly might've worked with Knox Thornton or Shelby, but right now, we can't prove that."

"We should at least cite him for speeding and reckless driving, just because it will feel good."

"Sure, why not?" Garza said. "As far as O'Brien and Craddock, how do those two pinheads always get mixed up in everything? Here's the funny thing. They basically kidnapped Thornton, and we could charge 'em with it, but Thornton committed a felony when he fired a shot into the trailer, and they witnessed it."

"Which means they had the authority to take him into custody," Marlin said.

Nicole eased into the left-hand lane to go north on MoPac into the heart of Austin.

"Right," Garza said. "And then they were supposed to get him in front of a magistrate 'without unnecessary delay'—that's the exact phrase in the code—but 'not later than 48 hours.'"

Marlin was reading between the lines. Garza and Deborah

Timms had plenty of wiggle room in this situation. They could file charges, or they could choose not to. Did O'Brien and Craddock deserve it? Maybe not. After all, Thornton had been trying to kill O'Brien. Would a Blanco County jury ever convict him for taping a would-be killer to a chair? The chances were virtually zero. They'd laud him as a hero instead, a brave man who was using his Second Amendment rights to stand up against a common criminal. Hard to argue against that.

There was still one very large question that remained unanswered.

"I know you hate loose ends as much as I do," Marlin said.

"Grant Bender, right?" Garza said.

"Yep."

Garza took a long breath. "Well, I don't know what to say about that. With Thornton dead, we may never know what happened there. We have Thornton's Beretta, and he might've used that to kill Bender, but we have no way of proving it. And I have to be honest—since Bender was probably killed in San Saba County, and his body was found in McCulloch County, it's real easy to say, 'Hey, it ain't our problem.'"

"True," Marlin said.

"Still," Garza said. "It would be nice if we could—"

Marlin's phone beeped.

"Hang on a sec, Bobby. Phil is calling."

"Sure thing."

Marlin switched over and said, "What's the news?" His entire body was tense.

Phil Colby said, "She's out of surgery and stable. Everything looks real good, John. She's going to be okay."

CHAPTER THIRTY-SIX

Four days later.

At eleven in the morning on Tuesday, Shelby was replacing a cracked ceramic tile beside a bathroom sink and wondering where he might go for lunch. The choices were limited. Good, but limited. First, though, the tile. Almost done. Just the grouting.

He had been here for only four days, but he liked the arrangement. Pedro, Vicente's brother, owned a tiny inn, and now Shelby was working there in exchange for a few pesos a week and a room. The room was hardly larger than a storage closet—but he didn't need anything more.

On the plus side, the work wasn't hard—sweeping, mopping, minor repairs, running errands—and Pedro was a nice enough guy. He hadn't asked any nosy questions. He didn't seem at all interested in Shelby's personal life or his reason for being here.

Shelby and Pedro would sit on a small balcony overlooking the Pacific at the end of the day and drink beer together, sometimes with a few of Pedro's friends, and after sundown they might go out to eat at one of the nearby restaurants.

Shelby liked what he had seen so far of Barra de Potosi—"Barra," as the locals called it—although there wasn't much to see. The population was fewer than a thousand people, not counting tourists, and there weren't many tourists to count, despite being just 30 miles from Ixtapa and 20 miles from Zihuatanejo.

It wasn't your typical Mexican getaway spot, with trendy nightclubs, flashy discos, and garish T-shirt shops. You weren't going to leave with a souvenir margarita glass or braided hair or a story about hooking up with a couple of drunken sorority girls.

In other words, it was perfect.

Seriously, Shelby wondered why he hadn't come here years ago, of his own accord, without a reason to flee from home. It was just so damn peaceful. The pristine white beach was lined with palm trees. There were more species of birds than Shelby could count or identify, of all colors, shapes, and sizes. You could kayak or snorkel in the lagoon or swim in the ocean.

Only four things would make this paradise even better.

First, if only April were here with him. She'd love Barra, and he could picture her splashing around in a bikini, lounging in a hammock, or walking with him to the bakery for a fresh loaf of bread. She wouldn't even have to work. They'd live in the cramped room together and get by on his small income.

Second, if he would stop having withdrawal symptoms. They weren't as bad as he'd feared, because he'd never had an uncontrollable habit, but they weren't pleasant, either. He'd ride it out. Get a fresh start. He had no choice.

Third, he couldn't stop thinking about the man he'd killed in Saltillo. It wasn't Shelby's fault, and he didn't necessarily feel guilty about it. Just remorseful. It was a shame, that's all, and Shelby wished he could change it.

And fourth, if only the sheriff in Blanco County would stop calling. Shelby was considering tossing the phone—but where would he get another one? There were no electronics stores in Barra de Potosi. There was no place to pop down and grab a new iPhone or even a cheap throwaway. Besides, the phone represented his last connection to his old life, and he wasn't quite ready to cut that cord for good. Soon, maybe, but not yet.

Shelby had saved all of the sheriff's voicemails, although he wasn't sure why. What Shelby knew, although he hadn't confirmed it from any other source, was that Knox was dead. That was the first thing the sheriff had told him. *You can come on home now*, the sheriff had said. *Come on back and let's talk about what happened to April. Let's get this mess sorted out.*

Yeah, right.

Going home was out of the question, even if he knew he wouldn't get charged with anything. But that didn't mean he couldn't make things right, or at least try.

One day later.

When Marlin and Nicole stepped into Lauren's hospital room, she was sitting on the edge of the bed, wearing sweat pants and a T-shirt, and looking as healthy and fit as could be.

"Oh, hey," she said, smiling. "I wasn't expecting you so soon."

Nicole was ahead of Marlin, so she hugged Lauren first, and then Marlin did the same.

"You look great," Nicole said. "I mean, wow, what a difference."

This was the second time Marlin and Nicole had visited. He had expected the first meeting between Nicole and Lauren to be awkward, but it had been anything but. They'd warmed up to each other in no time.

"Thank you," Lauren said. "I feel so much better. Just got back from a stroll of the scenic hallways. They want me up and moving around. Slowly, but moving."

"Is there pain?" Nicole asked.

"Some. It's not too bad. I'll have a nice scar from the surgery, so my days as a bikini model are over. Y'all have a seat."

Marlin and Nicole each took a chair near the large window overlooking the parking lot three stories down. Lauren slowly eased herself back into bed.

"When are you getting out?" Nicole asked.

"Supposedly tomorrow morning. They're monitoring my blood work and all that stuff, but if everything holds, yeah, tomorrow."

"Do you have someone to take you home?"

"Uh, well, I—"

"Phil's coming to pick her up," Marlin said.

Lauren gave him a surprised look that seemed to say, *Oh, you know that already?* Nicole turned toward him, too, with a raised eyebrow and an amused expression.

"We talked earlier today. No big deal," Marlin said, knowing they'd both understand he was making light of his earlier reaction to the relationship between Phil and Lauren.

They both smiled, and Nicole said, "Do you have enough food at the house for the next week or two?"

"I think so," Lauren said. "I can go to the store if—"

"You need to focus on getting well," Nicole said. "How about if I come up on Thursday or Friday and see how you're doing? I'll bring some things with me."

"That's very sweet," Lauren said. "I appreciate it."

As the two women continued to make plans, Marlin couldn't help but marvel at Nicole's attitude in what could very easily be an awkward situation. She was truly something special.

When they were done with their arrangements, Lauren said, "So...what's the latest? You said you had some news."

Marlin said, "We tracked Shelby Roach's burner phone across the Mexican border. After that, well, you know the cell companies down there don't have to comply with our warrants, and they sure aren't going to bother cooperating just for the heck of it—not for a guy like Shelby Roach. So he could be anywhere by now, down there or even back in the States. There's just no way of knowing. But I do have something interesting to share with you. Yesterday afternoon, someone sent an email to all three sheriffs in Blanco, San Saba, and McCulloch counties. Bobby forwarded it to me."

Marlin opened the email on his phone and handed it to Lauren, so she could read it for herself.

This is Shelby Roach and I want to set some things straight. You probably figured out what happened that night on that ranch, but I'll tell you anyway. The bull got ornery and gored April. She was hurt bad and I tried to scare it away with a warning shot. The bull kept coming so I had to shoot it. But then it fell on her and I couldn't get her out from under. She was dead without question and I panicked and ran. I feel bad about it but there's nothing I can do about it now except send an apology to her parents. I'm sorry. I loved her and miss her every minute of every day. As for Grant Bender, last year he and Knox had an argument. Doesn't matter what it was about, but there was three of us there, plus Grant, and Knox made me and another guy kick Grant's ass. That's all it was supposed to be, but Grant fell back and smashed his head on a rock. He was really messed up. Me and the other guy wanted to take him to the hospital, but Knox walked over and shot him in the head before we could even do anything about it. Then he told me to get rid of the body. I didn't know what to do with it so I stuck it in my freezer. That's where it was until last week before I left town, I decided it was time to get rid of it before my mother or the cops found it. I sank it in the lake but I guess it didn't stay down. I wished I had the guts to tell the cops earlier what happened but I was afraid Knox would kill me too. So that's everything I have to say. I have

not been read my rights and if you ever find me I won't repeat any of this without talking to a lawyer first. Right now I'm trying to help you figure things out and make sure nobody thinks I'm a murderer. Do not reply, I won't get it, because I tossed my phone into a river. Goodbye.

"Think it's legit?" Marlin said when Lauren was done reading.

"I do, yeah," Lauren said. "Who else would've sent it? And if it was him, why would he lie at this point? Underneath all his problems, well, I'm not going to say he was a decent guy, but he wasn't a hardcore scumbag like Knox. This is the kind of thing he'd do—confess to his sins once he knows he can't get in trouble for them."

"And now that Knox Thornton is dead."

"Right."

"The other guy he mentions…gotta be Colin Kelly, huh?"

"Yeah. Probably. No way to be positive, and he'll never admit to it. We're going to search Roach's place later."

"Let me know what you find, okay? I hate to miss that."

"Will do," Marlin said. "And there's one other thing. Bobby asked DPS to send a team from the crime lab to analyze the scene at O'Brien's trailer."

"To see which one of us killed Knox Thornton," Lauren said.

"Right."

"And?"

"We both hit him several times," Marlin said. "No way of knowing who actually killed him."

CHAPTER THIRTY-SEVEN

Bobo had never gotten a clear story about the shootout in Blanco County—the news reports raised more questions than they answered—but the bottom line, as far as Bobo could tell, was that it was good news, at least for him. The man Colin Kelly was so afraid of was dead, which meant Colin had nothing to be afraid of, which meant Bobo didn't have to worry about Colin any more. Or Derek.

Just the cops.

Two detectives—one from San Saba County and one from Leander—had come to see Bobo a few days earlier, wanting to talk. Of course, they immediately asked about some cash that had allegedly been contained in a suitcase that Colin Kelly had pawned at Bobo's shop. Did Bobo know anything about that? They said it would be very helpful if he did.

Bobo played it cool. Said he'd heard all that stuff before, from his former employee Derek and some big steroid junkie named Colin, and they'd even accused him of taking the money. But he hadn't of course. That's what he told the detectives. He ran an honest operation, you see. He was a straight-up businessman. A pillar of the community, despite the unfair reputation that was strapped across the back of every pawnshop in the country.

When the cops got a little more aggressive, that's when Bobo said, "Hey, I'm done here. You got more questions, talk to my attorney." And then, later, he asked his attorney to contact those cops' bosses and make it clear that if they harassed Bobo again, he would file a lawsuit. Not three hours after that, the mayor of Leander called Bobo personally to apologize for any inconvenience. The mayor wanted to make it clear that he was committed to fostering a business-friendly environment in Leander. Bobo had accepted his apology with grace and understanding.

In the next few days, Bobo had been very selective with customers, turning down any item that might be hot, just in case the cops were setting him up. He had nothing to worry about. He was in a great mood. Business was good. A little slow lately, but good.

The shop was empty when two customers came in on Wednesday afternoon. Couple of rednecks. Grimy. Like they'd been working with concrete all day. One was average height and skinny. The other guy was big. Every bit as big as Colin Kelly. Maybe bigger.

"Can I help you gentlemen?" Bobo asked.

"Need an engagement ring," the skinny one said. "Something real sharp."

Bobo moved toward the jewelry case, saying, "What'd you have in mind? Diamond? Or something non-traditional?"

"Diamond."

"What kind of cut? Round? Oval? Princess?"

"Marquise. That's what she wants, whatever that is."

"She has great taste. I only have a couple, but they are all very high quality. Any particular size in mind?"

"Got something around a carat?"

"I do, right over here," Bobo said, thinking a slow day like this could turn around quick with a big sale. He removed the ring from its display and handed it to the skinny man.

"Nice," said Skinny.

"Excellent color and clarity," Bobo said. "VVS."

"PBS?" Skinny said.

"VVS," Bobo said. "Very, very small inclusions."

"All righty. How much you want for it?"

"Four thousand dollars," Bobo said, which was an absolute steal, but he'd take even less, if push came to shove, because he'd paid so little for it.

Skinny let out a whistle. "Dang."

"It's an investment for a lifetime," Bobo said.

"Or until we get sick of each other," Skinny said, and he and his friend guffawed. Bobo joined in.

"In which case you could resell it," Bobo said, "probably at a profit."

"Can you come down a little?" Skinny asked.

"I could do thirty-five hundred, but that's the bottom line."

"Well, shit," Skinny said. "Here goes nothing." He pulled a big roll of cash from his pocket and began peeling off $100 bills. "There you go," he said. "Thirty-five hundred."

"You need a receipt?"

"Yeah, for insurance and all that."

"No problem at all," Bobo said. He grabbed a receipt pad. "Gonna need your ID."

Skinny slapped his driver's license on the glass, and Bobo jotted down his name, address, and so on, and then wrote a brief description of the item being purchased.

Skinny was studying the diamond more closely. "Crazy that a little rock is worth so damn much."

"It is, isn't it?" Bobo said. "And here you go." He slid the receipt across the counter with a big smile. "Thank you very much for your business. I wish you and your bride years of happiness."

Then something odd happened. The big man took the ring and the receipt and exited the shop. The skinny guy stayed where he was.

"Something else I can help you with?" Bobo said.

"You bet there is," Skinny said. "That diamond you just sold me is hotter than a pepper sprout."

Bobo's smile began to melt. "I don't know what—"

"Don't talk," Skinny said. "Just listen. There are two ways we can play this. First one is, I get the cops down here right now and report the crime, and they find a bunch of stolen stuff in your store. More jewelry. Some electronics. Maybe a gun or two. If we go that route, you're basically screwed. Probably jail time, unless you wanna spend a shit ton on lawyers."

Who was this guy? Who sent him?

"And the second way?" Bobo said. His voice was a squeak.

Skinny grinned. "Easy. I trade you the ring for the cash that was in those suitcases."

Bobo was smart enough not to say, "What cash?"

Four minutes later, as Red exited the pawnshop and made his way toward his truck in the parking lot, he had to resist the urge to run.

Holy guacamole. It worked!

He was carrying a duffel bag—not a suitcase—that Bobo had retrieved from the storage room. Apparently, he'd had it stashed back there in plain sight all this time.

Red could see that Billy Don was in the driver's seat, with the engine already running, ready to haul ass. The one time Red would allow Billy Don to drive his truck. Get while the getting was good.

Now they would go meet up with Derek, who had told them which items in the shop he suspected were stolen. For that, half of the cash was his. Red had been tempted to point out that it should be split three ways, because there were three of them, but he'd decided that might be pushing his luck.

Marlin and Bobby Garza accompanied two deputies from the San Saba Sheriff's Office when they served a warrant on Eunice Roach, giving them the authority to search Shelby Roach's cabin and the freestanding walk-in freezer on the Roach ranch—the one Shelby's dad has used years ago in his deer-processing business.

They started with the cabin, and it quickly became apparent that Roach had destroyed anything that might implicate him in any crime. Some loose ashes in the fireplace, along with a lingering odor of smoke, told them that Roach had burned some papers before he'd left town. After three hours, they had found nothing of value except one handwritten note that read:

Tony—1/2
Lisa—1/4
Eddie—Full
Tim—1/2
Arturo—1/2

They interpreted the note to mean that Tony wanted half a gram of meth, Lisa wanted a quarter, Eddie wanted a full gram, and so on. But that couldn't be proven by the note alone. Unfortunately, it was vague and would be worthless in a court of law.

Honestly, though, none of them much cared about the note. Their goal was to find any evidence supporting Roach's tale about the murder of Grant Bender, and the subsequent disposal of the body.

So they moved on to the walk-in freezer, hoping it would prove to be more fruitful ground. Henry Jameson, the forensic technician, joined them at this stage, to ensure that any evidence would be handled exactly right.

The aging freezer measured 12 feet by 12 feet and was designed to stand alone, outdoors, but someone years ago had built a small roof over the unit to shield it from the elements. The roof extended about 10 feet past the front of the freezer. That way, if it was raining, a hunter could back up to the freezer and unload a deer or pig without getting drenched.

One of the deputies cut the padlock off the handle, and then Henry Jameson popped the door open and looked inside. Marlin could see over Henry's shoulder, and everything appeared as he expected.

"Wow," Jameson said.

The floor of the freezer had been stained a dark rust color from the blood of thousands of animals over decades. None of the blood looked fresh. At least three dozen large cardboard boxes were stacked against the rear wall.

"What do you think?" Marlin said.

"I can pull some swabs," Jameson said, "but I don't think any of them will be useful. Cross contamination."

Marlin and the deputies left him to his work, and when he was done, the two San Saba County deputies entered the freezer. It was too small for Marlin and Garza to join them inside, and this was their turf.

One of the deputies said, "This box says 'Ryan' on it. This one says 'Arturo.'"

The other deputy used a pocketknife to slice the tape sealing the top of one of the boxes. He looked inside. Then he lifted out a small package wrapped in white freezer paper. It appeared to weigh about two or three pounds.

"'RE,' the deputy said, reading the writing on the package." He lifted another package. "'FM.'"

Marlin shook his head. This wasn't what he'd expected.

"Ribeye and filet mignon," he said. "Roach was rustling cattle and selling the beef."

"That explains why we never caught him selling any cattle at market," Lauren said an hour later when Marlin filled her in by phone.

"Also explains the note we found," Marlin said. "Arturo wasn't buying half a gram, he was buying half a cow."

"I've never run across an operation like that before," Lauren said. "A freelance butcher. But beef is pricy nowadays. Even if he was selling it at fifty cents on the dollar, he was still making a good chunk of money."

"He had the butchering skills and equipment, so why not put 'em to use?" Marlin said.

"Think he was selling meth, too?"

"No way of knowing at this point. The scale and baggies in his Ranchero say yes, but that's all we have right now."

"Any sign Bender's body was ever in the freezer?" Lauren said.

"Nope. He could've been wrapped in a tarp or stored in a big ice chest. Shelby was the only person who went in there, according to his mother. He told her he earned extra cash by butchering deer and wild pigs now and then. That's why he kept it running—and locked up—year 'round."

"Too scared to do anything with the body," Lauren said.

"Or maybe thinking it could be used against Knox Thornton as evidence later, if it came to that," Marlin said. "Problem is, the shots to Bender's head were through and through. No slugs to work with. We'll be searching Thornton's place tomorrow, and if we assume that was where Bender was killed, maybe we'll get lucky and find something useful. But I gotta be honest and say I'm not holding out much hope."

Lauren let out a sigh of exasperation.

"How you feeling?" Marlin asked.

"Pretty damn good," she said. "All things considered."

"I enjoyed working with you," he said. "And, you know, uh, I'm sorry you got shot."

Lauren began to laugh, and then he did, too, and they both continued for half a minute. Then she said, "Yeah, so am I. Not just the getting shot, but the working together."

CHAPTER THIRTY-EIGHT

One week later.

Red was nervous on the plane, not just because it didn't make sense that anything so heavy could fly through the air, but because they were on their way to Vegas and there was no backing out now. They were really going through with it.

"Look how cute it is," Billy Don said for the fourth or fifth time, holding the miniature bottle of bourbon in the palm of his hand. "Only problem is, they don't hold near enough."

Red had had five of those little bottles himself, on the rocks in a little plastic cup, but they hadn't taken the edge off just yet. So much money was on the line. Or would be, very soon. Crazy. He was putting his life savings—his future—in the hands of Billy Don. Insane. Idiotic.

"Can I get y'all anything else?" the flight attendant asked.

"Couple more of these," Billy Don said, holding up his empty bottle.

She nodded, agreeable as can be.

Those bottles were costing a stupid amount, but Red couldn't imagine going without a little bit of hooch right now. He'd worked himself into a high state of agitation in the past week. He should've just sprung for the higher-priced flight and gone the day after they'd gotten the cash from Bobo, but Red hadn't been able to talk himself into it. Just a matter of principle.

Red eased back into his seat and tried to relax. His arm itched where the bullet furrow was still healing up.

"Hey, I been thinking about something," Billy Don said in that quiet voice that most people seemed to use on an airplane. "What if I freeze up?"

"What do you mean, freeze up?"

"What if I sit down at the blackjack table and my mind won't work right?"

"Billy Don, so help me God, if we get over there and you can't—"

"Relax," Billy Don said, grinning. "I'm just kidding. It's all gonna be fine. You really are uptight."

Marlin and Phil Colby sat on Marlin's front porch at dusk, each with a cold bottle of beer in hand, and enjoyed the cool air. Normally, at this time of year, the temperature could easily be hovering in the nineties during the day and the eighties in the evening, but it had been an unusually agreeable May so far.

"What exactly is Bunco?" Colby said, after they'd been sitting silently for a few moments. Marlin had told Colby earlier that Nicole had gone to play Bunco at a neighbor's house that evening.

"Some sort of dice game," Marlin said. "That's all I know. And Nicole said it doesn't take any skill whatsoever."

"How many players?"

Geist, Marlin's pit bull, was nosing around in the grass nearby.

"Eight, I think."

"Can you imagine how loud that house is?"

"Next time, she's supposed to host it here."

Colby looked at him. "Well, good luck with that."

"I'll probably bail out for the night."

"You can hang out at my place."

"I'll do that." Then, after a moment, Marlin said, "Sometimes they need a substitute player. Maybe Lauren would be interested."

A screech owl trilled in the oak trees not far from the porch. Marlin had built several owl houses and hung them around his seven acres. He had seen two wide-eyed fledglings in the opening of one house the previous week.

"I bet she would," Colby said.

"I'll mention it to Nicole," Marlin said.

It would be good for Lauren to make some new friends in the area, seeing as how, just two days earlier, Bobby Garza had hired her as the new chief deputy, replacing Bill Tatum. She had checked with Marlin beforehand, flat-out asking him if he'd rather she not apply for the job. He'd told her Blanco County would be lucky to have her.

She'd be moving down in a month. He knew she'd use her remaining time in San Saba County to keep digging into the Grant Bender case, hoping to bust Colin Kelly for his participation—but it didn't seem likely. The search of Knox Thornton's trailer the previous week had turned up nothing implicating him or Shelby Roach or Colin Kelly in the Bender homicide, and no documentation of Thornton's cohorts in the alleged meth operation. The only evidence of any crime that the deputies found was the stolen livestock trailer that Roach had left at Thornton's place. Sometimes that was the way it worked out. Now that Thornton was dead and Shelby Roach was nowhere to be found, did it really matter? Well, yeah, it did, but sometimes you had to let it go.

"You want another beer?" Colby said.

"You bet," Marlin said.

Two days later.

It had been a hell of a ride, with Billy Don proving he really did know how to play blackjack, and now it had all come down to this.

On their third night in Vegas, at 11:42 p.m., Billy Don shoved it all—approximately $142,000 in chips—onto the blackjack table in front of him.

The crowd pressed in tighter, getting rowdier than ever.

Red, standing over Billy Don's left shoulder, was about to vomit.

The blackjack dealer called out to the pit boss, who sauntered over.

Trina, Red's gorgeous and temporary girlfriend, made a wisecrack about the pit boss's tan, but Red could hardly smile.

The pit boss nodded his approval for the bet, and the crowd got even louder.

The dealer did what dealers did. She dealt.

Five of spades for the tubby dude.

Queen of hearts for the sorority girl.

Nine of clubs for the Arab guy.

Two of diamonds for Horace Norris.

And then—*bam!*—king of spades for Billy Don.
Oh, thank you, God. Thank you.
The dealer gave herself a card facedown, then started the second round of cards.
Tubby dude got another five.
Sorority girl got a nine to go with her queen.
Arab guy got a six, for a total of fifteen.
Horace Norris got a seven, so he was sitting at nine.
Billy Don got a four. Damn. Not good.
The dealer gave herself a second card, face-down, and flipped her first card up. It was an ace. Crap. She peeked at her second card but did not flip it over. That meant she didn't have a blackjack. Good news.
She pointed at tubby dude, who took a six and stood. Stupid.
Sorority girl said she would stand.
Arab guy took an eight and busted.
Horace Norris hit, got a jack, and stood on nineteen.
Billy Don had to hit. That was the smart play. Even Red knew that by now. Billy Don tapped the felt. Red held his breath as the dealer dealt another card.
It was a two.
Now Billy Don had sixteen. A horrible hand. Any smart player knew you had to hit it, even though the next card would almost certainly put you over 21.
So Billy Don tapped the felt again.
Red could hardly stand it. Why hadn't they stopped with $72,000 each? Why the hell had they gotten greedy? So dumb.
The dealer slapped the card down. An ace.
Seventeen. Oh, sweet Jesus. Seventeen.
"Stand," Billy Don said.
Now it came down to luck.
The dealer used her ace to flip her hole card over, and Red was fully expecting to see a face card, which would end the game.
But it was a three.
Red let out a nervous giggle.
The dealer gave herself another card. Another ace.
Now she had fifteen.
This was unimaginable.
The pit boss was watching with interest. He couldn't believe what he was seeing.
The dealer gave herself a fourth card.
No frigging way. This couldn't be real, because she'd just dealt

herself a third ace. A six-deck shoe contained 24 aces, but the odds that four of those aces would show up in one hand—and three for the dealer—boggled Red's mind. His stomach was bucking and heaving.

"This is insane," somebody said.

"Never seen anything like it."

Now the dealer had sixteen—or six if she counted the aces as ones, which the rules allowed. She pulled another card and slapped it on the felt. A jack.

Her total remained sixteen. She drew another card.

For the briefest moment, just a fraction of a second, the crowd fell silent.

Then they erupted into a cheer.

Want to know when Ben Rehder's
next novel will be released?

Subscribe to his email list.
www.benrehder.com

Have you discovered Ben Rehder's
Roy Ballard Mysteries?

Turn the page for an excerpt from

GONE THE NEXT

GONE THE NEXT

1

The woman he was watching this time was in her early thirties. Thirty-five at the oldest. White. Well dressed. Upper middle class. Reasonably attractive. Probably drove a nice car, like a Lexus or a BMW. She was shopping at Nordstrom in Barton Creek Square mall. Her daughter — Alexis, if he'd overheard the name correctly — appeared to be about seven years old. Brown hair, like her mother's. The same cute nose. They were in the women's clothing department, looking at swimsuits. Alexis was bored. Fidgety. Ready to go to McDonald's, like Mom had promised. Amazing what you can hear if you keep your ears open.

He was across the aisle, in the men's department, looking at Hawaiian shirts. They were all ugly, and he had no intention of buying one. He stood on the far side of the rack and held up a green shirt with palm trees on it. But he was really looking past it, at the woman, who had several one-piece swimsuits draped over her arm. Not bikinis, though she still had the figure for it. Maybe she had stretch marks, or the beginnings of a belly.

He replaced the green shirt and grabbed a blue one covered with coconuts. Just browsing, like a regular shopper might do.

Mom was walking over to a changing room now. Alexis followed, walking stiff-legged, maybe pretending she was a monster. A zombie. Amusing herself.

He moved closer, to a table piled high with neatly folded cargo shorts. He pretended to look for a pair in his size. But he was watching in his peripheral vision.

"Wait right here," Mom said. She didn't look around. She was oblivious to his presence. He might as well have been a mannequin.

Alexis said something in reply, but he couldn't make it out.

"There isn't room, Lexy. I'll just be a minute."

And she shut the door, leaving Alexis all by herself.

~ ~ ~

When he first began his research, he'd been surprised by what he'd found. He had expected the average parent to be watchful.

Wary. Downright suspicious. That's how he would be if he had a child. A little girl. He'd guard her like a priceless treasure. Every minute of the day. But his assumptions were wrong. Parents were sloppy. Careless. Just plain stupid.

He knew that now, because he'd watched hundreds of them. And their children. In restaurants. In shopping centers. Supermarkets. Playgrounds and parks. For three months he'd watched. Reconnaissance missions, like this one right now, with Alexis and her mom. Preparing. What he'd observed was encouraging. It wouldn't be as difficult as he'd assumed. When the time came.

But he had to use his head. Plan it out. Use what he'd learned. Doing it in a public place, especially a retail establishment, would be risky, because there were video surveillance systems everywhere nowadays. Some places, like this mall, even had security guards. Daycare centers were often fenced, and the front doors were locked. Schools were always on the lookout for strangers who —

"You need help with anything?"

He jumped, ever so slightly.

A salesgirl had come up behind him. Wanting to be helpful. Calling attention to him. Ruining the moment.

That was a good lesson to remember. Just because he was watching, that didn't mean he wasn't being watched, too.

2

The first time I ever heard the name Tracy Turner — on a hot, cloudless Tuesday in June — I was tailing an obese, pyorrheic degenerate named Wally Crouch. I was fairly certain about the "degenerate" part, because Crouch had visited two adult bookstores and three strip clubs since noon. Not that there's anything wrong with a little mature entertainment, but there's a point when it goes from bawdy boys-will-be-boys recreation to creepy pathological fixation. The pyorrhea was pure conjecture on my part, based solely on the number of Twinkie wrappers Crouch had tossed out the window during his travels.

Crouch was a driver for UPS and, according to my biggest client, he was also a fraud who was riding the workers' comp gravy train. In the course of a routine delivery seven weeks prior, Crouch had allegedly injured his lower back. A ruptured disk, the doctor said. Limited mobility and a twelve- to sixteen-week recovery period. In the meantime, Crouch couldn't lift more than ten pounds without searing pain shooting up his spinal cord. But this particular quack had a checkered past filled with questionable diagnoses and reprimands from the medical board. My job was fairly simple, at least on paper: Follow Crouch discreetly until he proved himself a liar. Catch it on video. Testify, if necessary. Earn a nice paycheck. Continue to finance my sumptuous, razor's-edge lifestyle.

~ ~ ~

You'd think Crouch, having a choice in the matter, would've avoided rush-hour traffic and had a few more beers instead, but he left Sugar's Uptown Cabaret at ten after five and squeezed his way onto the interstate heading south. I followed in my seven-year-old Dodge Caravan. Beige. Try to find a vehicle less likely to catch someone's eye. The windows are deeply tinted and a scanner antenna is mounted on the roof, which are the only clues that the driver isn't a soccer mom toting her brats to practice.

Anyone whose vehicle doubles as a second home recognizes the value of a decent sound system. I'd installed a Blaupunkt, with Bose speakers front and rear. Total system set me back about two grand. Seems like overkill for talk radio, but that's what I was listening to when I heard the familiar alarm signal of the Emergency Alert System. I'd never known the system to be used for anything other than weather warnings, but not this time. It was an Amber Alert. A local girl had gone missing from her affluent West Austin neighborhood. Tracy Turner: six years old, blond hair, green eyes, three feet tall, forty-five pounds, wearing denim shorts and a pink shirt. My palms went sweaty just thinking about it. Then I heard she might be in the company of Howard Turner — her non-custodial father, a resident of Los Angeles — and I breathed a small sigh of relief. Listeners, they said, should keep an eye out for a green Honda with California plates.

Easy to read between the lines. Tracy's parents were divorced, and dad had decided he wanted to spend more time with his daughter, despite how the courts had ruled. Sad, but much better than a random abduction.

The announcer was repeating the message when my cell phone rang. I turned the radio volume down, answered, and my client — a senior claims adjuster at a big insurance company — said, "You nail him yet?"

"Christ, Heidi, it's only the third day."

"I thought you were good."

"That's a vicious rumor."

"Yeah, and I think you started it yourself. I'm starting to think you get by on your looks alone."

"That remark borders on sexual harassment, and you know how I feel about that."

"You're all for it."

"Exactly. Anyway, relax, okay? I'm on him twenty-four seven." Crouch had taken the Manor Road exit, and now he turned into his apartment complex, so I drove past, calling it a day. I didn't like lying to Heidi, but I had a meeting with a man named Harvey Blaylock in thirty minutes.

"Well, you'd better get something soon, because I've got another one waiting," Heidi said.

I didn't say anything, because a jerk in an F-150 was edging over into my lane.

"Roy?" she said.

"Yeah."

"I have another one for you."

"Have scientists come up with that device yet?"

"What device?"

"The one that allows you to be in two places at the same time."

"You really crack you up."

"Let me get this one squared away, then we'll talk, okay?"

"The quicker the better. Where are you? Has Crouch even left the house?"

"Oh, yeah. Been wandering all afternoon."

"Where to?"

"Uh, let's just say he seems to have an inordinate appreciation for the female form."

"Which means?"

"He's been visiting gentlemen's clubs."

A pause. "You mean tittie bars?"

"That's such a crass term. Oh, by the way, the Yellow Rose is looking for dancers. In case you decide to —"

She hung up on me.

~ ~ ~

I had the phone in my hands, so I went ahead and called my best friend Mia Madison, who works at an establishment I used to do business with on occasion. She tends bar at a tavern on North Lamar.

Boiling it down to one sentence, Mia is smart, funny, optimistic, and easy on the eyes. Expanding on the last part, because it's relevant, Mia stands about five ten and has long red hair that she likes to wear in a ponytail. Prominent cheekbones, with dimples beneath. The toned legs of a runner, though she doesn't run, but must walk ten miles a day during an eight-hour shift. When Mia gets dolled up — what she calls "bringing it" — she goes from being an attractive woman you'd certainly notice to a world-class head turner.

On one occasion, she revealed that she has a tattoo. Wouldn't show it to me, but she said — joking, I'm sure — that if I could guess what it was, and where it was, she'd let me have a look. Nearly a year later, I still hadn't given up.

"Is it Muttley?" I asked when she answered.

"Muttley? Who the hell is Muttley?"

"You know, that cartoon dog with the sarcastic laugh."

"You mean Scooby Doo?"

"No, the other one. Hangs with Dick Dastardly."

"I have no idea what you're talking about."

"Before your time, I guess. Are you at work?"

"Not till six. Just got out of the shower. I'm drying off."

"Need any help?"

"I think I can handle it," she said.

"Okay, next question. Want to earn a hundred bucks the easy way?" I said.

"Love to," she said. "When and where?"

3

Harvey Blaylock was maybe sixty, medium height, with neatly trimmed gray hair, black-framed glasses, a white short-sleeved shirt, and tan gabardine slacks. He looked like the kind of man who, if things had taken a slightly different turn, might've wound up as a forklift salesman, or, best case, a high-school principal in a small agrarian town.

In reality, however, Harvey Blaylock was a man who held tremendous sway over my future, near- and long-term. I intended to remain respectful and deferential.

Blaylock's necktie — green, with bucking horses printed on it — rested on his paunch as he leaned back in his chair, scanning the contents of a manila folder. I knew it was my file, because it said

ROY W. BALLARD on the outside, typed neatly on a rectangular label. I'm quick to notice things like that.

Five minutes went by. His office smelled like cigarettes and Old Spice. Rays of sun slanted in through horizontal blinds on the windows facing west. As far as I could tell, we were the only people left in the building.

"I really appreciate you staying late for this," I said. "Would've been tough for me to make it earlier."

He grunted and continued reading, one hand drumming slowly on his metal desk. The digital clock on the wall above him read 6:03. On the bookshelf, tucked among a row of wire-bound notebooks, was a framed photo of a young boy holding up a small fish on a line.

"Boy, was I surprised to hear that Joyce retired," I said. "She seemed too young for that. So spry and youthful." Joyce being Blaylock's predecessor. My previous probation officer. A true bitch on wheels. Condescending. Domineering. No sense of humor. "I'll have to send her a card," I said, hoping it didn't sound sarcastic.

Blaylock didn't answer.

I was starting to wonder if he had a reading disability. I'm no angel — I wouldn't have been in this predicament if I were — but my file couldn't have been more than half a dozen pages long. I was surprised that a man in his position, with several hundred probationers in his charge, would spend more than thirty seconds on each.

Finally, Blaylock, still looking at the file, said, "Roy Wilson Ballard. Thirty-six years old. Divorced. Says you used to work as a news cameraman." He had a thick piney-woods accent. Pure east Texas. He peered up at me, without moving his head. Apparently, it was my turn to talk.

"Yes, sir. Until about three years ago."

"When you got fired."

"My boss and I had a personality conflict," I said, wondering how detailed my file was.

"Ernie Crenshaw."

"That's him."

"You broke his nose with a microphone stand."

Fairly detailed, apparently.

"Well, yeah, he, uh —"

"You got an attitude problem, Ballard?"

"No, sir."

"Temper?"

I started to lie, but decided against it. "Occasionally."

"That what happened in this instance? Temper got the best of you?"

"He was rude to one of the reporters. He called her a name."

"What name was that?"

"I'd rather not repeat it."

"I'm asking you to."

"Okay, then. He called her Doris. Her real name is Anne."

His expression remained frozen. Tough crowd.

I said, "Okay. He called her a cunt."

Blaylock's expression still didn't change. "To her face?"

"Behind her back. He was a coward. And she didn't deserve it. This guy was a world-class jerk. Little weasel."

"You heard him say it?"

"I was the one he was talking to. It set me off."

"So you busted his nose."

"I did, sir, yes."

Perhaps it was my imagination, but I thought Harvey Blaylock gave a nearly imperceptible nod of approval. He looked back at the file. "Now you're self-employed. A legal videographer. What is that exactly?"

"Well, uh, that means I record depositions, wills, scenes of accidents. Things like that. But proof of insurance fraud is my specialty. The majority of my business. Turns out I'm really good at it."

"Describe it for me."

"Sir?"

"Give me a typical day."

I recited my standard courtroom answer. "Basically, I keep a subject under surveillance and hope to videotape him engaging in an activity that's beyond his alleged physical limitations." Then I added, "Maybe lifting weights, or dancing. Playing golf. Doing the hokey-pokey."

No smile.

"Not a nine-to-five routine, then."

"No, sir. More like five to nine."

Blaylock mulled that over for a few seconds. "So you're out there, working long hours, sometimes through the night, and you start taking pills to keep up with the pace. That how it went?"

Until you've been there, you have no idea how powerless and naked you feel when someone like Harvey Blaylock is authorized to dig through your personal failings with a salad fork.

"That sums it up pretty well," I said.

"Did it work?"

"What, the pills?"

He nodded.

"Well, yeah. But coffee works pretty well, too."

"You were also drinking. That's why you got pulled over in the first place, and how they ended up finding the pills on you. You got a drinking problem?"

I thought of an old joke. *Yeah, I got a drinking problem. Can't pay my bar tab.* "I hope not," I said, which is about as honest as it gets. "At one point maybe I did, but I don't know for sure. Probably not. But that's what you'd expect someone with a drinking problem to say, right?"

"Had a drink since your court date?"

"No, sir. I'm not allowed to. Even though the Breathalyzer said I was legal."

"Not even one drink?"

"Not a drop. Joyce, gave me a piss te — I mean a urine test, last month, and three in the past year. I passed them all. That should be in the file."

"You miss it?" Blaylock asked. "The booze?"

I honestly thought about it for a moment.

"Sometimes, yeah," I said. "More than I would've guessed, but not enough to freak me out or anything. Sometimes, you know, I just crave a cold beer. Or three. But if I had to quit eating Mexican food, I'd miss that, too. Maybe more than beer."

Blaylock slowly sat forward in his chair and dropped my file, closed, on his desk. "Here's the deal, son. Ninety-five percent of the people I deal with are shitbags who think the world is their personal litter box. I can't do them any good, and they don't want me to. Most of 'em are locked up again within a year, and all I can say is good riddance. Then I see guys like you who make a stupid mistake and get caught up in the system. You probably have a decent life ahead of you, but you don't need me to tell you that, and it really doesn't matter what I think anyway. So I'll just say this: Follow the rules and you can put all this behind you. If you need any help, I'll do what I can. I really will. But if you fuck up just one time, it's like tipping over a row of dominoes. Then it's out of your control, and mine, too. You follow me?"

~ ~ ~

After the meeting, I swung by a Jack-In-The-Box, then sat outside Wally Crouch's place for a few hours, just in case. He stayed put.

I got home just as the ten o'clock news was coming on. Howard Turner had been located in a motel in Yuma City, Arizona, there on business. Police had verified his alibi. He had been nowhere near Texas, and the cops had no reason to believe he was involved.

So Tracy Turner was still missing, and that fact created a void in my chest that I hadn't felt in years.

~ ~ ~ ~ ~ ~

ABOUT THE AUTHOR

Ben Rehder lives with his wife near Austin, Texas, where he was born and raised. His novels have made best-of-the-year lists in *Publishers Weekly, Library Journal, Kirkus Reviews*, and *Field & Stream. Buck Fever* was a finalist for the Edgar Award. For more information, visit www.benrehder.com.

OTHER NOVELS BY BEN REHDER

Buck Fever
Bone Dry
Flat Crazy
Guilt Trip
Gun Shy
Holy Moly
The Chicken Hanger
The Driving Lesson
Gone The Next
Hog Heaven
Get Busy Dying
Stag Party

Printed in Great Britain
by Amazon